MURDER
on
BEARSKIN NECK

AN ANNIE QUITNOT MYSTERY

GUNILLA CAULFIELD

Rockport is a real New England town. This book, however, is a work of fiction, and all active characters, locations and events are either the products of the author's imagination, or else are used fictitiously. Any resemblance to actual persons or events is coincidental.

Dedication

For Stephen Rask, Rockport Public Library Director Emeritus, and for all my old friends and colleagues at the library, especially Linda, June, Diane, and Jane and Boyd.

For all the loyal friends and patrons of the Rockport Public Library.

And for my invaluable editor, Emily, sine qua non.

PROLOGUE

"There is something in the wind."
(from *Shakespeare's Richard III*)

Star Island Park, in the picturesque little seaside fishing village of Rockport, Massachusetts, (not to be confused with the picturesque little seaside fishing village of Rockport, Maine) could be a contender in the *Guinness Book of World Records* for the smallest park in the world. The park juts out over the rocks on the harbor side of Atlantic Avenue, and is a favorite location of the artists for whom it was created. You might just be able to squeeze two compact cars onto the grassy spot—after removing the huge, flat boulder that takes up part of the space, that is, and being careful not to go over the steep edge and ending up in the harbor.

The boulder is at this moment occupied by Priscilla Pettengill, N.A., A.W.S., who is leading her class of hopeful watercolorists. There are, of course, better vantage points for catching the sunrise along the shoreline—the Headlands just up the street, or the end of Bearskin Neck across the harbor, to name two—but that is not what Priscilla is after.

"The *light!* We must capture the *light!*" she exhorts her bleary-eyed students, who are usually sound asleep at this uncivilized hour. They have already sketched out the scene on their oversized watercolor pads. The T Wharf juts out into the middle of the harbor, with the Sandy Bay Yacht Club at the end. The weathered building is topped by the familiar golden seagull weather vane, glinting in the morning sun. Further out, nearing the curved stone jetty that protects the harbor, a few lobster boats are chugging along on their way out to pull traps. Just below Star Island Park itself there is a small landing where a group of sleepy youngsters are raising sail on their turnabouts, getting ready for the first classes of the day. Soon the little sailors will be out on the bay, where they will practice *turtling* and learn how to right the boat and get back in.

"Hurry now, the light is fleeting! See how it catches on the weather vane…. Oh, look, now it's hitting the sails!" Priscilla smoothly and skillfully bathes the sails in golden sunrise hues while her students painstakingly daub theirs with orange splotches. A sudden wind fills the sails and the children shriek and laugh, trying to control their little floating nutshells.

A tourist out for an early walk stops to watch Priscilla's class. He leans on the fence and makes an encouraging comment to one of the students, a pretty blonde with a maximum of painting equipment and a minimum of talent, who gives him a scathing look in response. He shrugs and continues on his walk. Turning the corner onto Mount Pleasant Street, he walks by a blue gate with an open view across the harbor and out to sea, and stops there to enjoy the fullness of the sunrise. Midway out in the harbor, warmed by the early rays of the sun, is Motif # 1—the red fishermen's shack that is the emblem of Rockport. This morning, three hopeful fishermen are posing in front of it on the solid granite wharf, mirrored in the calm water. The tourist lifts his head to sniff the morning air. The scent of roses draws him on. He finds the source and, after looking to see if anyone is watching, picks a partly open bloom as he passes by and sticks it in his lapel. He is sporting a new straw hat and a suit that is just a bit cityish for around here. A little further down the street he sniffs the air again—*aaah, bacon and coffee*—and stops in at Flav's Red Skiff for breakfast.

CHAPTER 1

"Hung be the heavens with black, yield day to night"
(from *Henry VI*)

Murder is a rare event in Rockport. People who listen to their scanners for some excitement usually have to settle for reports about fender benders, flooded basements, teenage pranks, and the occasional break-in at one of the great summer homes that stand empty in the winter.

Annie Quitnot doesn't own a scanner. She listens to small bits of news on NPR with her morning coffee, and after putting the dishes away she scans the headlines of *The New York Times* online. In a small town like this, all the local news eventually filters down to her, a fact she frequently regrets.

Sally Babson *does* own a scanner. Sally is Annie's "coffee mate," and when she calls, breathless with news, Annie sighs.

"Did you hear who's been murdered?" Sally asks, keeping Annie on tenterhooks instead of offering the information up-front. This is the game she plays and Annie knows she has to play along; Sally is a good friend, and Annie doesn't want to spoil her fun.

"No, Sal, who?" she says, trying to sound curious. She nestles the receiver between neck and shoulder while she tries to gather her curly red hair and squeeze it into a barrette at the nape of her neck.

"Carlo Valenti, that's who!" says Sally.

This does shock Annie. In fact, it leaves her speechless. She lets the barrette slide out of her hand, and grabs the receiver tightly. Panic tugs at her sleeve, and she has to sit down.

"I don't believe it," she says, almost in a whisper. *Not Carlo.* "Are you sure? I mean, who told you?" Annie instantly regrets asking. She *does* want to know, but she does not want to listen to rumor and speculation.

"Meet me at the coffee shop and I'll tell you what I know," Sally says. *Yes, and then we'll get to hear what everyone else knows, too,* Annie thinks. The coffee shop (which in the old days was named "Oleana's" and is still referred to as that by some old timers) is the best place in town for news of the gossipy variety. It opens at six thirty in the morning and seats fifteen customers—less when the stools at the counter get loose and are "temporarily" removed, a time span that sometimes runs to months.

Annie sighs again. "Give me a few minutes, Sal. I have to fix a sandwich for lunch."

She hangs up and looks around, disoriented. Then she picks up the barrette and goes over to the oval mirror that hangs next to the computer in her tiny alcove to put her hair up. The face in the mirror is so pale you can see every freckle, and the green eyes are large and desolate. She tries to smooth out some of the wrinkles in the soft linen pantsuit she likes to wear to work. Ironing is not high on Annie's list of favorite activities, and besides, linen is supposed to look that way. Comfortable. Like the flip-flops, which she just remembers to kick off before stepping into a pair of more acceptable sandals. Annie has an impressive number of flip-flops standing at the ready—under the bed, at the back door, in the hall and in other places where they may be discovered by an occasional sweep of the broom. Next to going barefoot, there is nothing more comfortable than flip-flops. No official dress code is enforced in the library, but flip-flops are out. Distracted, she glances out through the window, without even noticing the view of the harbor.

When her parents died in a boating accident ten years ago, Annie inherited the home where she has lived most of her life, the Hannah Jumper House. Her parents bought it in the days before Rockport properties became far too expensive for a single librarian to own, and Annie knows full well how fortunate she is to have it. Her father spent most of his life working in the local forge, and her mother was the branch librarian in Pigeon Cove, on the northern tip of the island. No doubt the last fact eventually influenced Annie's choice of profession, although she started out in rather bohemian fashion, as an artisan in a little shop on Bearskin Neck.

Hannah Jumper, in whose house Annie resides, was a red-headed, outspoken seamstress. She is famous for making Rockport a dry town by organizing a raid one summer morning in 1856, during which she and her cohorts hacked asunder all the kegs and barrels of rum in town with their hatchets, no doubt making grown men cry. Hannah is either revered or reviled, depending on your point of view. Now and then the liquor issue comes up for a vote again, and some people tape their old "HANNAH LIVES!" bumper stickers back on their cars. So far, the "drys" have it. Actually, liquor was allowed in town the year after Prohibition. However, beer drinkers soon found a convenient place to relieve themselves—a lane which became known as "Diamond Spring Alley" after a favorite brand of beer—and by the end of the year the locals had had enough and the town became dry again.

There's a rumor that kegs of rum were buried in Hannah's basement, but Annie has made some small excavations down there without finding any evidence of it. The low, white-painted house with its roof of thick wooden shingles sits snugly right on the harbor, surrounded by a white fence with a blue gate.

An old-fashioned rose blooms outside the living room window, and an apple tree that bears the loveliest yellow apples in late summer grows outside the dining room. Annie lives alone in the main part of the house for most of the year. In the summer, she rents out the studio attached to its southern corner to a couple of New York artists. The doorways in the house are low, the walls lean and the floors dip, the wind whines in the windows, and the walls creak in stormy weather—but Annie wouldn't want to live anywhere else.

After gathering her wits enough to remember that she is supposed to meet Sally, Annie hurries into the kitchen, which is galley-sized and has a small window with a view of the harbor beyond the patio outside. She puts rosemary ham between thin slices of French peasant bread, then hesitates for a moment before she spreads Cholula hot pepper mayo on the bread instead of the pesto she'd really like—but she is considerate of her patrons, who may not appreciate a reference librarian with garlic breath. She slips the sandwich into a square plastic tub. In a small town like this you have to mind your trash, and Annie keeps hers to a minimum. No baggies. When her lunch is fixed and she is dressed and ready to go, she slumps down in a chair by the kitchen table for a long moment, staring out over the harbor without really seeing it. There is a look of puzzlement and anxiety in her face.

Once upon a time, in what now seems a long-ago past, Annie and Carlo were lovers. Was it only five years ago that Carlo left for Europe? They were in their mid-thirties, then. Annie is forty now: in other words, well on her way to spinsterhood. But back then, before she started working in the library, she owned a little shop on the Neck where she made and sold jewelry, handmade paper and other artsy objects. She sat in the tiny space, hammering silver and threading beads, making macramé planters using old glass insulators and talking to people. Annie has always loved talking to people, both locals and strangers. That was her problem, really. She never did have a sense for business. She was too willing to share, show how she made things, tell people where they could get supplies to make their own. Not surprisingly, she made more friends than sales. But those were the years when she knew Carlo, in the biblical sense.

It takes a determined effort for Annie to finally leave the house, but she knows Sally must be impatiently waiting for her by now. Before she leaves she makes sure the coffee maker is turned off and shuts the door to the little alcove next to the kitchen where she sleeps.

Still in a daze as she passes through the dining room, she picks up a stack of books from the table and goes to put them back on the shelf in her living room library. She goes through the front hall, where she latches the low door that leads to the upstairs. The narrow stairs behind the door go both ways, left and right, each to a separate upstairs bedroom. In order to use the stairs, you first have to crouch to get through the door, a feat many of her guests have had trouble with, especially after a glass or two of wine. Perhaps that's why someone added the narrow back staircase that leads from the living room up to the master bedroom. Annie continues into the living room, where bookshelves cover the walls. She gives her favorite Shakespeare volumes a caressing look as she passes by the large section devoted to his work. "Willie," as she thinks of the Bard, is a personal and treasured friend.

The expanse of bookshelves takes up most of the wall space, except for the fireplace area with the stormy seascape over it, painted by a former owner. The harbor end of the living room is a step down, and has a large picture window with what is arguably one of the most charming and picturesque views in town. For instance, right out there on a wharf in the harbor is Motif #1, the old red fishing shack believed to be the most painted and photographed subject anywhere—after, possibly, the pyramids.

Augustus, Annie's dachshund, who is named after Augustus Finknottle of *Jeeves and Wooster* fame, is happy in his basket by the fireplace. Gussie is snoozing happily at the moment. Now and then his legs move frantically, as though he's chasing something, and he whines and snarls a little. Augustus is elderly and doesn't move much these days. But he's the only family she has now and probably the only family she ever will. *Let's not go there,* she thinks, and is immediately disgusted with herself for using one of those current clichés.

"Good hunting, Gussie," Annie says as she passes him. She has dragged her feet long enough. Before the feeling of panic has a chance to take hold again, she leaves the house through the back door, which she always keeps unlocked, and reaches the street through the little alley between her house and the gallery next door.

CHAPTER 2

"Give every man thy ear, but few thy voice
Take each man's censure, but reserve thy judgment."
(from *Hamlet*)

The coffee shop's specialty is *Nisu,* a braided Scandinavian coffee bread, and Annie and Sally order it "with the works," which means the thick slices of it will be toasted, slathered with butter, and heavily laced with cinnamon and sugar. The place is full, with customers standing in the empty spaces left by the two currently missing counter stools. There are three tables attached to the wall opposite the counter, each seating two, and one at the end that seats one—as long as you're willing to sit and look at the refrigerator. A couple gets up to leave, which is how Sally and Annie manage to get their regular table. The place is abuzz with the morning's rumor and gossip, and Sally is keeping her ears well pointed. Ned Mazzarini, a carpenter who was friendly with Carlo, has the most firsthand information, and is sharing it with Tommy Cameron, one of the local lobstermen.

"They found 'im out on the rocks, behaahnd the gallery. Body haahf in the wahtah—at fihst they thought he'd slipped and fell, his forr'ead's all stove in. But he was stabbed, too. Bled laahk a stuck pig. Good thing we don't live in Flor'da. Shaahks would'a got 'im. Amazin' the tide didn't get 'im neithah; it was real high this maahnin', but he was jammed between the rocks, ah guess." Not many Rockporters use the true North Shore vernacular any more, owing to the influence of radio and TV and the influx of new blood. But Ned's an old timer, Rockport born and bred, and rarely goes "across the cut"—that is to say, over the water that separates the island from the mainland.

Annie puts down her Nisu. She is not normally squeamish, but she can't take another bite while she is listening to this.

"Powah Maahgo's all broke down," Ned continues. "Came back from Baahston on the train this maahnin.' Too bad she had to see him lyin' out theah on the rocks laahk a dead fish. Who'd do such a thing to Caahlo?" Ned asks, looking around the coffee shop. Ned was a friend of Carlo's, and could be expected to be bewildered. Carlo wasn't born on the island, however—had in fact been a *furrinah* (Aytalian, to boot), and was as such automatically a bit suspect. An *ahtist,* too (ouch), and furthermore, he had been quick to speak his mind on sensitive local issues, especially ones to do with Bearskin Neck.

The stories of Carlo's many past feuds are recounted in the coffee shop for a while. For instance, there was the time he incensed the local artists with his stand when a town ban on schlock art was suggested. The term refers to cheap, trashy works painted for the tourist trade, and most often refers to those imported "original, signed oil masterpieces" painted abroad on assembly lines by dexterous hands: one worker specializes in backgrounds, the next one adds the sky, the next one the trees, and so on; and at the end, someone adds the final touches: people, flowers, and a signature. Carlo had brazenly suggested in one of his (frequent) letters to the editor that a lot of the *local* art was schlock art, too, and as such should be included in the ban. This had certainly not endeared him to the artists, nor to the director of the local art society, Avery Shattuck, who had written a nasty letter to the editor in response, blasting Carlo and calling him an anarchist (among other things), which Carlo had found absolutely hilarious.

Another time the town merchants had objected to some new, small bistros and eateries that served Thai, Italian, or other "foreign" foods, suggesting it harmed the Neck's quaint New England image and was not conducive to good tourist business. Carlo had suggested that anyone who wasn't a Native American ought to abandon the Neck and give it back to the original Natives who had been there first to fish and collect clams. *Xenophobia* was what he had called it. "All you people were immigrants once, somewhere back in your ancestry. Everyone in this country is a foreigner. The Chinese shopkeepers on the Neck are just as 'American' as you are. Besides, not all tourists are satisfied with 'chowdah' and 'Injun Puddin.' They'll just go elsewhere to do their shopping and eating."

The merchants had been up in arms, the local board of trade had kept out of the fray, and the townspeople had been divided on the issue. There were letters in the paper representing both sides, some of them in the nostalgic vein of "let's have the town back the way it was in the olden days, when Rockport was a quiet little fishing village." Then there were those from the other side, some even suggesting that the town should allow franchises (McDonald's, et al.) to "broaden the tax base."

There is always a lot of talk in this town about the tax base. Of course, when you broaden the tax base by building more homes and businesses, you also end up with an increase in population, which causes an increase in the budget for school, water and sewer, road maintenance, and so on, in an everlasting vicious circle that, naturally, ends up with a tax raise. Franchises had been anathema for years, and when Dunkin' Donuts finally opened next to the railroad station, families were split on the issue. It was father against son, in a renewal of the Civil War. In Rockport, these are serious issues, indeed.

Later, Carlo had actually joined sides with the artists and shopkeepers on the Neck. Real estate developers and speculators had begun to make overtures to property owners, and had tried to drop a "tempting" offer here and there. When they were turned down (the offers weren't tempting enough, perhaps), the developers started on a different tack by suggesting to the townspeople that the congestion on the Neck was a fire hazard, and the smelly old fish shacks an eyesore and probably a health hazard as well.

The speculators' idea men had produced smart renderings of how Bearskin Neck might look if they got their hands on it. Clusters of condos (dressed with faux weathered New England shingle siding and richly surrounded by weeping trees and fluffy shrubbery) would house upscale shops on the street level. The Neck would be turned into a mall; in fact, one of the drawings depicted the walking street turned into a glass-roofed arcade. So, why were the shopkeepers against this delightful scenario? Because they could see the handwriting on the wall: they would not be able to afford the rent. They could hardly afford it as it was.

That time Carlo had been on the forefront of the opposition, again writing letters to the editor and putting signs in front of his gallery objecting to big money development of the Neck. While this had improved his relationship with the art community, it had at the same time alienated and angered local developers and speculators—especially a ruthless and ambitious developer by the name of Frederick Smythe. (In school, he had been Freddie Smith, but apparently that was not sufficiently upscale for a real estate developer.) "One day, if Smythe has his way," Carlo once said, "all of Rockport will be beige."

Smythe spends his time buying up properties left and right, gentrifying and condominiumizing wherever he goes. This morning a rumor circulates in the coffee shop that Smythe recently made what he called a "generous offer" to Carlo for his "shack." Which Carlo refused. And then Smythe went and bought a few of the old fish shacks alongside Carlo's, and let it be known that he was planning to tear them down. Which, of course, incensed Carlo, who promised to stop him.

It stands to reason that he might have had enemies as well as friends, some of the customers in the coffee shop think. Others hide behind their morning papers while pretending not to listen. When Ned has no more to tell, he takes his coffee and donuts to go. Now that people have heard as much as seems to be known, a few other customers—mainly townies at this time of day—also begin to break up and make room for new ones. Annie checks her watch.

"Got to go, Sally." Annie suddenly can't stand sitting there, hearing people talk about Carlo as if he were just a stranger in a news story.

"Why? You've got half an hour." Sally is pointing to the big round clock that hangs on the back wall over the microwave, the waffle iron, and the two toasters that often emit curls of black smoke.

"I know, but I promised to get some information for Dot Bradley. And if I don't get it done before the library opens, you know how it goes. Half the morning will pass before I get to it, and Dot's supposed to stop in before lunch."

What Annie needs most desperately is to hide, to be by herself, and a half-hour alone by her desk is the best she can do before the library opens, when patrons will beleaguer her with their requests. Annie's best working time is in the morning; by early afternoon her brain suddenly planes out and hits a restful spot, and then, just as she comes out of it, the school kids arrive with illegibly scribbled research projects they will need guidance with.

Sally nods and stuffs the last piece of Nisu in her mouth. A few buttery crumbs stick to her chin, and when Annie points it out, Sally laughs and wipes them off.

"Can't take me anywhere, huh?" Sally has curly black hair and looks younger than she is. She dresses like a teenager, in short skirts or shorts, and likes wearing a multitude of jangling silver bangles. She is working in a gift shop on the Neck in the summer, which keeps her in coffee money and, more importantly, helps her relieve the tension stemming from having twin teenage boys who get into endless trouble. The gift shop doesn't open until eleven, like most of the shops in the tourist mecca called Bearskin Neck, so she'll have to occupy herself until then. She's not going home, that's for sure. When she left the house, Ben and Brad were already fighting over whose turn it was to use the computer. If she earns enough money this summer Sally intends buy a second one so they'll each have their own. Of course, then they'll find something else to fight about. Oh, well. While she waits for the shop to open, maybe she'll stroll by Carlo Valenti's gallery on the neck. *Just for a look,* Sally thinks.

CHAPTER 3

"Rest, rest, perturbed spirit!"
(from *Hamlet*)

Annie hurries over to the library and goes in the back way, past the row of bloomed-out Kwanzan cherry trees and up through the reading garden, to avoid the patrons already waiting by the front entrance. Normally she is happy to stop and chat with them. Some kind patron will always hold the door for her while she rolls in the book-return bin, and if the weather is foul she will let the patrons into the vestibule where they can read local announcements on the bulletin board while they wait for the main doors to open. But today she is distracted—and besides, she *does* have work to do—and her time has already been shortened by the visit to the coffee shop.

After unlocking and pushing up the grilles at the circulation desk, she goes over to the reference area, which is her beloved second home. Annie's favorite quick-reference books sit crammed together in rough Dewey order on the desk, supported by a pair of bookends in the shape of hands copied from a Michelangelo sculpture. *If you were to put the bookends together, they would form a pair of praying hands,* she thinks. Is anyone praying for Carlo, or are they all just abuzz with the news?

She slumps down in her comfortable leather swivel chair, a donation from a generous patron, and picks up the note from Dot Bradley. Dot left it a few days ago, saying she'd stop in today for the information, but Annie has been too busy to deal with it. *Dot's a sweet girl,* Annie thinks, *I just wish she had a little more self-confidence.* In her mid-thirties, Dot is a pudgy and fairly unattractive girl. Bad skin, blond hair that is thinning on top, a fact which she tries to hide by wearing a baseball cap, letting the long ponytail stick out through the hole in the back. She is a private nurse with one of the local agencies, and a favorite with the elderly patients. Dot's grandfather, who dotes on her, brought her up after her parents died. The son, George died suddenly of a heart attack, and his wife Lily followed him, less than a year later, probably of a broken heart. Judge sent Dot to nursing school, perhaps in the hope that it would toughen her up a little, and has supplemented her income since then.

Annie reads the note again.

Annie,

My grandfather gave me a watercolor for my birthday. It's by Grant Heyward, who was Josie Mandel's husband. Grandpa is coming to my house for lunch next week, and I'd love to sound like I know something about Heyward when I thank him. Grandpa always treats me like I'm an ignoramus. So, can you give me some info on Heyward? Mostly biographical stuff, when he was born and married and died and went to school and stuff like that. You know my Grandpa; he'll pump me.

Thanks, Dot.

Yes, Annie knows Dot's grandpa, Judge Bradley. A bit of a curmudgeon, Annie has always thought, cantankerous and overbearing. Ironically, he also happens to have saved Annie's brother's life a long time ago when Justin fell overboard during sailing classes and nearly drowned. Judge (everyone calls him "Judge," as though it were his name) is one of the more illustrious members of the Sandy Bay Yacht Club, an avid and still—although at least a decade into retirement—skilled sailor. Judge Bradley was a crusty, egocentric character even back then, and whenever he and Annie meet these days (he comes to the library religiously when the latest issue of *Ocean Navigator* is due) he still asks about Justin, indirectly reminding her of the debt. Justin, who is Annie's only living relative, is married and lives in New Mexico now, and Annie hasn't seen him for a couple of years. They were close as children, with Justin, being the big brother, looking out for her. The fact that she ended up with the house had probably contributed to the sudden estrangement that followed their parents' deaths, but their once chafed relationship has been repaired since then, though kept up mostly via phone calls and e-mail.

Annie, who will always feel beholden to Judge, is determined to get some ammunition for poor Dot. Annie always thinks of her as "poor Dot," as the girl won't make a move without checking with Grandpa, and will probably never be able to leave the nest and fly out on her own. What Dot calls "my house" in the note is a small cottage on the back lot of her grandfather's property. And, as far as Judge treating Dot as an ignoramus—it's probably only a sign of "tough love" on his part. He has been like a father to the girl, and in his gruff way obviously loves her.

It would, of course, have been easier to gather a wealth of material if the artist had been Winslow Homer, Marsden Hartley, Fitz Henry Lane or Edward Hopper—or any of the many other famous artists who came to Cape Ann to paint in the past. But Annie knows her sources, and starts digging. Right now, anything that will deaden the pain of old memories will serve, and when Annie gets her teeth into a task, everything else gets pushed out of her mind. And yet, underneath her busy archival search, she senses a restless search of a different kind.

CHAPTER 4

"The seeming truth which cunning times put on
to entrap the wisest."
(from *The Merchant of Venice*)

When Dot has not come in by two o'clock, Annie calls her.

"Oh, Annie, sorry. I was just leaving. I'm going out for the afternoon with a friend. Is it okay if I pick the stuff up another time?" Dot asks, sounding anxious to go.

"Sure, Dot. Are you okay? You sound like you have a cold."

"Oh, I do, so I didn't want to pass it on to you or my patients, you know…but I'm fine to go out," she adds.

"Okay, Dot," Annie tries to calm her. "You said you needed this in a hurry, that's all. Wasn't Judge coming over for lunch? Anyway, just give me a call and I'll bring it to you, or else come in and pick it up when you can." She shakes her head, a little annoyed at Dot but at the same time hoping the poor girl will have a good time. Good for Dot if she feels secure enough to get away from Grandpa for a day. With the poor girl's low self-esteem, it surely can't be easy for her to live up to Judge Bradley's expectations.

Annie puts the material in a large envelope. It includes the short biography of Grant Heyward, who turns out to have been the nephew of Brent Heyward, the wealthy owner of Heyward chain stores. After starting out as a stained glass artist, Grant moved to Rockport with his wife and took up painting. He exhibited at the Rockport Art Society but died fairly young. His widow, Josie Mandel (Josie kept her maiden name) later became a legend of nearly Hannah Jumperish proportions. After receiving Grant's inheritance when Uncle Brent died, Josie Mandel became well known as the Perle Mesta of the Rockport art scene, throwing famous parties and taking many budding artists under her wing. Along with Grant Heywood's biography, Annie has also made Xerox copies of a few of the artist's works, mostly watercolors, some of them quite nice.

Annie puts the envelope in her "ready for pick-up" file and goes downstairs to the staff lunchroom—affectionately known as "the dungeon"—in the basement of the Rockport Public Library. The dungeon has a rough, freestone wall, part of the original foundation. The small windows are actually located above ceiling level, and a deeply angled window ledge reminiscent of medieval castle windows lets dim light down into the room. The dungeon has amenities not found in its castle cousin, notably a microwave, which is known to emit unlibrary-like odors when certain staff members heat up their chowder or Chinese leftovers.

The library is the best place in town for news of the more serious and factual variety. The Main Desk library assistants act as veritable tourist guides in the summer, and during the rest of the year the library staff—aside from guiding the town's regular cadre of voracious page turners—lend assistance to a constant stream of people hungry for information: ordinary residents with curious minds, authors looking for interesting facts, local historians, amateur genealogists...not to mention schoolchildren needing help with their homework.

Some years back, when the library was still housed in the old Carnegie building, (yes, indeed, financed by the same Andrew Carnegie who built libraries all over the country) news came about a million-dollar bequest to the library by Franz and Luisita Denghausen. Franz and Luisita, legendary names in Rockport art circles, were Rockport residents except in the winter, when they lived at the Ritz-Carlton Hotel in Boston. Luisita was born to wealth, her father being the Boston multimillionaire Charles Leland, and Franz and Luisita became generous benefactors, leaving a great legacy of gifts to many institutions.

The trouble with the million-dollar bequest to the small town of Rockport was that the Smithsonian, which had already received ten million dollars in the Denghausens' will, contended that they should have Rockport's million, too. At that, the townspeople rose up in rebellion. The media loved every minute of it: television crews descended on the library in droves, and even *The Wall Street Journal* went on to describe the town's plight. Rockporters mobilized to fight the great Smithsonian. They wrote letters to newspapers and politicians, and cancelled their memberships and subscriptions with the institution. Finally, smarting from the bad publicity, the Smithsonian Institution gave up. The small town of Rockport had become the mouse that roared! That's how a great old granite building, which started out as a cotton mill and later—after a devastating fire—was refurbished and turned into the Tarr School, finally became the town's beautiful new library.

Annie had been part of the human chain that passed books from the old library to the new over neighbors' lawns, across the churchyard, and down the street, up the library steps, and right inside onto the new shelves. Later there was a festive dedication, with Roger Mudd as invited speaker. He had lauded the town on its great achievement of "whipping the Smithsonian." Various important townspeople and selectmen had also gone up to the podium to speak, eager to be part of the great success story.

In addition to the dungeon, the library basement, or "Lower Level," as the staff is instructed to call it, houses the staff room and the "morgue," where magazine back issues and duplicate copies of books (the Harvard Classics, for instance) are stored. The rest of the lower level is dedicated to the Local History Room, which has sections on genealogy and local biography as well as on fisheries, granite quarrying, and other island industries—art, of course, being one, and a fairly large section at that.

The mention of Grant Heyward's connection to Josie Mandel told Annie where to start, and from there she found all she needed, even if most of the information was on Josie. *If all searches were that easy,* she thinks. She puts her sandwich in the microwave for a quick zap, which scents the room (pleasantly) with a fragrance of rosemary and hot pepper. Then she sits down at the round table and, at last, allows her thoughts to return to Carlo.

CHAPTER 5

"If thou remember'st not the slightest folly
that ever love did make thee run into,
thous hast not loved."
(from *As You Like It*)

Carlo's gallery was located a couple of doors away from Annie's on the Neck, and when they closed up shop at night they would meet, though never openly. In a small town like Rockport, a girl wants to watch her reputation. Annie had originally thought him considerate when he went along with keeping their relationship sort of quiet. For the two years they were together, they usually met at home, her place or his. Sometimes they went out of town, frequently to Boston, to eat or take in a play. Annie worried that Carlo's motives weren't quite that noble, that maybe keeping their affair private also allowed him to remain "eligible" in the eyes of other attractive females. The trouble with Carlo was that he was excessively attractive himself. A big man, both in personality and physique, with a well-sculpted face that remained tanned year-round, and a broad, manly chest for a woman to rest against. The translucent blue eyes were accentuated by dark, expressive eyebrows and wavy, brown hair, which had a tendency to curl at the nape of the neck in humid weather. My Hemingway, Annie thought. As far as Annie was aware, back then nobody had known that Carlo and she had a thing going—not even her closest friend in those days, Clare Draper. Annie wonders that Clare never suspected anything. Clare's a smart girl in many ways, but also a little scatterbrained. She is the cataloguer in the library, and very competent, so she can obviously concentrate when she needs to. Probably suffers from some form of attention deficit disorder, Annie thinks, which often seems to be paired with a unique ability to hyperfocus. Right now Annie is tempted to go up and confide in her and cry on her shoulder. But no, it's too late. Clare would certainly hold it against her that she hadn't told her back then. And what good would it do? Carlo is gone, and Annie can't bear the thought of talking about him, even with Clare.

In the company of others, Carlo and Annie simply turned up as friends, and were part of the bohemian local art scene that existed outside the establishment—the establishment being the Rockport Art Society. Like other art associations and academies, past and present, the RAS has rules about who can belong. A jury will judge the work and determine if the artist passes muster. There are always some, especially among those not accepted, who claim that acceptance comes down to politics and *whom you know,* as well as to the institution's idea of what "art" is. Many artists try diligently, year after year, to be accepted at the RAS. Others—amateurs and Sunday painters, for instance—don't bother, knowing they don't measure up. Then there are the perennial outsiders, many of whom consider themselves above any such small-town clique, and follow in the footsteps of artists the world over who have rebelled against the establishment. To those who *do* belong, there are many benefits: the camaraderie, the ambiance of the exhibition space, and of course the famous Summer Concert Festival, beloved by townies and summer people alike.

During the years they were together, Carlo was an ardent lover and full of unforgettable surprises, both sublime and ridiculous. Like the time he insisted that Shakespeare was better in Italian. To prove it he bought her an old volume that included *La Dodicesima Notte, Romeo e Guilietta,* and *Come vi Piace,* and started declaiming in a loud, theatrical voice, *"Romeo, Romeo! Perché sei tu, Romeo? Ah, rinnega tuo padre!... Ricusa il tuo casato!... O, se proprio non vuoi, giurami amore, ed io non sarò più una Capuleti!"* (*O Romeo, Romeo! Wherefore art thou, Romeo?...*) which had sent her into paroxysms.

Carlo set his own sights high and staked out great plans for the future. He had lived the first twenty years of his life in Europe and longed to get back there, back to *Torino,* where he was born and grew up, and on to Paris, Venice, Rome. "I don't intend to be stuck in this little town forever," he said, appalled at the thought of having to paint seascapes and quaint village scenes and other tourist potboilers for the rest of his life— *potboiler* being a word the artists in the colony use to describe the paintings that "pay the bills." Carlo insisted that *potboiler* was just another euphemism for schlock art. No, he was determined to become part of the *real* art world.

One of the things Annie found interesting about Carlo was that no matter how European he was—which showed in many ways, one being that stereotypical need to sit in coffee shops late into the night and have serious philosophical discussions— he also seemed endearingly American. Open, generous, independent, fearless, determined. And ambitious.

In those days, Annie slept in the large upstairs bedroom in the Hannah Jumper House that looks out over the harbor. She remembers nights there, lying next to Carlo, listening to the wind whipping the lines against the masts, the tinny, pinging sound from the aluminum masts and the castanet-like snapping from the wooden ones. This is why Annie no longer sleeps upstairs; the sound still pains her. Downstairs in the little alcove it's quiet, with an old grapevine and a tangled shrubbery of lilacs and honeysuckle outside to damp the sounds from the harbor.

Then one day, Carlo finally made good on his plans and went back to Europe, where he ended up teaching at the American Academy in Rome. He sent her letters in the beginning, giving exalted reports on life in Italy, even asking her (though somewhat casually) to come and join him. But there was never any sign of real commitment, she thought. Annie had not wanted to be reduced to a status of permanent girlfriend, or to live in the shadow of Carlo, who was larger than life. Oh, but she had agonized over it, and had waited, hoping for…well, not necessarily an offer of marriage, but a definite indication of a deep and lasting affection, and a need of her.

And then, after the years of being away, Carlo had returned, bringing a nubile young art student by the name of Margo DeVoe with him like a trophy. How could he? Was he just trying to exhibit his virility, to show Annie what she was missing—and what she could have had if she had followed him to Europe like a loyal dog? Oh, and it had worked. She still remembers the stark feeling of jealousy, the blood boiling at her temples at the sight of him, prancing about with his new girlfriend.

◦✵◦

Now Annie sits alone in the library dungeon, crying heedlessly. Her body trembles from delayed shock of the news, and from reliving memories long buried. She finally blows her nose in a napkin and walks over to the counter to wash up. She fills her hands with cold water, bends over the little sink, and dabs her cheeks, trying to wash the mascara off so she won't look like a raccoon when she goes back upstairs. When she turns around, the library director is standing in the doorway, mildly amused until he sees her swollen face. Duncan Langmuir is a man of intellect, humor, and courtesy, but right now he is at a loss. Crying women are not normally part of his day, and he frowns slightly.

"Is everything all right?" he asks, stupidly. Obviously, everything is not all right.

"Yes, Duncan, everything's fine," Annie answers, equally stupidly. Then, to her shame, she breaks down again and sobs desperately.

"Carlo?" he asks. He has seen Annie cry once before, a few years ago—the day Carlo Valenti left for Europe. Carlo, an avid reader—*wasn't Hillerman one of his favorites?*—came in to say good-bye to the girls at the front desk. His step was light and jaunty as he walked out the front door. Duncan saw Annie slip downstairs, and when she returned to her desk a while later, her face was flushed and swollen, just as it is now. Annie didn't tell him much then, but he ventured a guess and she nodded—again, just as she is nodding now. Later, when she knew him better, she told Duncan a little about Carlo and herself. And the day Carlo got the prize at the Biennale, and it was all over both the national and local front pages, Duncan came down from his office to make sure she was all right. Since then, he has been an understanding and compassionate Father Confessor, always keeping Annie's confidences to himself. Now he goes and puts a fatherly arm around her shoulders.

"Want to take the rest of the day off?" At first she shakes her head vigorously; then the shake slowly turns into a nod.

"Oh, Dunc." She feels like leaning her head against him but senses that this would be overstepping a boundary. Duncan Langmuir may be sympathetic, but he is also reserved and correct, and she does not want to presume on his kindness. "You know, I don't...didn't..."

"You don't have to explain, Annie. Just take the day. You can make it up."

Annie has begun to calm down, and the flames on her cheeks are fading.

"I'll go up and distract them at the desk while you sneak out the back way," Langmuir says.

Gratefully, Annie puts on her linen jacket and takes the tan leather portfolio out of her locker, which she never keeps locked, on principle. Maybe this trust is a remnant from those bohemian days when she trusted everyone. Well, she certainly trusts her colleagues at the library, and they are the only ones with access to the dungeon.

True to his word, Langmuir is keeping everyone at bay as Annie slips out the back door. The library garden, with its shaded benches and plantings of modest native flora, suddenly blur in front of her eyes as tears well up again. She stumbles down the walk, hurrying to get off the library grounds before she runs into anyone who'd recognize her.

CHAPTER 6

"O swear not by the moon, th'inconstant moon,
that monthly changes in her circled orb,
lest that thy love prove likewise variable…"
(from *Romeo and Juliet*)

As soon as she steps inside the house, Augustus trots gin-
gerly across the floor to meet Annie, who picks him up and
brings him with her into the kitchen, where he gets one of his
special treats from a little crock marked, in blue glaze, "Gussie's Goodies." It was made especially for Augustus by Clare.
Clare, apart from being a scatterbrain, is a girl of many talents
She is not only the cataloguer at the library, but she is also a
member of the Beautification Committee and the Affordable
Housing Advisory Committee, an Animal Rescue volunteer, a
justice of the peace, and a creditable potter in her spare time.

Annie and Clare grew up together in the Cove. They both
went to the Pigeon Cove School, and in the afternoons they
played on Pingree Field and explored the wilds of Dogtown.
Annie's father was working at the Tool Company then, which
in those days was a noisy and lively place. The thunder of the
drop forges could be heard all across town, but especially around
Pigeon Cove. Across the street from the factory was the local

store, and kitty-corner from it lay the Story Library, the Pigeon Cove branch of the public library. Today the Tool Company is closed and the building stands unused, the Pigeon Cove School was turned into condos as soon as the large new community school complex uptown was finished, the little store has burned down, and the Story Library has been closed and turned into a private residence.

Clare was Annie's bosom buddy all the way through high school. She was a softhearted girl, picking up strays and injured birds; and even now she has three cats that she's gotten from the shelter and a scrawny, raucous cockatiel named Pavarotti that likes to hang upside down from his perch and screech. Clare accompanied Annie the day she picked up Augustus, and is Gussie's "favorite aunt." After school, Clare lived and worked in Boston for a few years and they lost touch, but since her return they have been friends again, and colleagues besides.

I should have stopped in on Clare to tell her I was going home, Annie thinks now. Up in the library's Tech Services, Clare will be wondering what happened. They had planned to take their midafternoon coffee break together in order to go over the list of reference books that Annie needs most urgently. As usual, Clare has a backlog of books to be cataloged. Instead of calling Clare to explain, however, Annie sinks down in the lumpy, blanket-covered easy chair in front of the fireplace, with Gussie in her lap.

What was it she tried to tell Duncan? That she no longer was in love with Carlo? Or that she never loved him? Did she? She has refused to think about it for such a long time. *They were the happiest years of my life,* she thinks now, desperate to give her feelings free rein before they retreat into the shadows again.

She felt so alive, then, before Carlo left. But that was five years ago. Has she been alive since?

When her jewelry business (predictably) failed, she closed up shop. Tossing about for something else to do, she walked into the library to check the newspapers for job opportunities, and happened to see a notice on the bulletin board about an opening for a substitute on the circulation desk. The words *helpful, friendly*, and *serving the public* had appealed to her, and she applied and got the job. Not having to deal with her failing business left her free to enjoy the relationship with Carlo, and she threw caution to the wind and began to assume that theirs was a lifetime commitment. The day Carlo told her he was leaving, she was devastated.

Since then, Annie worked hard to educate herself and has finally ended up at the Reference Desk. It suits her exactly. All the traits that made her unsuitable to run a business are exactly right in reference; if anything, she has to watch out for giving more help than is required or asked for. By now, Annie considers the library her second home, and she is well known by everyone in town—well, every reader, anyway. Rockporters are avid bookworms, and nearly everyone goes to the library.

Carlo rented out the gallery space on the Neck while he was away, and he never got rid of it. Annie nursed a nagging hope that this meant he would eventually come back; she just never figured on him bringing someone with him. On his return, he immediately moved back into the little living space above the gallery, and Margo moved in with him. That same week Annie went to a get-together at Clare's, and Carlo and Margo showed up. At the sight of him, Annie quickly retreated to the back of the room, trying to find a way to sneak out unseen, but Carlo caught her eye and made his way over. Gently, step by step, he backed her out into Clare's kitchen, where he took her hands and pulled her close.

"Anna, *carissima,* I have meessed you so," he said, exaggerating his accent in the way she used to find so seductive while bending forward to kiss his favorite freckle on her neck. "Will you be home later, after the party is over? Can I come and see you? It's a moonlit night...so lovely..."

Oh, how dare he! She pushed him away in disgust at such a casual and banal suggestion after being gone for years...or maybe it was in fear of her own feelings, which had been quivering hotly just under the surface since she caught sight of him. If he had "meessed" her so, why hadn't he called? Why hadn't he come to see her as soon as he got back? And how could he approach her like this, with a new girlfriend in tow?

"You animal," was all she said. He seemed stunned by her reaction and, apparently thinking she didn't mean it—was she simply acting coy?—pulled her close again and began to say something else. Just then Clare walked in, and Annie left abruptly. Margo was standing just outside the door, an odd smile playing on her face, and turned away as Annie passed her. That was the last time Annie ever talked to Carlo. But why? What was she afraid of? Her own feelings for him? Was it jealousy, after all this time? The art crowd parties were never the same without him, yet now that he was back, she couldn't make herself go. Was it because he always had that girl in tow? Clare seemed puzzled and asked why she never showed up, but

Annie wasn't able to tell her. After all, if she kept it a secret while it lasted, what earthly use would there be to tell anyone after it was over?

A realization suddenly hits Annie with full force. *If anyone found out about Carlo and me now, wouldn't they connect me to the murder?* Wouldn't they wonder if she, in a fit of jealousy, killed Carlo?

CHAPTER 7

"'Tis in my memory lock'd,
and you yourself shall keep the key of it."
(from *Hamlet*)

Annie sighs and gets up and puts the sleeping Augustus down in his basket. What is she to do to keep from going crazy? Looking for a distraction, she goes out to her studio (when she was doing her jewelry she called it "the smithy"; these days it's "the bindery"), which is located in a separate small outbuilding with a rickety porch that overhangs the harbor. She used to rent out the little studio as a kitchenette in the summer, and use the large studio attached to the other side of the house for herself; but when she started working at the library, she decided to rent out the larger studio instead, since she could get twice as much for it. Since then, she's found the little studio quite satisfactory.

One corner is still dedicated to jewelry making. Rats' nests of silver wire in various gauges huddle among collections of beads. There are small jars of amber, jade, lapis lazuli, and carved cinnabar; larger jars gleaming with Czech glass beads and Venetian millefiore; all lined up on the workbench. The bench also holds a small anvil, a gift from her father on her fifteenth birthday. The jewelry corner has been gathering dust lately, and she walks past it over to the bindery section.

Actually, it was Carlo who got her started in bookbinding. Annie had been into papermaking and marbling in order to provide cheap gift-wraps for her shop, when Carlo asked her to mend an old book he had. The book needed the torn marbled endpapers replaced and a bit of glue to restore the spine.

"Ah, bellissimo, cara," he had said when she handed it to him. And that's all there was to it. She had fixed his book, and kept going from there.

Floor-to-ceiling racks on the far wall hold screens of many sizes that Annie uses for papermaking; all with a brass wire "Q" neatly embroidered in one corner to create her personal watermark. Jars with dried onionskins, rose petals, lavender seeds, tealeaves, and other odd bits are kept in a wall cupboard between windows that look out into the yard through foliage and fragrant blooms of pink eglantine.

The long worktable is divided into three stations: cut and fold, sew and finish, and a pasting area. Annie rattles around in the room, trying to steer her brain away from the only thing it wants to concentrate on.

Who killed Carlo?

No, she mustn't think about Carlo, especially about Carlo being dead. She came here to forget, to let him slip under the surface of her consciousness, the way a shrouded body silently slips into the deep blue fathoms. Annie throws herself into a project that will occupy her, mind and body, until she is mentally ready to accept his death.

Paradoxically, the project will end up being something that touches on Carlo, something that will celebrate his life.

The specifics will come to her once she gets her hands busy. She clears off a large work surface, covers it with a plastic shower curtain, and lifts up the big wooden marbling tray. She will start her new project by making a special pair of matched end-papers. In the haphazard way of a practiced chef, she processes Carragheenan moss—Irish seaweed that acts a thickener—and some water in a blender before adding it to the large pot of water on the stove. In twelve hours, she will again add more water, and the "size" will be ready. Then she will start the marbling.

What next? Annie looks around in agitation. *She must keep busy, and not think.* She finds the paper she is looking for: oatmeal colored, with little inclusions of rosemary needles (for remembrance) and tiny pink gillyflower petals (for bonds of affection.) She folds the papers two sheets at a time. Once they are sewn together, that will be the thickness of the book.

Suddenly she feels exhausted and covers the table with a large, clean sheet to keep dust and spiders from falling on her project. She checks the burner, turns off the lights, and goes back out in the yard, trembling slightly after the concentrated effort.

Maybe I'll take a walk. Let the wind blow through my hair, she thinks. Annie finds that walks calm her when she is upset—which isn't often. The year after Carlo left, she took a lot of them, trying to forget him. Now it seems she will have to start over again. But it's not the same, is it? Back then, there was always the *possibility* that he might return. Now there is nothing left to still the agitated beating of her heart. Not even hope.

CHAPTER 8

"Like a red morn, that ever yet betoken'd
Wrack to the seaman, tempest to the field."
(from *Venus and Adonis*)

Annie leaves through the kitchen door. It is late afternoon, and the weather is changing. "Sunshine in the morning, sailor's warning" seems to be holding true today. A wind has come up suddenly, and there are whitecaps on the swells in the bay. Annie has sauntered up Atlantic Avenue to the Headlands, and now stands on the highest point. From here you can look out to the open sea, the sea that claimed her parents. Annie had stood here then, waiting, just as the fishermen's wives of old had done, her eyes trying to penetrate the heavy fog, hoping to see her father's small motorboat returning to harbor. When the family still lived in Pigeon Cove, he'd had a one-string permit for lobstering, but had given it up when they moved in-town. That day, her parents had just gone out for a pleasure trip, armed with a picnic basket. It was their wedding anniversary. An unexpected gale, followed by the dense fog, turned the 'sunshine in the morning' into a hazardous situation all too familiar to people living on the seashore. It was three days before their bodies were found. Annie and her brother scattered the ashes right off the Headlands. For a long time Annie was not able to go back out onto these rocky ledges to look out over the cruel sea. The pain was simply too unbearable. But today she feels closer to her parents here than anywhere else.

Now she turns to look at the harbor and Bearskin Neck. "Babson, Babson killed the bear, with his hands I do declare," it says on the old sign above the Pewter Shop. Babson was one of the first settlers, and this is supposed to be how Bearskin Neck got its name. Well, so goes one legend, anyway. Annie's eyes are drawn across the harbor, past the small yachts and sailboats that dot the surface, riding on the chop coming in through the narrow inlet between the Headlands' jetty and the tip of the Bearskin Neck breakwater.

From where she stands, she can see the back of Carlo's gallery and the screened porch where they could sit in privacy and have a long, cool drink in the evening while they watched the boats return to harbor. Rockport may be a dry town, but Annie and most of the people who live here are no teetotalers. Many people who vote against making "likker" legal do so mainly to keep the gentle, old-time atmosphere of the town unchanged. Bars and package stores would, according to some, bring noise and carousing, neon signs, (which are still illegal in town), and beer cans strewn all over the place. It is also pointed out that the teenagers' summer jobs as waiters in restaurants—one of the few opportunities available for young people in the town— would be limited to those over eighteen, which is the required age for being able to legally serve alcohol. Be that as it may, Gloucester, with which Rockport shares the island, is only a five-minute drive away; and some of the package stores even deliver. So "demon rum" runs freely in Rockport anyway.

Carlo's gallery is taped off all around with yellow tape. Officer Hale is standing on the lawn, looking out over the harbor. He turns his head toward the Headlands, and Annie wishes she had some shrubbery to sink back into. Instead, she turns and walks across the cliffs, following an indistinct path across granite ledges down toward Old Garden Beach. The waves are crashing over Big Haystack, a large rock that nature has planted there to test kids, providing them with a challenge to climb the steep, slippery sides to reach the top. Another rock, dubbed Little Haystack, is totally submerged. Right now nobody is in the water, which is getting quite rough. All the small boats still out on the bay are heading toward shore.

When a sudden gust rips at her loosened hair and floppy linen pants, Annie turns out of the wind. A skindiver appears on the ramp up from the beach, carrying a net bag with some dark green shapes in it. "Lobstah dinnah" coming up. The shellfish constable, who often sits nearby in a van, isn't here today to check if they're legal size. Some of the lobstermen claim that divers raid their traps, but the divers insist that it's easier to pick the lobsters off the ocean floor than it is to try to get them out of the traps. Lobstering is the last remnant of what used to be a thriving fishing industry in Rockport. The once great Gloucester fishing fleet is also a memory, although Gloucester-ites continue to sport a harbor that looks as though they expect the situation to be reversed at any moment.

Annie walks up Harraden Avenue and takes a right turn. When she reaches the top of Atlantic Avenue, she sees two police cruisers leaving Carlo's place. *I should have taken a walk somewhere else*, she thinks. However, as she makes her way along the street, she can't help turning her head towards the Neck whenever she comes to an open space between the houses. Carlo's place seems to have been deserted, but the yellow tape is still up, flapping in the stiff breeze.

She enters her yard through the blue gate, walks along the false bamboo hedge over to the fence, and looks out over the harbor. The water is rough all the way into the inner harbor wall at the edge of her yard. Waves are breaking on the rocks below her, casting their salty spray in her face. As usual, she goes in by the kitchen door. This is how she misses the envelope that is taped to the front door.

CHAPTER 9

"Go hence and have more talk of these sad things.
Some shall be pardon'd, and some punished."
(from *Romeo and Juliet*)

After changing into T-shirt and a pair of comfortable flannel pajama bottoms, Annie calls the library. Penny, one of the part-time library assistants at the circulation desk, answers, her voice bright and eager. Annie asks for Clare.

"Is this Annie?" Penny says, the voice suddenly hesitant.

"Yes, Penny. Is Clare there?"

"Um, well, let me check." Penny covers the receiver while she checks. It's taking her a long time. Maybe Clare is in the dungeon, or in the director's office, or on the toilet. When Penny finally comes back on the line, she starts by clearing her throat.

"Ahem. Annie? Are you still there?" Penny sounds officious.

"I'm still here, Penny."

"Aah, well, people have been here looking for you...."

"What 'people' is that, Penny?" Annie asks.

"The police," Penny says softly, and Annie imagines her holding a hand over the receiver.

"The police? What about?"

"They didn't say. Mr. Langmuir told them you weren't feeling well and had gone home. They came back and said you weren't home, either. Where are you calling from, Annie?"

"From home. Maybe you'd better connect me with Mr. Langmuir, Penny."

"He's gone for the day. Do you still want to talk to Clare? She just came back from the coffee shop."

"Please. Thanks, Penny."

"No problem. Hope everything's okay."

"I'm sure it is, Penny."

Clare's voice when she comes on is slightly breathless. "Hi, Annie. I was wondering what happened to you. Weren't we going to meet this afternoon?"

"Yes—sorry. I wasn't feeling well, so Duncan let me go home. What's going on over there?"

"Going on? You know me, all alone up in my hidey-hole. I never hear anything. Do you mean about Carlo? I can't imagine who would want to kill him, Annie. Why? I mean, we all loved Carlo, right? I just can't understand it. I thought it was great— everyone did—when he came back. You know, parties were always so much more fun when he was there. Don't you agree? Oh, God, Annie, I don't want to start getting maudlin, here," she says. "So, anyway, are you okay?" Clare sounds solicitous.

"I'm fine. Nothing contagious. I'd love some company, though. How'd you like to stop over after work? I'll supply a glass of something cold and give you my short list of book preferences—those *Elder Law* books, for instance. I've got the list here at home."

"Oh—sure, Annie." Clare hesitates a moment. "I'll be over around seven, say?"

"Fine. Thanks, Clare." Annie hangs up and goes to check if there's anything edible around that doesn't need to be cooked. There's a knock on the door, and she slips into a purple silk kimono with an embroidered dragon on the back, and remembers with a sudden pang that it was Carlo who gave it to her. Years ago she admired it in the window of the Chinese shop on the Neck, and when she went upstairs that night, the kimono was draped across the bed. She ties the belt with a violent tug and slips into a pair of flip-flops on the way to the hall, shaking her head at a fleeting image in the mirror. Her curly, windblown hair stands out like a red tent around her head. She usually gathers it into a loose knot for work—without ever succeeding in achieving the stereotypical, sedate image of a reference librarian: tightly wound topknot, steel rimmed glasses, tweed skirt and sensible shoes—but there's no time to do anything about it now.

When she opens the door, Officer Hale is standing outside.

"Oh, hi, Billy," she says.

Officer William Hale is in his thirties, tall and blond, ruddy-faced. Must be some Scandinavian blood in there somewhere, Annie thinks. Works out, judging by the muscle mass. He's always been helpful to Annie, as when she ran out of gas on Nugent's Stretch recently.

"Hello, Miss Quitnot."

"*Miss Quitnot?* What ever happened to Annie? What can I do for you, Billy?" she says.

"I just have a couple of questions. May I come in, or would you feel more comfortable coming down the station?"

"The station? Why, what for?"

"I see you're not dressed. Do you want me to wait outside while you get dressed?"

"No, no. Come on in, Billy."

"Oh, I almost forgot. I found this taped to your door," he says, and hands her an envelope. Annie puts it on the dining table on the way to the alcove, where she quickly changes back into the comfortably wrinkled linen pantsuit she wore to work earlier. Officer Hale waits in the hall while Annie gets dressed. As soon as she gets outside she realizes she's still wearing her flip-flops. Oh, well.

The ride to the little granite building on Broadway that houses the police station takes only a couple of minutes. It would probably have taken four minutes to walk. Soon, the Rockport police will move into their new headquarters on Upper Main Street, palatial in comparison, where they'll be able to screen every car that comes into town. Unless the driver is aware of the back roads, of course.

Before they get out of the cruiser, the officer turns to Annie.

"Miss Quitnot…it would be better—when we get inside, I mean—if you would address me as Officer Hale," he says. Then he steps out and holds the door open for her. Annie is too flustered to notice the man with a camera sitting a van in the parking lot. She and Officer Hale walk into a small interview room with a wooden table and chairs. Annie nods to Chief Murphy, who sticks his head in the door for a moment. When he disappears, he leaves the door open. Officer Hale pulls out a chair for her.

"Please take a seat. Now, Miss Quitnot, can you tell me where you were this morning between three and seven?"

"In bed, of course," she says, but it suddenly hits her why she is here. That's the kind of question the police ask of a murder suspect.

"I don't suppose there's anyone who can verify that?" Officer Hale asks.

"No, I live by myself. What makes you think I had anything to do with it?"

Officer Hale studies her face for a moment. "Anything to do with what?"

"Carlo's murder. That's what this is all about, isn't it?"

"We've had two people come forward suggesting you as a suspect."

"What? Who?" she stammers, stunned.

"I can't tell you that."

"So much for the right to face your accuser."

"This is not a courtroom. Let me ask you this then, Miss Quitnot: did you kill Carlo Valenti?" Officer Hale asks, his voice neutral, as if she were just a stranger.

"Of course not, Billy! For God's sake, you know me! What kind of insanity is this?" Annie starts rising from her chair in agitation.

"Please sit down, Miss Quitnot. You must understand, we have no choice but to act on it when someone comes forward and makes an accusation that sounds credible."

"Credible! Why would I want to kill Carlo?"

He looks at her levelly. "People kill for all kinds of reasons. Jealousy, for instance."

"This is crazy. Am I under arrest?"

"Not at the moment. Am I to understand, then, that you *deny* killing Carlo Valenti?"

Annie feels tears well up in her eyes again. Fiercely she fights them off. "Of course I deny it! Don't you have to have some evidence before you arrest someone?"

"Like I just said, Miss Quitnot, you are not under arrest. However, for the moment we must ask you not to leave town."

Annie does not smile or nod to either Officer Hale or Chief Murphy before leaving the station. She is both incensed and terrified, not to mention mortified. And what's happened to Billy? The chief must have given him some severe instructions. So, the chief must think she's a plausible suspect. Who would have suggested it to him? *Two people?* And now she has to *run* home, or she'll miss Clare again. It is three minutes before seven.

Clare is late, however, and Annie has time to change back into the T-shirt and pajama bottoms. She sets glasses, ice, and tonic on a tray, and gets the gin (Gordon's, of course, like in *The African Queen*) from a cupboard that also holds a bottle of rum (with a homemade label that says "Hannah Jumper's Private Stock") and a half full bottle of Punt e Mes—a bitter Italian vermouth that was Carlo's favorite; the bottle should have been thrown out long ago. Years, in fact. Annie puts the tray on the dining table. That's when she sees the envelope that Officer Hale handed her earlier. She rips it open, unfolds the note, and reads the message, which is printed in capital letters:

I KNOW ALL ABOUT YOU AND CARLO.

CHAPTER 10

"A glooming peace this morning with it brings:
The sun for sorrow will not show his head."
(from *Romeo and Juliet*)

*R*EFERENCE LIBRARIAN QUESTIONED IN VALENTI
SLAYING, the headline reads. There is a picture of Annie, wild-haired and disheveled-looking, being led by the arm
into the police station by Officer Hale. The brief article is full
of salacious bits of information. *Onetime lovers...jealousy possible
motive,* etc.

"Oh, Gussie, who's doing this to me?" Annie hugs Augustus, who snarls sympathetically. Where are they getting their
information? From the same person who wrote the note? Who
could it possibly be that knew about Carlo and her?

By the time she stopped by last night, Clare knew that the
police were looking for Annie. *Penny's doing, no doubt,* Annie
thinks. So, naturally, Annie was forced to tell her about the
visit to the police station. Clare shook her head sympathetically, and then tried to make light of the whole thing, telling
Annie to forget about it—the police were probably questioning
half the town's population by now. *Easy to say yesterday, when she*

knew nothing of Carlo's and my relationship, Annie thinks. Will Clare be as confident today, after reading the paper?

Annie has lain awake most of the night, alternately crying at old memories that haunted her, and worrying about her predicament. *Two people have come forward,* Billy Hale had said. Who on earth could they be? Duncan and Josie were the only people who knew about her relationship with Carlo. Annie had confided in Duncan, and Josie had once intimated that Carlo had told *her*—but neither of them would have called the police. And now she has to get ready for work. After the newspaper article, the worst part will be facing everyone in the library. Especially the director. Duncan Langmuir likes to keep the atmosphere in the library calm and pleasant—"it should be an *oasis* for the townspeople," he frequently reminds the staff—and discourages gossip and scandals and anything else that might upset this soothing ambience. Now the library's very reputation is on the line because of her. Funding a necessary increase in the library budget (without which state funds will be withheld) might be denied at town meeting, donations might dry up…. Maybe she should take some time off until the whole thing gets cleared up? She will talk to Duncan about it.

It never occurs to her that she might be *forced* to take a leave, but that is what confronts her when she arrives at work. Apparently a discussion has taken place. It is not clear to her who was involved—whether the police had anything to do with it, or the library trustees, or the town selectmen, or people working at the library, or patrons—but a suggestion has been made that Annie should be suspended with pay for the time being. In his office up on the second floor, Langmuir closes the door that is always left open and assures her that he intends to disregard the suggestion; but Annie calmly says she will accept it, telling him she was already considering taking some time off voluntarily.

"Call in a substitute. I'll stay away. It's better than having the whole town come in and gawk—and I have a feeling that's what will happen, now that the word is out. I'd love to know who suggested my name to the police, though. I just can't imagine who would have."

"Annie, I'm so sorry about all this," Duncan says. "You know you have my full confidence. If there's anything I can do, I'm just a phone call away. All right? Promise you'll call if you need anything?" Annie nods and takes the elevator down to the dungeon to collect her personal belongings from the locker. While she waits for the elevator to come, she sees the children's librarian, Stuart Cogswell, at his desk. She sticks her head in the door.

"Hi, Stu," she says. He looks up and gives her an automatic smile, the kind that has no warmth or sincerity behind it.

"Annie. How are you?"

"Fine, thanks. How's Ariel?"

"She died yesterday. Found her floating belly-up, dead."

Annie walks over and looks into the fish tank. Ariel was a popular angelfish that had developed a wobbly swim, probably an air bladder problem. There is only one fish left in the aquarium now, a neon tetra named Flounder.

"Sorry, Stu. The kids will be upset."

"Right." Cogswell seems preoccupied, and Annie retreats toward the door.

"Just stopped in to say bye, Stuart. Taking a few days off."

"Sounds like a good idea, under the circumstances." He picks up a folder and opens it, as though he has more important things to do than chat with Annie. She takes the hint but has one more thing to say.

"Just wanted to say that if any of the kids have a reference question and need some help, please tell them they can call me at home," she says, and gets another automatic smile.

"Well, now. Thank you for the offer, but I'm afraid I can't take you up on that."

"Why not, Stu?" Annie asks.

"How do you think the parents would react if I told the kids to call someone who...aah..."

"...might be a murderer?" Annie finishes for him in disbelief." You can't believe that, Stuart!"

He gives her a supercilious smile. "Doesn't matter what I believe, my dear Annie. People read the paper, you know. But I thank you, as I said, for the offer. Now, I'd better get busy. Hope this blows over quickly."

"Thanks for your confidence," Annie hisses under her breath as she steps into the elevator.

In the dungeon she empties her locker, then checks the fridge for any leftovers she may have stashed in there that might grow strange molds in her absence. She hears footsteps, and Esa Kauppila walks in. Esa is the library janitor, a sweet boy of Finnish ancestry. He is not really a boy—being nearly Annie's age—but still looks and acts like one. He has the high cheekbones and deep-set blue eyes of the Finnish, but not the liveliness; Esa has been shortchanged as far as wit and intellect goes. But he is good at his job, friendly, and helpful; and he always looks out for Annie, keeping her desk clean and her leather chair polished.

"I know you didn't do it, Miss Annie," he whispers, even though no one else is there. Annie gives him a sad but grateful smile and tilts her head a little, touched by his loyalty.

"Thank you, Esa. I was just leaving; I'll be gone for a few days. Take good care of the reference department for me." Esa smiles and nods eagerly.

Annie feels a strange bitterness as she goes up the stairs and casts a last look toward her desk before stepping out into the broad sunlight. She's filled with misgivings. She can't even deal with the shock of Carlo's death, and now, on top of it, she has to cope with people thinking that she killed him.

CHAPTER 11

"Let there be gall enough in thy ink."
(from *Twelfth Night*)

Annie goes straight home and takes Gussie out for a "walk," which means she is carrying him like a baby, letting him down now and then to sniff around for messages from his friends. When he is finished with his business, they go back home and Gussie, exhausted, lies down for a nap. Annie goes out to the bindery and checks on the *size*. When it is properly adjusted, she pours the liquid into the marbling tray.

All preparations are made. Annie has tested that the size is the right temperature and that the inks have the proper amount of oxgall in order to float and spread properly on the surface. Now she dips little wisps, broken off from her corn broom, in the ink and splatters it evenly over the surface, one color at a time, watching it spread. She has chosen dark green, magenta, turquoise, vivid yellow, burnt orange, and white. When the surface is completely covered in what is called the "Turkish Stone" pattern, she picks up her *rake,* pulls it down across the surface the long way, and then the long way in the opposite direction, a small distance over. She continues raking and combing in a precise order until she has the pattern she wants, a

"Bouquet." Annie takes one sheet of the treated paper and lays it down slowly and evenly over the surface so she won't cause any ripples, then carefully picks it up with thumb and forefinger from diagonally opposite corners. She rinses it and scans it quickly to make sure it is good, then proceeds immediately to make a second one, as similar as possible to the first one.

Annie spends the next hour making additional papers with other patterns – "Peacock" and "Snail" and some freehand designs. Then something changes—the temperature or the humidity, or maybe there's too much oxgall in the ink. She runs into problems with air bubbles, and with the ink not spreading; and then, when she thins the ink, it spreads too much. Maybe it's not the temperature, the humidity or the ink. Maybe there's some kind of black cloud floating above her head.

She goes back in to check on Gussie, who is snoring happily, and decides to get out of the house for a while. Dogtown is a great place to go when you want to be alone. It makes up the center of the island, consisting of three thousand or so acres of woodland dotted with old granite quarries and water reservoirs that mirror the sky, shiny eyes of the forest. The early settlers are long gone from here, along with their cattle and even the dogs that gave the area its name. If you are a stranger and want to explore the woods, you'll need a minimum of three things: a map, a water bottle, and a machete—at least if you plan to go off the beaten path. The woods are riddled with catbrier and other nasty underbrush. And then, of course, there are the bug-ridden swamps.

Annie is familiar with the woods, after walking them for years. There are many ways to get into Dogtown, old fire roads and walking trails; some marked, some not. Some trails peter out and lead nowhere. Today she decides to go up Summit Avenue, across Hospital Hill, and into the woods toward Briar Swamp. She crosses the WPA dam that runs alongside the swamp, where she spots a scarlet tanager. The woods are quiet now, not like early in the morning when they are full of birdsong. She sits down on the edge of the Toneatti boardwalk, a wooden walkway at the edge of the swamp, and pours coffee into the thermos cup. The pitcher plants are blooming, and she watches as a small insect tries to crawl out of the pitcher. The little beetle's progress is hampered by the fine hairs that grow on the plant's inside wall, ingeniously pointed down and trapping the prey forever. *Poor thing. Trapped, just like I am.* She puts her finger inside the pitcher and tries to help the little creature to crawl out, but instead he falls into the water, doomed. The enzymes instantly start to dissolve it, and soon the plant will absorb it. She doesn't want to draw another simile here. Instead, she gets up and puts the thermos in her backpack.

Annie continues her walk past Whale's Jaw, one of the big rocks called *erratics* dumped by the glacier. Whale's Jaw actually used to look like the wide-open jaws of a whale until a hiker decided to light a campfire beside it, which caused the lower jaw to crack and fall down. The day after it happened Annie went up to look, and found herself peeking under the broken rock to see if the hiker's feet might be sticking out somewhere.

She jogs across blueberry-covered hills, down into ravines and gullies where streams flow and ferns grow. The image of Carlo dances cruelly in front of her—the sturdy frame that could still run silently on the forest trail; those strong, swaying arms holding branches aside for her; the back of his neck running with sweat, the hair curling at the edges. Finally, she ends up over in Pigeon Cove. Pigeon Cove is said to have received its name from a large flock of unfortunate pigeons that washed ashore there in a storm. The Cove is officially a section of the town of Rockport, although the "Covers" (pronounced to rhyme with "rovers") don't think so. They consider it going "out of town" when they head for downtown Rockport, which they do reluctantly. It goes both ways, of course—many downtowners think of the Covers as some strange form of Canadians. The Covers are a breed of their own, and sometimes talk of "seceding" from Rockport. These days, this kind of talk is mostly in good fun, but you can sense a certain amount of rivalry between the different cultures on the island even now, several generations removed from the immigrant fathers.

The island was named "Cap aux Isles," *Cape of Islands,* by Champlain. Later it was renamed "Cape Ann" in honor of America's colonial queen, Queen Anne. Among the early immigrants were Scandinavian stonecutters, Finns and Swedes and Norwegians, many of whom settled in the Cove. The north side of Front Beach used to be called "the Finn end," and Forest Street was long known as "Finn Alley." The Swedes and the Finns had their own churches in the old days, where they showed up sober on Sundays.

On the southern part of the island lived the Gloucester fishermen, who were mainly Portuguese—many from the Azores—and Italians. The descendants of the Italians still speak Sicilian, which they pronounce Sicili*án*. You can still hear Sicilian spoken if you go into some of the bakeries or coffee shops in downtown Gloucester. The fishermen celebrate St. Peter's Fiesta in June of each year. The celebration lasts through five days of "spirited" feasting, ending on the last day with an outdoor Mass and followed by the Religious Procession: the marching of the statue of St. Peter through the streets, accompanied by a parade of carnation-covered cars; and the Blessing of the Fleet (or remnants thereof) at Stacy Boulevard. The Fiesta includes a gaudy and noisy carnival in St. Peter's Square, the Seine Boat Races, and the ever popular "Greasy Pole" event, which is traditionally won by someone of Italian ancestry with a name like Brancaleone, Misuraca, Favazza, Giambanco, Curcuru, or Frontiero. Young men walk out on the greasy pole, which sits permanently installed high above the water at Pavilion Beach, with a flag attached at the end of it. The horizontal pole is thickly covered with gobs of black axle grease, and the challenge is to be the first one to make it to the end of the pole and grab the flag. Before the competition starts, the young macho men of Gloucester usually imbibe enough so that they will feel no pain when they fall and hit various parts of their anatomy on the pole. There are rafts of boats in a circle underneath, ready to rescue anyone knocked senseless. It is a tradition that nobody is supposed to win in the first round, but after that it's a free-for-all. Sometimes it takes six or seven rounds, with ever-more trembling legs increasing the risk of injury to the family jewels.

There was also an Irish contingent in Rockport that caused a ruckus every payday—and let's not forget the Polish. These days, there is a plethora of Russians, Bulgarians, Hungarians, Japanese, Chinese, Koreans, and Middle Easterners moving in. Rockport is becoming quite the cosmopolitan place.

Well, Annie herself is a mixture of Irish, Italian and English, which may account for her red hair and quaint name, her emotional temperament, and her passion for Shakespeare.

Her mother was an immigrant, born in Ireland, and her father's family came from England, although there must have been an Irishman somewhere back there, too, since the name Quitnot is Irish. Annie's paternal grandmother was Italian, which gave Carlo a great deal of satisfaction. She remembers suddenly how Carlo once tried to figure out the exact proportional mixture of Irish and English and Italian their children would have, if— and here Annie collapses and sinks down on a boulder, unable to keep going.

CHAPTER 13

"For he being dead, with him is beauty slain
And beauty dead, black chaos comes again."
(from *Venus and Adonis*)

When she is able to resume her hike, she heads north. After a while the woods thin out, and Annie reaches an open area of hayfields and paddocks. She walks through a gently sloping meadow, edged with buttercups and rustling pods of bloomed-out lupines. In the distance there is an old, well-kept house surrounded by barns, a flower garden, and a large orchard; and when Annie gets closer she sees Josie Mandel sitting in the shade of an apple tree—two gnarled figures grown old together. Annie waves when Josie turns towards her, and the old woman squints, trying to see who it is. Not wanting to be rude, Annie walks up to the fence.

"Hi, Josie. It's Annie Quitnot. I don't know if you remember me." Josie looks ancient today, her face creased and leathery, but there are still hints of the beauty she once was. Josie spends much of her days outdoors, tending her garden. Her hair, which still has streaks of black in the gray, is gathered in a bun at the back of her neck. She has a kind of ageless beauty that reminds Annie of Georgia O'Keeffe. Annie hasn't seen Josie up close since her days with Carlo, who had been one of Josie's protégés. Josie had financed the buying of his gallery, which had only been an old fish shack at the time. Carlo lived in it while he fixed it up. Once he and Annie became lovers, he had been happy to eat—and sleep—at Annie's place.

"Of course I remember you, Annie. Won't you stop in for a while?" Josie says. Annie reluctantly opens the gate. If Josie hasn't heard about Carlo, Annie doesn't want to be the bearer of bad news.

Josie is still sharp as a tack, however, and has read the paper. Which means that she also has read about Annie. Her old but alert eyes study Annie's face while they both start off with platitudes: "Oh, isn't it terrible," and "How could something like that have happened here?" and finally, "Of course I know you didn't do it, dear." Then Josie looks away, focusing somewhere in the distance.

"I always thought he was my...best investment, you know. That he would go places, make it big." She pinches her lips together in a straight line, as though she is trying to keep them from trembling. Annie, who has had enough of crying and is trying to get away from her own emotional turmoil, nevertheless bends down and puts her arm around Josie.

"But he did, Josie! He was very successful in Rome—had a good reputation at the academy there. And the prize at the Biennale, that was a very great achievement. He had a couple of shows on Newbury Street in the last few years, even though he himself wasn't in the country; you must know about that."

"Of course, dear. He's been up here often since he returned, and I know all that. You know, when he first came back, he was talking about opening a local art school for young kids, "*catch them before they learn wrong,*" he said. When I told him that they have classes for kids at the Art Society, he looked sort of disappointed; but then he said he was talking about a *real* art school, not just a week or two of summer classes. I don't think he thought of himself as any great success in the art world—and that's what counts, you know. I wish he hadn't brought that Margo with him." Annie doesn't want to think at all about Margo, even less talk about her.

"He was fond of you still," Josie continues, cryptically, looking up at Annie. "I'd like to show you something he gave me, Annie, and tell you what he said," she confides and starts to get up, but Annie doesn't want to hear this either. She feels sudden pain radiating like fire in all directions of her body, pounding her brain and tugging at her heart.

"Josie, let's not do that now. I'll come back soon and we can talk more about it, when we've calmed down a little. I don't want you to upset yourself." Josie nods, and Annie sits down and listens numbly to the old woman, who now seems to be talking to herself, reminiscing, oblivious of Annie's presence.

"Would you like a cup of coffee?" Josie says finally. "Dot should be here anytime to take my blood pressure, and she usually stays for a cup."

Annie shakes her head. "Maybe next time, Josie. Dot's a sweet girl, isn't she? Her grandfather just gave her one of your husband's watercolors, she told me."

"How nice. Yes, Judge bought several of my husband's art works. It gave Grant a real boost at the time. Well, don't be a stranger, Annie," Josie says.

"I promise to stop by again real soon. Right now I do have to get back."

Annie waves from the gate, then follows the dirt road down the hill, weaving her way along the side streets down to Granite Street, where she crosses Keystone Bridge—the "demarcation line" between Pigeon Cove and Rockport. Some people think it's amazing that nobody has set up a tollbooth on the bridge yet.

Annie stops on the middle of the bridge and looks out over Gull Cove. She wonders what it was that Josie wanted to tell her. What could Carlo possibly have said about her? That he was feeling sorry for her? Did he comment about her looking older, or about her not having found anyone else, after being deprived of her great lover? Had he told Josie that he invited Annie to join him in Italy, but that she refused? Oh, she really didn't want to know. She couldn't stand the idea that Carlo may have pitied her.

When Annie gets home, she stops in only long enough to see the answering machine blinking. She ignores it, goes out and gets into her car, an old blue Chevy with rust spots (which she carefully paints over every year in order to get her sticker renewed). She just wants to run away from it all. Going up South Street and past Lane's farm, she keeps going along the ocean side of the island, past the beaches. Cape Hedge and Long Beach, which she can see from the road, are wall-to-wall with sunbathers and beach umbrellas and kite fliers. Suddenly she notices a flashing blue light in her rear view mirror, and pulls over to the side of the road. Officer Hale walks up to her window.

"What did I do now?" she asks, exasperated. "I know I wasn't driving too fast. My car knows the speed limit on this road real well, Billy."

"No, Miss Quitnot, your speed was fine. Where are you headed?" *Miss Quitnot, again. This is getting tiresome,* she thinks.

"Grocery store—my fridge is empty," she says.

"You weren't trying to skip town, by any chance?"

"Skip town?" she says, incredulous. Officer Hale points to the Gloucester town line sign up ahead. "I thought skipping town meant leaving the state, or the country, or something like that," she says feebly when the light dawns.

"We do have a grocery store in Rockport, you know."

"I can't show my face at IGA" (she pronounces it *iggah,* like most locals do) "right now."

Officer Hale studies her for a moment.

"Well, as long as you promise just to go to the grocery store. If your car isn't back at your house in a couple of hours, I'll have to report it. Orders."

Annie tries to say thank you, but chokes on it, and as soon as the officer steps away from her car she peels out and speeds off down the street. *What am I going to do,* she thinks, trying to steer out of a wild skid. *Who did this? Who killed Carlo…and is someone trying to frame me?*

CHAPTER 14

"Three-pil'd hyperboles, spruce affectation,
Figures pedantical."
(from *Love's Labors Lost*)

"Annie, where are you? We're waiting for you," Duncan Langmuir says. He sounds a little impatient. "Didn't you get my message?"

"Oh, sorry, Dunc, there must be twenty messages on my phone. I listened to a couple, and then I just erased them all."

"That bad? Anyway, we're all sitting here with our coffee. Are you coming?"

It's Thursday, librarian coffee night, and this week it's Duncan's turn. She had totally forgotten, of course. Every week they get together for an informal and mostly social cup of coffee, sorting out the problems of the world and discussing good books.

"If you really want me to come I can be there in five minutes." Annie sounds reluctant.

"Of course we do," Duncan says, emphatically.

Duncan lives in a great Victorian house—complete with a widows-walk, making it one of the early captain's houses—in the center of town, not far from the library. Due to his enormous collection of books, which are resting on gleaming floor-to-ceiling mahogany shelves in the great room that takes up most of the first floor, the librarians sometimes refer to his home as the *branch library* (not to be confused with *the library annex,* which is the book hut next to the swap shop at the dump, where townies with dump stickers on their cars can drop off or pick up books for free).

How Duncan came by this house is a story he has told the staff piecemeal at their Thursday get-togethers. However, since Stuart joined the library, Duncan—and Annie, too—have been less forthcoming with personal information. The rest of the members of the group don't appear to notice the difference, but Annie misses the easy congeniality of the early days. Stuart puts a damper on the proceedings with his supercilious air and snide comments.

Duncan Langmuir was born in Iowa, fathered by a vacationing English don from some London college. The father went back to London—without marrying the mother—before the baby was born. He did, however, confer on Duncan his last name, and sent money regularly for his keep. Duncan played in the sunny Iowa cornfields until he was ten, when his mother died in a car accident. The father promptly imported the boy to London, sight unseen, brought him up, and saw to his education. Later, Duncan started out as an assistant history professor at Oxford, but his love of books soon pulled his career in a different direction, and he ended up in libraries. In his late thirties he took a vacation in the States, wanting to take a look at his roots and perhaps searching for another turn in the road. Finding Iowa not as he remembered it, he flew east on a whim, to visit the Boston Public Library and see the Puvis de Chavannes and John Singer Sargent murals that he had read about, murals and frescoes being Langmuir's other special interest.

Before moving to the States, Langmuir had made several trips to the European continent to see ancient Italian frescoes "in person." Some day, he thought, he would like to go back to Italy—to revisit Turin, where he had eaten the best food he could ever remember; then continue to the Tuscan countryside: to the stark valleys, *the country of the pointed cypress trees* that he had fallen in love with; and finally on to Florence and Venice to see his favorite frescoes again before they were lost to humanity. *We can fly to the moon, but we can't salvage our own history,* was his comment.

While he was in Boston, an "opportunity he could not refuse" presented itself at the library. He remained there happily for a few years, living in a small, second-floor flat on Exeter Street. He learned that Bostonians summered either on the South Shore or on the North Shore, and after trying both, he decided that he preferred the North Shore. When his father died, Duncan turned his inheritance into a healthy down payment on the Victorian house in Rockport, intending it for a summer residence, and perhaps later on for retiring into. The directorship at the Rockport Library became vacant shortly afterwards, and as soon as he had been accepted for the post, the house became his permanent home. Once ensconced in Rockport, he decided that nothing could tempt him away, and unless the trustees fired him (a circumstance which he would do his best to avoid), he would indeed end up retiring there.

Having used up his inheritance by buying the house, he has since lived frugally—as librarians generally do—in order to pay mortgage and taxes and make improvements on the house, much of which he has done with his own hands. His only frivolous expense is the monthly book purchase, when Toad Hall, the local bookstore, gets a visit. Now and then he adds some older volumes picked up during antiquarian forays.

"Come in, come in," Duncan says, greeting Annie warmly, squeezing both her hands in his. This is before they join the others, who are seated in the comfortably worn easy chairs and sofas around the room. To Annie, Langmuir is *"A proper man, as one shall see in a summer's day; a most lovely, gentleman-like man."* She likes to outfit people she knows with Shakespearean descriptions. The director is dressed in tan chinos and a slightly rumpled corduroy jacket. Despite his ascetic appearance and gentle manner, he is an energetic man and, as the improvements to his house show, capable of serious physical labor. His wavy hair is still a dark auburn, with just a sheen of silver at the temples. Langmuir's serious brown eyes study Annie intently before he leads her in to the room.

They are a small and intimate group, regular staff members only; substitutes and part-timers come and go and are not generally included, nor are the pages. Most of the people in the room have worked together for a number of years. Stuart Cogswell is the most recent of them, having joined the library only two years ago. Wearing a suit and tie, shoes impeccably polished, Stuart sits in the wing chair, which puts him somewhat above the rest of them. *Lording it over the group,* Annie thinks. Stuart's face has a faintly aristocratic air, with rather small eyes under wavy, ash blond hair and pale eyebrows; a long nose with narrow nostrils, as though he needs to shut out the smell of his surroundings, and thin, often pursed lips.

Clare, Annie's friend and the library cataloguer, has been with the library almost as long as Annie. Clare's cool blond looks are enough to make any woman envious. She has a slender body and a face like a Greek goddess, but seems in no way conscious of her beauty. She seldom uses make-up and dresses informally, most often in casual slacks and clingy, pastel-colored jersey tops. Marie, the dowager librarian, has been head at the Circulation Desk since time immemorial and is the second oldest of the group. With steel gray hair and a round, pleasant face, she is on the heavy side, and often huffs and puffs going up and down the stairs in the library. Marie is sharing the sofa with Maureen, the white-haired and perennially smiling outreach librarian, who, being in her late eighties, is by far the oldest staff member in the library. In fact, she is older than most of the elderly and housebound patrons she visits and brings books to, and is universally loved.

Sitting by the fireplace, Jean, the library assistant, has chosen a single chair rather than join the others in the sofa. Jean is thin and mousy, the picture of that stereotypical librarian that Annie is not, with steel rimmed glasses and sensible shoes. She does have lovely, violet eyes, and often dresses in purple, but this is unlikely to be noticed by anyone. The only missing member of the group, Duncan's able and efficient assistant, Geri, is out of town to attend a library consortium management meeting; and after that she is going to Florida on vacation.

Duncan pours Annie a cup of coffee, and as usual they all help themselves to the goodies—in this case Duncan's home-made cranberry teacake.

"Well, Annie, we haven't solved any of the world's problems yet. Maybe you can help," Duncan says, subtly lending Annie his support.

"I doubt it. I can't even seem to solve my own," Annie says, looking dispirited.

"Aah, the reference librarian is finally stumped," Stuart says with rather obvious glee. It is general knowledge in the group that Stuart would prefer the Reference Desk to the Children's Desk. He even suggested to Annie once that they should switch, on the theory that "women make better children's' librarians," at which Annie only laughed. She is far from laughing now.

"I haven't read the paper yet; do they have any other suspects?" Marie asks. Annie winces at the word *other*.

"Well, I'm still *at large,* as you see," Annie says, but then goes ahead and tells them how she was stopped by the police and told to remain in town. "I was hoping you could tell *me* the news," she adds. "The paper was sold out by the time I got to the store."

"Basically, there are no new developments," Stuart volunteers, with poorly concealed satisfaction. "Margo—you know I don't personally see any reason why *she* would be a suspect—but in any case, a witness saw Margo step off the eight thirty train, and then she went home to make the gruesome discovery. The girl has nobody, apparently, no family at all, and Carlo was her whole future. Poor girl, so young and vulnerable. She is very upset, of course, and who can blame her. She had been trying to get included in a show on Newbury Street, I understand. I suppose that's what she was returning from when she came back on the train."

Clare, after giving Annie a somewhat furtive look, gets up for more coffee. Stuart crosses and recrosses his legs and fastidiously flicks a dust mote off his sleeve. *"...full of maggot ostentation..."* Annie thinks. *Thanks, Willie, for another perfectly apt description.*

"Other than that, there wasn't much new, I think," Stuart continues obliviously. "Nothing seems to have been taken from the place, so they don't suspect burglary. And, ah well, too bad, no other former girlfriends hiding in the wings, either...that I've heard of, anyway."

Annie groans inwardly. "Great news. Thanks, Stu. I love how they put all this information in the paper. Sounds like *case closed,* somehow."

"Oh, I'm sure it's not as bad as all that," Duncan says. "We're all behind you here, and a number of patrons have called the library in support of you. Give the police time; something's sure to turn up."

"I agree with Duncan," Maureen says, smiling kindly at Annie, "and of course we all know you are innocent."

"Meanwhile, we don't have a reference librarian," Stuart says, and Annie senses immediately that he is angling for her desk.

"Jean is going to fill in for Annie," Duncan responds, "and we're getting a sub to take Jean's place at the circulation desk." Jean smiles nervously.

Good God, Duncan, why? Annie thinks. Jean is always trying to intercept and answer reference questions by herself at the Main Desk, rather than send patrons on to the Reference Desk. Annie can do nothing but sit and watch as Jean drags patrons around the stacks, trying to point out plausible titles or sections to them. Annie has tactfully tried to suggest that since they are always so busy at the Main Desk, Jean shouldn't waste her valuable time, etc., etc. She has even mentioned the problem to Duncan once or twice, but he has only nodded thoughtfully and sympathetically. *Well, maybe he wants Jean to know just what it's like to actually run the Reference Desk? She may be in for a surprise. Jean's very organized, I have to give her that...I just hope she doesn't start reorganizing my files. Another thing is, she's not much of a people person...but she'll do,* Annie decides.

"Actually, doesn't my degree make me the one more qualified?" Stuart asks, with a tinge of ice in his voice.

"Jean is the senior employee, and besides, it's not a permanent replacement," Duncan says with a meager smile, trying to hide his irritation.

"Yet," Stuart says. Annie looks at him, furious. She could strangle him—and suddenly she knows that that's just what he wants. He's baiting her, knowing her temper will flare up. She contains herself and leans back in her chair.

"So, what other world problems have you been working on tonight?" she asks, keeping her voice light. "Have we had any applicants for the page position yet? Lisa will be leaving when the school year starts. She'll be hard to replace, I'll miss her."

"We've had a couple of sign-ups, but I haven't interviewed them yet," Duncan says.

"Lisa's been great, we should have a little party for her before she leaves," says Maureen, probably already planning what to bake for the occasion.

The rest of the evening proceeds without incident, and Annie is relieved when they break up. All she wants is to go home and sleep. Of course, when sleep finally comes, it is disturbed by dreams. In one, Carlo is surrounded by floating goddesses in gauzy dresses. Annie wakes up in a sweat. *Who killed Carlo? I didn't do it, but someone did. Were there other secret girlfriends hiding in the wings? Someone who may have been jealous enough of Margo to kill Carlo? But then why hadn't she killed Margo, instead of Carlo?* Annie drops off again, but when she wakes up, the pillows are on the floor and the sheet is wound around her like a shroud.

CHAPTER 15

"Like to the lark at break of day arising..."
(from the 29th Sonnet)

Annie groans and rolls onto the floor, unable to unwind the sheet while lying in bed. Pale daylight seeps in through the alcove window, offering a dim improvement on the darkness of the night. When Annie finally is able to stand and stretch her aching body, her alarm—which plays Helen Vendler's dry-lipped but sensuous reading of the 29th Sonnet—bounces softly off the whitewashed walls, echoing in the shell spaces of her ears. Annie pulls on jeans and T-shirt, hops into the car, and inserts a tape into the deck, trembling a little as she does so.

> *"...It was the nightingale and not the lark*
> *That pierc'd the fearful hollow of thine ear.*
> *Nightly she sings on yond pomegranate tree.*
> *Believe me, love, it was the nightingale.*
>
> *It was the lark, the herald of the morn,*
> *No nightingale. Look, love, what envious streaks*
> *Do lace the severing clouds in yonder east.*
> *Night's candles are burnt out, and jocund day*

> *Stands tiptoe on the misty mountaintops.*
> *I must be gone and live, or stay and die..."*

Carlo's recorded voice, reading from Romeo and Juliet, is suddenly too rich for her, especially in the small space of her car, and Annie rolls down the car window. His exaggerated pronunciation of *"pomm-e granat-e"* makes her laugh (with the addition of one small sob), just as she did the first time he read it to her. *"Save your emoting for Ham-let,"* she had said.

She drives over to Pigeon Cove and up Landmark Lane, so called because of two tall elms, nicknamed "Loring and Rebecca" (also known as "the Sentinels"), that were once used as mariners' landmarks. Landmark Lane goes steep and straight up to the top of Pigeon Hill, which was part of the old Dogtown Commons, where cattle grazed in the old days. On many old maps and in old annals it was spelled "Piggon" hill. In 1712 the commoners met and decided that:

"all the Common that belongs to the town upon Piggon Hill is to lie comon still perpetually to bee for a sea mark, and that no trees shall be cut down upon the land that is reserved for said sea mark upon the penalty of 20 shillings for every tree that shall be cut downe, one half to the informer and one half to the poor of the town."

Well, the two elms have long since succumbed to old age, and the hill is so overgrown with trees that a mariner wouldn't be able to single them out anyway. On the other hand, if somebody cut all the trees down now, it would probably solve the heating problems for the poor of the town for years to come. Not too long ago, you could still stand on top of Landmark Lane and make out the coastline far up into Maine, but sadly, Annie thinks, no more.

She parks the Chevy on the meadow, turning in through an opening in the stone wall. This little meadow is where, until a few years ago, the local Scandinavians used to celebrate midsummer; it was, some said, the nearest they could get to a view towards the old country. The tradition has lately been moved down to Millbrook Meadow, the park across the street from Front Beach, where these hardy Northmen and -women now dance and cavort around the cross-shaped, flower-bedecked midsummer pole to the musical accompaniment of accordions, fiddles, and buxom Finnish singers. The celebration concludes with feasting on hot dogs and strawberries with cream. These days the meadow up on Landmark Lane is covered with tall grass, and the hole for the midsummer pole is long overgrown. Annie leaves the car at the edge of the meadow and goes for a run in the woods, where she sees not a single human—only birds, squirrels, deer tracks, and the tip of a foxtail. Afterwards she drives back home, thankful for the brief respite. She parks the car in the garage that leans precipitously on the studio end of the house and makes a run for the safety of the back door.

Out in the bindery she continues working on her project. She has spent the day trying to keep Carlo out of her mind, but he is pushing his way back in. Now she imagines hearing Carlo's voice: *"Calma te, Anna. Take it eesy! Don't get so upset, cara...."* He knew her well, of course. Compulsively attacking a project is Annie's way of dealing with stress or emotional turmoil. She takes out the sewing frame, collects the *signatures,* attaches the cloth tapes to the frame, and marks the folded edge of the signatures with the locations for the stitches.

Annie has made books that took several long evenings to finish sewing together. Since this book does not have too

Gunilla Caulfield

many pages, it only takes her a few hours to sew, including the occasional rest stop to stretch and relax her fingers. When the sewing is completed, she cuts the tapes off the frame, leaving a couple of inches on each side of the work. She draws the tape smooth so that there is no bunching between the threads, and makes sure the back is square.

Suddenly she hears the telephone ring and, forgetting her resolution, quickly rushes inside the house to answer.

"Annie?" She hears Sally's voice, sharp and a little tremulous. "Hello? Are you there, Annie?"

"Hi, Sal, I'm here." Guilt racks Annie. *Oh, no, I should have called her.*

"Well! I've tried to call you a hundred times. You don't answer your phone, I guess. What's going on, Annie? Can't you tell me? I thought we were friends...."

"Oh, Sally, I'm so sorry. Of course we are. And I'm sorry I haven't called. But my life has been such a nightmare."

"I bet. I don't believe any of what I hear, of course, but... well, you've been holding out on me before, I see in the paper. You never told me about you and Carlo," Sally says, a little accusingly.

Annie hesitates before answering. It seems a private life is no longer a luxury she can afford. "That was before I really knew you, Sally. It was something I didn't want to think about or remember myself, so I never talked about it with anyone. Honest, Sal. Nobody knew about it but Carlo and I."

"And whoever told the paper, right?"

Annie has to agree with this irritating truth. However, Sally has a big heart, and Annie is forgiven. "Want to go out for a sandwich?"

"I don't think so, Sal…."

"Of course, you can't show your face anywhere! How about we go up the line?"

If you live in Rockport, to go "up the line" is to go "across the cut" and then south, toward Boston. If, on the other hand, you go across the cut and then north, you're traveling "down Maine" direction. This is sometimes a little confusing and hard for people who don't come from Cape Ann to figure out.

"Can't do that either, Sal. Can't leave town, you see. Why don't you come here. I'm sure I've got something we can make a sandwich with."

"I have a better idea. I'll bring something," Sally says.

Annie goes back out to the bindery and covers the worktable with the sheet again. When Sally comes (through the back door—she is thrilled with the idea of being in on something secret) she's carrying a big brown paper bag with a plastic bag inside, which contains two freshly boiled lobsters from Roy Moore's on the Neck.

"Johnnie just pulled them out of the cooker," she says proudly. "Got you a couple of smoked mackerels for supper, too, I know how you like those. And some shrimp for our appetizer."

Annie is ready to cry at such proofs of friendship. They decide to sit outside and eat their lobsters "in the rough." Not quite as rough as behind Roy Moore's, maybe, where you are invited to sit on smelly wooden crates looking out at the fish shacks in the back and suffer (or enjoy) the fragrance of tar and hulking old lobster pots. Annie's granite patio, on the other hand, is hidden from view of passersby, snugly placed in the corner between the house and the studio.

Annie fixes them each a Tom Collins to go with the shrimp, which they eat out of the little paper box that comes complete with cocktail sauce and slice of lemon. Then they crack the lobsters, which they both expertly devour, chewing every last bit of meat out of the knuckles, sucking the juice out of the legs, and licking the morsels and "lobster butter" out of every crevice. After that, Annie eats her tomalley—the "green stuff," which is actually the liver, found in the carapace—and reaches for Sally's, too. Sally won't touch the stuff.

"What's the matter, you don't like your loblolly?" Annie says, ribbing her. "Loblolly" is what some long-ago visiting Welshman called the green stuff. This was also the origin of the name "Loblolly Cove," a little known fact, but one that Annie likes to keep alive in her official position as town reference librarian. She has a host of obscure facts that she likes to foist upon people this way.

"If you like it so much, why don't you bottle it and sell it? You might make a fortune," Sally says, making a disgusted face as Annie sucks the last of the loblolly out of the lobster body.

"It's been done, otherwise I might. Used to order it at the Union Oyster House for an appetizer. They probably still have it, but I haven't been there for a while." She hasn't been there because that was where she and Carlo often used to go when they sneaked off to Boston for gallery or museum events. But Annie doesn't explain this to Sally.

"Avery Shattuck came in to the coffee shop this morning. Sat down at the counter. Some wise guy asked him if he was glad to be rid of "the anarchist." You should have seen him. I thought he was going to choke on his donut. Asked for a lid for his cup and took his stuff to go. Everybody chuckled once he was out the door." Sally looks gleeful.

"Poor Avery. No sense of humor, that's his problem. But you know, for a while after that letter he wrote, a lot of people thought that Avery ought to resign. It was not an action worthy of a person in his position, they said. Also, they felt it had made him and the society look sort of ridiculous. Well now, if he'd been the director of the MFA, I might have agreed, but I thought it was really a tempest in a teapot. I'm sure he's regretted that letter many times, though," Annie says, giggling.

"I bet. I remember now that the society's funding dried up for a while, but I don't know if the letter had anything to do with it or if it was just the economy. Anyway, I heard that Lew Falco is challenging Shattuck for the directorship," Sally says, sipping on her Collins.

"Oh? Well, having the letter brought up again won't help poor Avery, that's for sure. I know that he approached Josie Mandel at one point. For funds, I mean. But she turned him down flat. Told him she only supports artists directly. I don't know what he was thinking; I mean, it was well known that Josie was 'the anarchist's' backer."

"I know. She only helps those *avant-garde* artists, though, doesn't she?" Sally is quite conservative in her taste in art. She prefers painters like Sargent, Homer and Whistler, not to forget her favorite, Mary Cassatt. Nothing abstract, thank you very much. "Oh well, Shattuck is sort of a stuffed shirt. Maybe they need some new blood at the RAS," Sally says, while putting the lobster remains into a trash bag. "The other thing I wanted to tell you is that I saw Margo on the neck, while I was waiting for the lobsters." She lowers her voice as though afraid someone might be listening in. She's been saving this little tidbit for dessert.

"Oh?"

"Yeah, with a real grieving widow look. She was wearing *normal* clothes, not her usual artsy-craftsy stuff—you know what I mean, those long flouncy skirts and that flowered peasant scarf she always wears—and she was looking kind of haggard. She was trying to get into the house, but Officer Elwell wouldn't let her in. She said all her stuff was in there, and she needed to get things. But he said it was still a crime scene, and she'd have to wait."

Annie considers this. Where has Margo been staying, then, if not above the gallery? Probably one of the artists in the group has taken her in. Unless she has friends in Boston? That's where she was the night Carlo was murdered, anyway. Why had she gone in to Boston alone? If it were for a gallery opening, or to try and arrange for a show, surely Carlo would have gone with her. Annie realizes she doesn't know much about "poor Margo" other than what she's heard through the grapevine. Margo is not from New England, so having her own friends in Boston seems unlikely. As far as Margo's talent as an artist—well, Annie has seen a couple of Margo's collages. Pale and lifeless versions of Carlo's work in a different medium, Annie thinks cattily, probably not good enough to warrant a show on Newbury Street. Margo had seemed to Annie to be totally dependent on Carlo. Whenever she had seen them (rushing to avoid them, of course), Margo had been right at Carlo's heels. Wouldn't she have had him along for support, whether for a social evening or to try and get her work shown?

"So, then she left?" Annie asks.

"Well, actually, Ned Mazzarini was there, boarding up Carlo's windows for the cops. Ned was done, I guess, and he must have offered her a ride, because she got in the car with him and they drove off. Carlo's car wasn't in his space, I noticed, or else Margo would probably have used that." Carlo's old, green Scout. Annie remembers lazy rides in it up along the coast, or sometimes inland for mountain hikes, with an "Italian lunch" of bread and cheese and wine in a basket. Carlo had taken out the rear seats and built a flat bed to hold large paintings for delivery to his customers, which frequently also became their bed, (somewhat uncomfortable, she remembers), on a lonely side road by the sea or in the hills. *The Scout must be a veritable antique, now.*

"Probably impounded," Annie guesses. "And whatever happened to Leo, I wonder?" Annie had given Carlo a black lab puppy, which he had named Leo, (short for Leonardo, of course) and which he had taken with him to Europe. She had been amazed when Carlo brought Leo back with him, now a full-grown and still lively dog at seven.

Sally looks thoughtful. "You know, there was a black lab sniffing around Dock Square when I was passing through on my way here," she says.

Annie laughs. "Plenty of black labs in Rockport— almost as many as goldens, I'd bet," she says, dismissing Sally's notion.

Annie can't see any sinister connection between Margo and Ned Mazzarini and decides to drop the whole thing, since Sally has no more information. They finish their drink and embark on another, and Annie feels better than she has in days. Before she leaves, Sally threatens to come by and just barge in if Annie doesn't keep in touch, and Annie hugs her and promises to call, and thanks her again for the bounties of the sea.

"And watch out for Billy Hale, he's probably lying in wait for anyone coming from my house…and you've been drinking, too!" Annie adds, looking a little concerned. "Maybe you'd better stay a while, and I'll fix us some coffee?"

Sally hesitates, then shakes her head and makes a face. "The boys will kill each other. Gotta go home and see what they're up to. I'll be okay."

CHAPTER 16

"O sleep! O gentle sleep!
Nature's soft nurse, how have I frighted thee,
That thou no more wilt weigh my eyelids down
And steep my senses in forgetfulness?"
(from *Henry IV*)

Annie hasn't heard from the police all day Friday and considers it a good sign. This is the optimist's way of looking at it. The phone has also stopped ringing incessantly, so she has put the answering machine back on. She looks up Ned Mazzarini's number and dials it. He also has an answering machine, of course, and she leaves her name and number. If he's anything like the other tradesmen in town, it may be a day or two until she hears back from him. Considering the state of the economy, it's amazing how many people in this town can afford to have stuff done to their property. Or maybe that in itself is a sign of the poor economy, Annie thinks: people can't afford to buy a bigger or newer home, so they enlarge or fix up the one they live in. She looks over at a long crack in the living room ceiling. That crack had been there five years ago. She still remembers Carlo's comments about it. *"Ma-donna, what are you waiting for? Your own private Grand Canyon?"* Or another time, *"Cara mia, you already have two staircases, are you looking for a place to hang a rope ladder?"*

There's more: the leaky windows on the back side of the house need to be replaced, the floors should be refinished, and the upstairs walls whitewashed. All these things she has put off, oblivious to the passing of time. Oh, well. Maybe she'll spend the rest of her life in jail and not have to worry about it.

Amazingly enough, Ned calls her back within an hour.

"What can I do yah faw, Annie?" he asks. He is expecting a lucrative job, she supposes.

"Hi, Ned. Just a quick question for you—someone said they saw you drive Margo from the Neck this morning. Could you tell me where she's staying?" Annie figures the direct approach is best.

"Ah. Thought yah maaht want me to do them back win-dahs. Gonna give yah a haahd taahm next wintah, them win-dahs. Fihst staahm, yah gonna wish ah'd 'a don'em faw yah."

"Wish I could, Ned, but they'll have to wait a while. Maybe in the fall. Hope we have a long summer first."

"So don' I." (This is a common way of stating agreement here.) "Well, Maahgo, eh? Powah thing. Ah let 'er outta' the caah on the cawnah of Granite an' Haven, laahk she as't. No aah-deah wheah she's stayin'. She jus' waved an' smahled real brave an' said she had to call someone abaht the funr'l. Well, Annie, yah change yaw mind abaht them windahs, yah call me."

"Thanks, I sure will. And Ned, thank you for calling me back so fast. By the way, did Margo mention why she wasn't using Carlo's car?"

"She said she didn't know wheah it was, that Caahlo must'a paahked it somewheahs else."

"Of course. Thanks again, Ned."

The funeral, Annie thinks when she hangs up. She feels a stab of guilt—she hasn't even thought of the funeral. But why should *Margo* have to arrange for the funeral? She's not a relative. Wouldn't they have to send Carlo's body home, to Italy? *This is too much.* Dread fills her, she's drowning in it, and in order to avoid thinking about it all she goes back out to the bindery for the next step in her project.

Annie whips the protective sheet off the work area. After gathering all the materials she will need, she starts by gluing on the headband and the mull. Then she cuts the boards: front cover, back cover, and a narrow one for the backbone. Since the book will be fairly large, she uses a heavy board, so it won't warp. Several hours later, when she has finished putting all the parts together, she puts the book under weights and lets it sit.

Annie has a beautiful, thin piece of honey-colored calfskin that she bought recently and has been itching to use, which will cover the book. It will be a fairly simple cover, with a French groove. *And gold tooling,* she thinks, which is not quite so simple. However, this is enough for today. Her body aches from top to toe—from the physical strain of working late, from grief and anxiety, and from not knowing whether tomorrow she will be sleeping in her own bed or in a jail cell. But at least these compulsive and perhaps useless tasks have taken her mind off things for a while. And another surely sleepless night has grown shorter.

CHAPTER 17

"O brave new world,
That has such people in 't!
(from *The Tempest*)

On Saturday morning, Annie decides to risk making a run for it again and go across the town line into Gloucester for a cup of chowder at Amelia's. You can certainly find good chowder in Rockport—at the Fish Shack right down in Dock Square, for instance, or at Ellen's or Brackett's or the Chowder House on the Neck, or even over at the Lobster Pound for a sunset cuppa chowdah by Folly Cove—but she is not prepared to eat surrounded by staring townies. She is getting good at sneaking out now, and pulls her floppy straw hat down to her eyebrows as she drives up South Street toward Thatcher Road, hoping Officer Hale won't lie in wait this time. The straw hat would do her no good regardless; he'd recognize her old Chevy anytime.

Once at Amelia's, she takes her chowder to go and walks over to Good Harbor Beach with it. Sitting in front of the fragile dunes (planted sparsely with thin, spiky grasses, which makes the sandy humps look like a herd of elephant babies) she gets pelted with sand and salty spray. The wind has picked up even more, and there are people out there surfing now. This is a favorite spot for surfers on the island; no other beach is quite equal to it if the wind is right. Long Beach comes in a close second, especially the southern end. Today the waves are good enough for some of the surfers to get up for a good long run before they sink back into the froth.

The chowder is gritty from sand blowing into it. When Annie is done, she reluctantly returns to the car. She would like to continue over to Wingaersheek Beach and walk around among the dunes there; the high dunes have the whitest and finest sand on all the North Shore. But that would mean going across the cut. Too risky. Thankfully, she doesn't get caught by the police on the way home this time, and heaves a sigh of relief as she drives down the hill to her house. After parking the car in the garage, she pulls the door down, which takes some effort. *Soon the garage will need the support of the door just to keep it standing,* she thinks.

When she gets to the kitchen door she finds it wide open, swinging in the wind. Must be the storm. Hoping the hinges aren't bent, she shuts the door carefully and rattles the knob a few times to see if it will stay shut. It feels solid. Then she hears a pitiful moan and turns around to find Gussie lying on the floor, yipping weakly. Annie bends down over him and sees blood trickling down his neck. She gives him a little nudge, but he makes no effort to stand, so she picks him up. It looks as though he's cut himself; there's a big gash across the back of his neck. She hurries over to the sink and dabs the wound with a paper towel to see how bad it is. Looks like it needs stitches. Annie puts the dog down on the little braided carpet in front of the stove and runs to get his carrier. She notices, almost absentmindedly, that the living room is a mess, too—furniture upset and pillows and candlesticks and knickknacks strewn all around—and stops for a moment in wonder. Maybe Gussie has had some sort of seizure? Then she remembers what she has to do, and runs for the carrier, which she keeps under the bar sink in the lower living room. She puts Gussie into it before going into the sleeping alcove for a blanket to cover him with, and gets another shock. The alcove looks even worse than the living room. The little Victorian desk across from the bed has been emptied, bills and other stuff she keeps in the cubbyholes are thrown all over the room, and the drawers are lying in a pile under the desk. Worse, her computer monitor lies destroyed on the floor. It looks like someone's used a sledgehammer on it. This is not Gussie's doing.

"What's going on here?" she shouts, but doesn't have time to worry about it and runs off with Gussie instead. She puts the carrier on the passenger seat and tries to pull open the garage door, which creaks menacingly. Finally, she manages to lift it far enough that she can drive the car out, although she hears ominous scraping sounds above her head. *Ugh, more spots to paint.*

The veterinarian's office is located on the "Back of the Cape," or the mainland side of the island. This means she has to drive through Pigeon Cove and Folly Cove, over the line again into Gloucester, and continue through a couple of Gloucester's "villages," past Annisquam and through Lanesville and Riverdale. Gloucester consists of a number of villages, most of them on the island, some across the cut on the mainland. Annie's arms shake as the shock of what has happened hits her, but she speeds along, jaws clenched, not even worrying about getting caught.

The veterinarian's office smells comfortingly of cedar chips, and Jenny, the girl at the desk, gives Annie a calming smile.

They are shown in right away, and Augustus gets a thorough check.

"Is it serious?" Annie asks anxiously.

"I think he'll recover okay, Miss Quitnot," Doctor Parker assures her. Annie has used Dr. Parker ever since she first got Gussie. He's an older man, very genteel, and still calls her by her last name. His manner is gentle and caring, and he handles Gussie with large, capable hands. Pushing the glasses off the top of his head down onto his nose, he studies the dog carefully. "He's old, of course. I still remember when you brought him in as a puppy. What happened to him?"

"Don't know, Doc. Got home and found him on the floor like this. The house is all torn up; I thought maybe he had some kind of seizure at first…"

The vet shakes his head. "I don't think so. Looks like he was hit with something. Maybe he fell down some stairs? He has a mild concussion, I'd say, and we'll keep him overnight to be sure. Is he more mobile than this, usually?"

Annie dissembles, doesn't really want to admit even to herself that Gussie is getting to be quite elderly—especially right now, with death hanging around her like a clammy sheet. "Doesn't move a lot these days, I'm afraid. Well, I usually carry him when we go for a walk," she admits, honestly.

"Yes, I see. He's got arthritis, of course. We'll start him on some pills. Make him good as new."

"Thanks, Doctor Parker. See you tomorrow then. In the morning?"

"Call first, to be sure."

CHAPTER 18

"O villain, villain, smiling damned villain!
My tables—meet it as I set it down,
That one may smile, and smile, and be a villain..."
(from *Hamlet*)

On the way back, Officer Hale is lying in wait. Annie thought it would be someone else, since she was going the back way. All the cops in town have a favorite spot to sit and wait for people to break the law. She knows some of their hiding places; for instance, Officer Elwell's places himself right by the information booth coming into town. He likes to sit there and read, and sometimes he even misses speeders going by. Maybe the books are too exciting, about police chases and things like that, she supposes. But Officer Hale moves around, obviously, and now he's caught her once more.

"Well now, Miss Quitnot. Sneaking out of town again?"

"Had to take the dog to the vet."

Officer Hale looks into the empty seats, then back at Annie, questioningly. "So where is he, then?"

"Had to leave him there overnight."

"That little dachshund? What's wrong with him?"

"Needed stitches."

"Did he have an accident?"

"Actually, I think somebody clouted him on the head," Annie says angrily.

"What do you mean, *think*? Why don't you tell me what happened," Officer Hale suggests, taking a waiting stance and pulling out a pad and pen.

"Well, I got home and found Gussie lying on the floor, bleeding. The back door was hanging open, and the house looks like a tornado's gone through. Maybe Gussie surprised a burglar or something, I don't know."

Ordinarily Officer Hale would have made a comment such as, "Maybe he fell off the threshold, haha," and the thought of the little dachshund actually attacking a burglar is of course amusing enough for a similar crack, but he restrains himself.

"Did you report this to the police?" he asks.

"No, I didn't have time. I just picked Gussie up and took him to the vet's."

"Was anything missing?"

"Missing? Oh, in the house, you mean. How do I know? Like I said, I didn't have time for anything."

"Why don't we go over to your place then, and let's have a look?"

"Fine. I'll meet you there." *Fine and dandy.* Annie can see the headlines now: *REFERENCE LIBRARIAN SUSPECTED IN VALENTI MURDER CLAIMS SHE IS BURGLARIZED. Caught defying police order not to leave town.*

The trustees will order Duncan to fire me now, Annie thinks.

At her house, Officer Hale examines the kitchen door. "I see no signs of forced entry, here," he says.

"I keep the door unlocked, Billy."

"Not advisable..."

"I know," Annie says impatiently. "It's just an idiosync—a thing I have." She slows down. "I've always trusted people, you know what I mean? That's one of the great things about living in a small town—you know and trust everybody..." Annie feels like crying, suddenly. She will never be able to trust everybody again.

Officer Hale appears not to notice her distress. "So, Miss Quitnot, can you tell if anything has been stolen?" He is looking down at his notepad while talking to her, as if he feels uneasy about questioning her. Annie is too incensed to notice, and afraid that she is sinking deeper into the quagmire every minute. When will it all end?

"No, I can't," she answers angrily, her voice too shrill, "I don't know that I have anything that anybody would want to steal. I don't own anything valuable that I can think of, except for my books, I suppose. But look how they've been thrown around—that's no booklover's doing!" She points to the volumes carelessly tossed about on the floor, and tries to pick a stack up, kicking a chair that is in her way. The chair topples and falls against the coffee table.

"Easy there, Miss Quitnot. Nothing else of value? Jewelry? Money? Do you keep any cash about?" He looks at her, trying to keep his questioning calm.

"What, Billy, do I look like someone who has cash to hide? I had my purse on me, with my wallet and passbook and credit card, and I certainly don't own any jewelry worth stealing. No, the most valuable things I own are my books, and most of them are only valuable to *me*. I'll go through them when I put them back, and let you know if anything is missing. My computer is kaput, of course, although actually it looks like the CPU might be okay. The monitor's been bashed in, and the keyboard is smashed, too."

"Let's go have a look-see." She takes him into the alcove, and Office Hale looks around, a little taken aback.

"Oboy, this doesn't look too good. Somebody would have to be pretty angry to do this. You sure you have no ideas?" Annie knows what he's fishing for: a connection to the murder. Officer Hale makes a few more notes. "Well, I'll have to report this anyway," taking a last look at the mess.

"Is it possible to keep it out of the paper?" Annie asks. "I'm going to lose my job if this keeps up."

Officer Hale looks at her, frowning. "I hope that's all you're going to lose, Annie," he says, earnestly, "and I seriously hope you'll keep your doors locked from now on." Annie senses that he is genuinely concerned for her. The chief must have really lit into him to make him act so *according to the book* until now.

"I guess you're right." Annie says, grateful and dispirited at the same time. As Officer Hale moves toward the door, she asks, "Oh, by the way, Billy, do you know what happened to Carlo's car?"

Officer Hale looks wary again. "What do you mean, *happened to it?*"

"I mean, I understand it's missing."

"Why are you asking about it?"

"Well, I think it's strange that Carlo was at his place, but not the car—if Margo took the train to Boston, I mean."

"It appears Miss DeVoe doesn't like city driving," Officer Hale says, carefully.

"That doesn't explain why the car is missing."

"Miss DeVoe *reported* it missing. Carlo may have parked it somewhere else, or it may be stolen. We're looking for it. That's all I can tell you. And I shouldn't even have told you that. Now, will you lock the door when I leave, please? I'll drive by later, on my way home. I think you should leave the light on by the front door, too, Annie."

She is touched by his concern, and it's good to hear him call her Annie again, even if he probably wouldn't do it within hearing of Chief Murphy. As she watches him leave, Annie thinks that tonight is one night she wouldn't mind some company. Maybe she should call Sally? But no, it's too late, and Sally has the boys to think of, and Matt will be annoyed. Matt doesn't like trouble with the authorities.

CHAPTER 19

"Silence that dreadful bell!"
(from *Othello*)

The storm intensifies during the evening. A sailboat that was anchored out in Sandy Bay—as usual in the summer, the harbors are full—tears loose and ends up on Front Beach. At the next high tide, the Coast Guard will come and haul it off. Another boat runs aground on Salvages, a frequent site of shipwrecks.

Annie sits exhausted in her living room, looking out over the harbor. There are no stars tonight, the sky is obscured by a sea fog that lies like a down comforter all the way in over the shore, and the darkness adds to her ominous feelings. The main harbor is still crowded with sailboats and motorboats belonging to the summer people. Rockport is chronically short of harbor space, and when a storm forces mariners to seek harbor, many have to be content with dropping anchor out in the bay. There are no natural harbors in Rockport, only those created by building jetties and breakwaters.

The Pigeon Cove Harbor is smaller, and full of fishing boats. Alongside the harbor lies the old Tool Company, a long, rusting hulk of a building on a narrow piece of land that borders the harbor. Annie has dubbed it "The Mustard Palace," as the whole, corrugated metal exterior has been sprayed with some material, which has turned the color of mustard. The result is ghastly, and Annie looks the other way whenever she drives by it. She prefers to remember it as it was in the days when her father worked there: a lively place, ringing with the clanging of the forge. Mothers warned their kids to stay away, and not stop to look in through the openings. White-hot pieces of metal could come flying out at any time to kill you, they said.

Tonight, more than ever, Annie misses her parents. She still remembers the day they went out in her dad's little motorboat, just planning to go on that small pleasure cruise. It was Sunday, her dad's day off, and the Story Library was closed. A few hours later the gale struck. It had not been forecast, just seemed to spring up out of nowhere, and was followed by a dense sea fog. Annie stood on the Headlands for hours on end, ready to catch sight of the boat as soon as it appeared. It never did. Annie had been thirty then, and hadn't met Carlo yet.

The present storm is just a mild summer gale, of course, but it is wreaking havoc all the same. Due to the mess in her sleeping alcove, which she is too tired to deal with after Officer Hale leaves, Annie decides to sleep upstairs. Also, were there to be another visit by the intruder, she would have a better chance at escape from the upstairs bedroom through the window across the side roof and down onto the patio. In the alcove, she'd be trapped. Not that she expects it to happen. Whatever it was the thief was after, she obviously didn't have any. Annie puts fresh sheets on the bed and brings up her favorite quilt for comfort. She doesn't even have Gussie, and misses him and imagines hearing him whining and howling for her. The house feels empty and cold.

Once in bed she becomes aware of every little sound. She cringes at the twanging and snapping and pinging of the lines against the masts. The wind rattles the windows, and water slaps noisily against the rocks down below. It has not started to rain, however, and the sound of the dry wind is alternately a shrill whistle and an insistent soughing sound that occasionally turns to a roar. Tomorrow all the harborside windows will be covered with salt. She twists and turns in bed, but after a while she falls asleep.

Annie dreams. In her dream she is standing behind Carlo, watching him paint in the studio above the gallery. Carlo did not paint in public; he couldn't stand having a crowd watching him. Many Rockport artists feel that *"plein air"* or *"al fresco"* painting, sitting in front of an easel in the great outdoors, is the only way, and enjoy parking themselves on their chosen street corner or popular sightseeing spot and listening to comments from passersby. But Carlo painted only in the solitude of his studio.

In Annie's dream, which mimics reality so closely that it might as well be a memory, he is working on a large canvas, as usual laid down flat on the wooden table that takes up most of the studio. Now and then he rests the painting vertically against the wall and stands back to look at it. Carlo thins his paints to a wash, which he keeps in an assortment of cups and pots on the table surrounding the canvas. In the dream, as Annie watches, he lays on a wash and smoothes it out with a sponge. He keeps a pile of cloths and sponges handy so that he won't need to clean them in between colors. When he has covered part of the canvas with a translucent layer of paint, he takes a bucket of sea sand, which he has washed to get rid of the salt, and sprinkles it over parts of the painting. Once this layer is dry and the sand firmly attached, he will add more layers of paint, and sometimes yet another layer of sand.

Carlo has finished the first layer and gently, so the sand won't get knocked off, puts the painting over in the racks to dry. He turns to Annie as though he has just noticed her presence—she knows that's not true; he is instantly aware of her when she comes into the room—and pulls her to him, roaring like a lion. He is always full of physical energy when he gets up from painting, and Annie, breathless in his embrace, has looked forward to this moment all day. But now something is wrong; horns are blaring....

Annie is suddenly awakened from her dream by the incessant honking of the town horn. A fire somewhere. She listens for the signal code. *1-3-1.* Bearskin Neck. She throws the covers off and hurries over to the window. There's a great glow over the Neck, and billowing clouds of smoke. Carlo's place is burning. The alarm has just finished sounding, but she can hear the wail of the fire engines already.

This is the great nightmare of every inhabitant on the Neck—fire. And so far, the storm still hasn't brought any rain with it, just relentless wind. The little shacks and cottages on Bearskin Neck sit crowded together like people in church pews on Christmas morning. Over the years, some of the shacks and houses have even been attached together, since they were built so close that nobody could squeeze between them to re-shingle or paint the sides anyway. Carlo's gallery stands on its own, but some of the neighboring shacks are only yards away. Annie sees sparks fly across the space and land on the neighbor's roof.

The fire squad has arrived. Dock Square is full of quickly parked trucks belonging to a large number of volunteers, who sleep with their fire-fighting clothes and boots laid out by their beds. Soon they are pumping water onto the roofs downwind of Carlo's. Lightning flashes across the sky far out at sea, and the thunder, though delayed, comes rolling in with loud booms and crackles. Suddenly the clouds burst open, and the long-awaited rain comes to the firemen's aid. Now the wind will begin to die down, too. But it looks like it's too late to save Carlo's place. Was the fire caused by a lightning strike?

Annie hears someone rapping on the door downstairs. Has the intruder returned? Silently, she slips downstairs. She walks into the dark living room and slowly eases over far enough to look out the window. Officer Elwell stands outside, shoulders hunched in the rain.

CHAPTER 20

"Time shall unfold what plighted cunning hides;
Who covers faults, at last shame them derides."
(from *King Lear*)

Annie is again brought to the police station for questioning. It's still pitch dark outside at three o'clock in the morning. She can tell they don't believe her. Chief Murphy himself has sat in on part of the interview. Officer Elwell has repeated the same questions over again—to trip her up, she supposes. Billy Hale isn't around, must be off duty. Would *he* believe her? Annie is getting impatient, angry and flustered, which only makes matters worse, as she finally completely loses her temper and lashes out at them.

"Now, Chief, why would I want to burn down Carlo's house? I'm in enough trouble, aren't I, since it seems you have already decided I'm your perpetrator in his murder." She spits out the word *perpetrator* with unnecessary vigor.

The chief studies her silently for a moment.

"Calm down, Miss Quitnot. We are following standard procedure, that's all. No one here at the station will make decisions on your guilt or innocence. That's for the courts to determine. But, since we have two witnesses in the case of Mr. Valenti's murder that came forward with information voluntarily, we have no choice but to follow up on any subsequent event that seems connected. The fire is just such an event."

In the end, they have to let her go. They obviously have no *evidence* that she set the fire, but again, she has no alibi. And they have obviously settled on her as their logical and only suspect, now. Whoever those two were that came forward to accuse her, they must be very "credible" indeed. What could they possibly have told the police, other than that she and Carlo had an affair? That, by itself, couldn't be enough to accuse her of murder. She knows she should try to get a lawyer, but some foolish hope that *it will all go away* still sustains her. And if she got a lawyer, they would probably suspect it was because she has something to hide. Isn't that the way it always appears? Anyway, she can't afford a lawyer, on her meager salary, so the case is closed on that idea.

She goes home and tries to catch a couple of hours of sleep, but to no avail. In the morning she calls Clare. Clare lives alone and has a guestroom; maybe she'll let Annie camp out for a few days? She could ask Sally, of course, but Sally's house is a nightmare of its own, with those boys. Sally and her husband also have widely differing ideas on how to deal with their unruly offspring, and constantly break out into loud and unsettling quarrels. Annie doesn't think she could handle the bedlam.

Clare picks up the phone just as Annie is about to hang up.

"Yes, who is it?" Clare sounds short, irritated.

"Hi, Clare...it's me, Annie. Sorry if I caught you at a bad time?"

"Oh, hi, Annie, no, no, it's fine." It doesn't sound to Annie as though it's fine; Clare's voice has an edge to it.

"How would you feel about a houseguest for a few days? I'm having a hard time being alone here with everything going on," Annie is feeling embarrassed, as though she is begging.

Clare hesitates. "Well...ah, any other time, Annie, because, as it happens, I already have a guest, a friend of mine from out of town. Sorry."

She doesn't sound really sorry, Annie thinks. It sounds like a convenient and quickly thought up lie, an excuse to turn Annie down. *Is she just afraid to get involved, or is it possible that Clare believes I actually killed Carlo?*

"It's okay, don't worry about it, I have somewhere else I can stay. Have a nice visit with your friend."

But the phone call unsettles Annie, and she doesn't want to risk being rebuffed elsewhere. Instead she calls the vet to see if Gussie can be picked up. At least he is loyal and trusting. When Jenny tells her Augustus is on the mend and may come home, Annie gets ready to leave, then checks herself. She dials the police non-emergency telephone number and asks for Officer Hale, but he is not in. She tells Officer Elwell that she has to go to Gloucester to pick up her dog from the vet's.

"One moment please, Miss Quitnot." She hears mumbled conversation before Chief Murphy picks up the phone himself.

"You may go, Miss Quitnot, but please return immediately."

Annie can't resist. "You mean, don't try to sneak across the cut?"

"This is a serious matter, Miss Quitnot."

"Sorry, Chief Murphy. I promise to come right back."

Gussie is indeed much improved. In fact, Annie hasn't seen this level of animation in a long time. Those happy pills that Dr. Parker prescribed must work miracles. She supposes they must have a component that dulls pain, since they really couldn't work that fast. Hopefully they are also curative, and will have a lasting effect. If they can make that kind of medication for people, why not for pets? Gussie jumps out of the carrier as soon as she opens it, and does a dance in front of her, albeit a little stiffly. He has a bandage around his neck still but otherwise seems whole and unhurt. Annie picks him up and does a little twirl herself. She smiles at Jenny and thanks Doctor Parker, who gives her a prescription for Gussie's "happy pills." Then she keeps her promise and goes straight home.

There is a message from Langmuir on the answering machine, asking her to call him. *Here it comes,* she thinks, *I'm fired.*

"Rockport Public Library, may I help you?"

"Penny, it's Annie, I'm returning a call from Mr. Langmuir."

"Let me see if he's free." Penny sounds cool.

Duncan sounds genuinely concerned when he comes on the line. "Annie, I just wanted to see how things are with you. Sorry about today's article in the paper. You must be upset, I imagine."

"Haven't seen the paper. You mean about the fire?"

"Well, that, too. If you haven't seen it, I'm sorry to have brought it to your attention."

"What is it, have they found me guilty or something?"

"No, no. Annie, I'm leaving the office in about five minutes. Okay if I stop by?"

"Of course, Dunc. I'd give anything to see a friendly face."

"Fine. Stay put. I'll bring the paper when I come."

CHAPTER 21

"Hysterica passio! down, thou climbing sorrow!
Thy elements below."
(from *King Lear*)

Duncan brings the paper and hands it to Annie. She glances at the front page and starts reading.

VALENTI WIDOW FEARS FOR HER LIFE

Margo Valenti tells police of her ordeal...married only the day before husband's shocking death...lost everything in fire...staying at undisclosed location for security reasons...feels threatened...

Annie bites her lip until it begins to bleed. As she continues reading article, she loses control and can't help letting out a groan of frustration, and Augustus comes running. He is yipping and growling ferociously, and jumps up to snap at Langmuir's pants, as though whatever it is, it's all the director's fault. The dog has managed to get the bandage off his neck, but there's no sign of new bleeding. Annie, distracted by Gussie's behavior, fights to get control of herself.

"Gussie, stop it!" She picks up the dog and strokes his back to calm him down. "Thanks, Gussie, but you got the wrong guy!"

Langmuir laughs a little and steps further into the room, giving Annie and the dog some space, which seems to suit Augustus.

"I don't believe it, Dunc. How could he go and marry that girl? She's only twenty-three years old! At least that's what they say. She's just a kid, for God's sake!"

Duncan eyes her speculatively. "Maybe he was, too, in a way. Some of these artistic types aren't very mature, I've found."

Annie wants to contradict him and object to this stereotyping, but she is too grateful for his support. "Anyway," he continues, "I suppose they've checked you out on the fire, too?"

"Yes. They've got me pegged, Dunc. How am I going to get out of this mess?" She offers Langmuir a seat. "Can I offer you a drink? Coffee? A sandwich? I'm not cooking, these days. I just grab whatever falls out when I open the fridge."

Langmuir studies her thoughtfully.

"Well, open the fridge and see what falls out, then. Better yet, let me open the fridge. You sit. Oh, I forget…where's the fridge?"

Annie laughs, a short, dry laugh, but she sounds a little less stressed.

"Out that way," she says, pointing. Duncan disappears.

"Ouch, what happened here?" he says, as if talking to himself. Annie suddenly remembers that she hasn't cleaned up the mess.

"Oh, God, Duncan, sorry. Forgot to tell you," she calls out, "wait a sec." She joins him in the kitchen. The door to the alcove is open, and she explains about the intruder and the attack on Gussie.

"No wonder the little thing is nervous. But Annie, this is no good. You can't stay here by yourself. There must be someone you can stay with," he says, looking seriously concerned now.

"I tried calling a friend. I think she was afraid, actually. I don't want to call anybody else and find that they're all afraid."

"I'm not afraid..." he says gently, looking sincerely at her, eyebrows drawn together in a small frown.

"...and I'm not moving in with you..." she replies, a little amazed at her own flippancy.

"That wasn't exactly going to be my next suggestion." He looks unperturbed and a little amused.

Annie puts her head in her hands. "I'm so sorry, Duncan, of course. I didn't mean to say that. I must be going out of my mind. I apologize."

Duncan smiles and puts an understanding hand on her shoulder. "No need. What I was going to say was: I'm going to rent a room for you up at the motel. It will be in my name. We can tell the police about it, so they won't think that you've flown the coop. What do you say? I'll go and get my car. Meanwhile, you turn on a couple of lights and leave the radio on. Pull the curtains closed. Go out the back way and see if you can get to Atlantic Avenue without being seen, and I'll pick you up there, just around the corner."

"I hope this isn't just a cheap pick-up," Annie says irreverently, then covers her mouth, aghast at having made yet another flip comment. She groans inwardly.

"That's the spirit, Annie. I'll pick you up around the corner in fifteen minutes."

"But wait, what about Gussie?"

This is a problem. No pets are allowed at the motel.

Langmuir thinks about this for a moment. "Well, he'll just have to come and stay with me. Will he accept that?" he says.

"After staying last night at the vet's, he'll either have a complete fit or he'll accept his fate and follow you around adoringly, especially if I pack some of these," Annie says, filling a plastic tub with treats from Clare's crock. She winces at the memory of Clare's rejection. "I'll be ready in fifteen minutes," she says. Unfortunately, she doesn't have a cent in her wallet, but she will insist on paying Duncan back for the motel room later.

The motel sprawls alongside the road coming into town, but it has a number of rooms out in the back that can't be seen from the street. Duncan has rented one of these and paid up for a week, so Annie is installed without having to show up at the desk.

There is an indoor swimming pool in the central building, popular with the local residents in the winter. "Little Florida," some of them call it. Many townies take out a membership and swim there all winter—and winter can last a long time in New England. Little Florida, filled along the side walls with potted shefflera plants—to resemble palm trees, presumably— and lined with lounge chairs, is always warm and humid. People who don't like warm and humid need not apply; they can join the Polar Bear Gang on Front Beach and go for a swim in the ocean on New Year's Day. Right now Annie wishes she could go for a long, relaxing swim, but that would mean either going outside and walking around the building, or through the corridors—either way, she would be liable to meet people who would recognize her. So, she has to settle for a shower instead. She makes sure that the door to her room is locked and that the telephone works before stepping into the shower. Afterwards she slips into a clean pair of pajamas. Then she flips on the TV. Which turns out to be a *big* mistake.

Rockport has made the national news. *Murder in New England.* The victim: a picture of Carlo, handsome, in a Hemingway-hero rugged kind of way, the internationally acclaimed artist. The suspect: a picture of Annie, wild-haired and disheveled-looking, town librarian and former lover. Then follows a short footage of the grieving widow fleeing reporters, with her hands shielding her face (and doing a poor job of it), blond hair flowing silkily over something black and sedate. And then the follow-up story: *The Fire.* The gallery ablaze, billowing clouds of smoke in flickering strobe lights, firemen struggling heroically to prevent the conflagration from spreading and devouring all of Bearskin Neck. Another short footage of the now crying widow, fearful, saying she's going into hiding somewhere. Then back to the suspect with a not-too-subtle footnote suggesting that Quitnot had already been intercepted at least twice trying to leave town.

Annie turns off the TV. She sees her image in the huge mirror across from the bed. She is white as a ghost. The phone rings, and it's Duncan, telling her not to turn on the TV.

"Too late. I saw it already." Her voice hardly carries. She wants to hang up and just lie down on the bed, but Duncan keeps talking, on and on, as if he were a Samaritan trying to keep a suicidal caller on the line.

"A thought just occurred to me...would you like me to call Clare, maybe have her come and visit?" He is trying so hard and being so thoughtful, and yet, after her last phone call to Clare, that is about the last thing that Annie could want. She sighs, hoping he doesn't hear it.

"No, no. Thank you, Duncan. I'll be fine, honest." Annie is trying to control her voice, to appear confident.

"I'll call you in the morning, then," he says, still sounding a little hesitant.

"Yes. Thanks. Thank you for everything, Dunc." She hangs up quickly, before she changes her mind.

CHAPTER 22

"I know a bank whereon the wild thyme blows,
Where oxlips and the nodding violet grows
Quite overcanopied with luscious woodbine,
with sweet musk-roses, and with eglantine."
(from *A Midsummer Night's Dream*)

"Don't worry, I called Chief Murphy. It's okay," Duncan says. Annie and Duncan are in his car the next morning, with a bag containing a full breakfast from the motel kitchen. Omelets, muffins, coffee, the whole nine yards. "Anyway, we're not going out of town. I'm just taking you to Halibut Point. Should be deserted at this time of the morning. It's past sunrise, so the sun worshippers will have left." Gussie is in the back seat and yips happily. Annie hopes it is because he is happy to see her.

You don't catch halibut at Halibut Point. The original name was *Haul about Point,* from the days of the old fishing vessels that had to "haul about" before continuing down the coast. Maybe they had some halibut in the hold, too, but chances are it was mostly cod—that "other white meat," a slogan that got the Gloucester fishing industry in hot water with the Pork People, who claim to have used the term first.

Duncan parks in the State Park lot, since he is a member of the Trustees of Reservations, and points to a sticker in the window to prove it. *Window stickers on cars ought to be outlawed,* Annie thinks, *along with bumper stickers.* Nothing but elitist status symbols. Life synthesized, entire philosophies reduced to short sentences. Invitations to road rage even, some of them. Duncan only has a few of the *status* stickers—WGBH, the Trustees, MFA—and then the more proletarian sort, six years' worth of Town Parking and Dump stickers. That's how old his car is. If he keeps it much longer, he won't be able to see out the rear window.

Annie supports NPR and WGBH and a few other well deserving institutions herself, but she always tells them to "keep the stickers and mugs and umbrellas and the discount card," stating she wants all her hard-earned money to go directly to the cause, not to some fundraising organization. They gracefully accept her money anyway, of course. They are not too fickle.

With Augustus on a leash, they walk through the long, natural arbor of climbing wild rose, bittersweet, catbrier, and woodbine. Some of the lianas that wind themselves around the trunks and strangle the trees are as thick as a man's arm. On the forest floor beneath this rampant growth are scatterings of tiny wildflowers that create a delicate background pattern. At the end of the arbor, Annie and Duncan arrive at Babson's Quarry, where they settle on granite blocks left over from the old quarrying days. Alongside the quarry stands an old watchtower, where long ago men stood looking for German submarines. From where Duncan and Annie sit they can see up the coastline and, since it's a clear day, even the Isles of Shoals and Mount Agamenticus up in Maine. An atmospheric mirage makes the Isles of Shoals shimmer and oscillate and look twice their height.

The quarry is filled with sweet water these days, to a level higher than the ocean that surrounds the park. Annie went swimming here back when she and Justin were kids, but now swimming is not allowed. The water is still, and the steeply quarried granite sides are mirrored on the surface in cubist fashion.

"Asparagus or mushroom-and-cheese?" Duncan asks.

"Oh, either one—asparagus, if that's okay. Pretty fancy," Annie says, digging in with a plastic fork. They eat and have their coffee, watching two herons fly overhead. Seagulls are performing their morning ablutions in a corner of the quarry, ducking their heads and fluffing their feathers, disturbing the cubist image. Gussie gets up and barks enthusiastically at the sight and gets a treat from Duncan's pocket.

"Annie, tonight is Poet's Night; I wasn't sure if you'd remember. Would you still be willing to help out?" Duncan says. "If not, I'll have to get someone else. I would have asked Geri, but she's on vacation, if you remember. Besides, poetry isn't exactly her thing."

Once a month the library allows would-be poets to share their work. Annie usually volunteers to introduce the poets and answer any questions that may come up. The poets have their own friends bring refreshments and make coffee in the library's large, brightly polished urns, so otherwise the affair is fairly simple.

"Oh, I don't know, Duncan. Do you think it would be a good idea? I do miss the library, but what if people get upset at my being there?" Annie is hesitant.

"I think it would do you good. They're poets, gentle people, not small-town gossipmongers. Anyway, I plan to be in my office, should there be a problem. And then I'll drive you back to your new home."

Annie nods slowly, still not sure. They get up and walk around the quarry and out onto the high promontory built on a mountainous pile of granite blocks. Despite signs warning of danger, people still try to scale the hill from the shoreline far below. Some years back a reckless climber was crushed to death by a rock fall. Today, a lone fisherman stands on the ledge below, at a safe distance from the granite slope, patiently reeling in his line. It is a brilliant, ethereal, blue-sky day. The storm has moved on, but lusty swells are still roaring ashore with a great deal of flying sea foam. Duncan and Annie, closely followed by an energetically cantering Gussie, walk back through the arbor, which is dripping with nectar and humming with bees. Duncan drives Annie back to the motel, where she gives Gussie a rough good-bye hug. She spends the afternoon napping and lazing about, trying not to turn on the TV. Instead, she goes through every flyer and magazine, even the *Rockport Anchor,* left there for the tourists. When she gets tired of leafing through pages, she lies down on the bed and tries to make sense out of what has happened.

Dispirited, she now understands why Margo is involved with the funeral arrangements. She is the wife! Annie thinks back to her last meeting with Carlo. Why had they never told anyone they were getting married? And under those circumstances, how could he try to make a play for her the way he did? Call her *carissima,* and ask if he could come over later, "on such a lovely moonlit night," if he was marrying Margo? Is that what he had become, just some kind of gigolo? In a way, she wants to believe it. It would hurt less then, the fact that he had been stupid enough to marry that Margo. And yet, she wants to remember him as the great love that he was, she can't give that up. She will probably never have another.

By late afternoon she is ready to climb the walls of the little motel room—and hungry, besides. The motel serves breakfast only, and she has not brought any food along. Good thing she had a big breakfast. She'll have to help herself to cookies and sweets from the refreshment table at the library tonight instead of having supper, unless she could somehow get back home to raid the refrigerator. But no, she would have to walk all the way across town to get home. Leaving the car in the garage to pretend she is at home is turning out to be a great inconvenience. After all the recent salacious news, she is not about to run the gauntlet just for something to eat. She'll wait until she gets to the library, hoping Duncan will be right about the "gentle people," and that none of the town gossips show up.

CHAPTER 23

"Reputation, reputation, reputation!
O! I have lost my reputation."
(from *Othello*)

Duncan picks her up, and they arrive at the library early. Esa must still be somewhere around, cleaning, since the grilles by the Main Desk haven't been pulled down yet. Annie walks over to Reference, feeling nostalgic. There is a vase of flowers on her desk, carnations and daisies and purple iris. A peculiar mix. Did Jean buy them for herself, Annie wonders, or were they put there by Duncan or the trustees to make the "new" reference librarian feel welcome? She feels a sting of jealousy.

"Hi, Miss Annie." Esa has come up behind her without her noticing. He cannot manage the name *Quitnot,* and so calls her Miss Annie. He also says *Miss Jean* and *Miss Marie.* Esa is somewhat more intimidated when it comes to the men, and Duncan Langmuir becomes *Mr. Lammer,* while Stuart Cogswell is *Mr. Swell.*

"Do you like the flowers?" Esa asks.

"They're very colorful," Annie says carefully.

"They're for you, Miss Annie. I bought them for you," Esa says proudly.

"You bought them for me? But Esa, flowers are so expensive. You really shouldn't have!" she says, touched all the same, and feeling momentarily guilty for her assumption that the flowers were for Jean.

"That's okay, Miss Annie, Mr. Swell gave me some money for...oops! It's supposed to be a secret!" he says, giggling and covering his mouth.

"A secret?"

"Yup. But it's okay, Miss Annie, 'cause it's a good secret, not a bad one." He smiles broadly, a Cheshire Cat grin. She could probably pry the secret out of him without difficulty, but that wouldn't be fair play.

"Well, Esa, thank you very much. And thank you for taking such good care of my area. It looks very neat. But now I think I'll have to go upstairs. The program's about to start. I hope to be back at my desk soon, Esa. I miss you all."

"And we miss you, Miss Annie." Esa turns on the vacuum cleaner and starts making a quite unnecessary pass through her department. It's neat as a pin already.

Annie goes upstairs and walks into the Friends' Room, where the evening's event is taking place. The seats are more than half-filled, which is pretty good for poetry. She settles herself quietly in the back row until it's time for the introductions, when she goes forward to give her little well rehearsed speech. There is no heckling, no rude comments from anyone in the audience, and Annie presents the first poet, who reads his three sonnets—a drippingly romantic set—and receives generous applause. Annie introduces poet number two, an elderly woman, dressed in black and wearing a great amethyst brooch pinned to her ample chest.

"Clustered condos cling
Like barnacles
To cliffsides;
Soaring seagull screech
And cry in air
At sunrise..."

Oh dear, Annie thinks, while smiling and nodding encouragingly to the woman, who is reading her poetry in a loud but quavering voice. At the end of this reading there will be an intermission, which Annie is looking forward to. Her stomach has begun to make unforgivable noises, and she is already eyeing the goodie-table. She has seen the cheese and crackers on the far corner, and someone has even made little cocktail sandwiches—*Bless her, whoever she is,* Annie thinks. *Or him,* she amends guiltily.

But she is also looking forward to the next reading. The locally revered poet Robert Morgan has promised to read a few of his most recent works, which, if true to form, will be replete with irony and caustic wit.

Annie has just taken a bite of a small ham-and-cheese triangle when she hears a whisper loud enough that she is convinced it is aimed for her ears.

"I can't believe she would show up here. I heard she was suspended!"

Annie glances around. She recognizes the woman instantly. The pinched face and normally loud and grating voice are unforgettable. Mrs. Ridley is one of those perennial professional volunteers—at church, at the art society, at the library. Mrs. Ridley is also one of those patrons who never owes a fine. "Oh, no, dear. That is a mistake. The librarian must have used the wrong date-stamp," or "No, no, you must have neglected to check it in the day I returned it," or "I never took that book out in my life. I don't read those kinds of books," or some similar excuse.

Annie steps away from the table, and when Mrs. Ridley has filled her plate and walks over toward her chair, she catches up with her.

"Mrs. Ridley, I couldn't help overhearing, and I wanted to assure you that I am only here to help out as a volunteer tonight. I'm not back at work," she says, and adds, "yet."

People are milling about in the room, and Mrs. Ridley and Annie are standing alone in the middle aisle. Mrs. Riddle gives Annie a sour look.

"Well, your presence here is unsettling, to say the least. Quite takes away the pleasure of listening to the readings."

"I'm very sorry you feel that way, Mrs. Ridley. I'll go and ask if Mr. Langmuir can find a replacement for the rest of the evening," Annie says, turning toward the door that leads out to the corridor.

"Oh well, don't bother. The harm's done." Mrs. Ridley snaps her neck, which signals the end of the conversation, and goes back to the refreshment table to pick up a drink. Annie has lost her appetite and drops the rest of her sandwich into the trash barrel on the way out of the room before walking over to the director's office. As usual the door stands open, and she walks in.

"I'm sorry, Duncan, but I think my coming here tonight was a mistake." She tells him about Mrs. Ridley.

"Oh, drat that woman!" Duncan says. "Well, you can sit in here, and I'll take your place until after the intermission. Then I'll drive you back. Did you get something to eat?" He looks at her and winces. "You never even got any lunch, either, did you? Well, let's go in together and you can fill up a plate. Enough so you can take some back with you to the motel."

Annie shakes her head quickly. "No, no, that's okay. I'm not going back in there. I don't want to cause a scene and make more trouble for the library."

Duncan nods thoughtfully and waves for her to take a chair before he goes into the Friends' Room to take her place. When the readings start up again, Annie can hear Robert Morgan's familiar, resonant voice:

LANDLUBBAH
He stands on the pier, wearing a bright yellow Mac,
Shivering slightly in the damp morning breeze.
Weighted down with gear—
Rod, bait, and creel.

"This is no river cruise, sonny.
If you catch one out theah,
She'll nevah fit in that pitiful basket.
But, anyways, you won't catch one. You see, that rod
Will be broke in hahf afore you land 'er."

After chuckles and applause, Morgan goes on to the next poem, but someone shuts the door and the poet's reedy voice fades away. Duncan returns shortly with a paper plate heaped with food and sweets and a couple of cans of soda. Annie smiles broadly.

"Now, if there's a only good movie on, I'll be okay," she says.

Duncan drives her to the motel and comes in to turn on the lights and check the room. He waits for Annie to get settled, putting her makeshift dinner on the dresser. As he is leaving, Annie follows him to the door. Before he opens it, he suddenly turns around and gives her a swift embrace, squeezing her elbows with surprising force before letting go.

"Annie..." he starts, but does not continue. Abruptly, he opens the door and leaves, shaking his head.

CHAPTER 24

"O, what may within him hide,
though angel on the outward side."
(from *Measure for Measure*)

In her motel bed, Annie dreams again. She dreams that Duncan is standing over her, watching her sleep. Suddenly he leans forward and brings his hands toward her neck. She wakes up in a cold sweat, her heart beating frantically. I'm going mad, she thinks. Why am I having a nightmare about Duncan? Duncan, who is the only person she feels she can really trust?

True, his unexpected embrace and abrupt exit caused her momentary anxiety. But Duncan shows empathy for all his staff, whenever they need it. He is not usually physical about it, though. These days you can get sued for harassment for embracing an employee; maybe that was why he left in such a hurry. In her current state, maybe she is simply unable to tell the difference between a supportive hug and an amorous embrace? *It was the way he squeezed my elbows,* she thinks, and then laughs a little hysterically at how foolish that sounds.

But...then the embrace was followed by that unfinished sentence, and his leaving so abruptly. Duncan is always in control, always correct and completely professional. Sometimes he may treat her differently than he treats the others, but she and Duncan have known each other a long time now and are naturally closer. They are also kindred spirits in many ways, sharing their love of Shakespeare and an interest in art and architecture—although her area of interest is modern art, while Duncan's is the ancient and renaissance eras. And just think of all his help and support since Carlo's death. Duncan told her to take time off even before she was a suspect. He even paid for the motel room out of his own pocket, and has already refused her offer to pay him back. Right from the start, he showed the other librarians that he had complete confidence in her, despite all he knew of her past.

At this point in her contemplation, Annie's eyes open wide. Duncan *did* know all about her past—even before it was plastered all over the front pages. He was the *only one* who did, except for Josie and, she now remembers, her brother Justin, whom she had called one evening just after Carlo left. She'd had some wine and started to feel very sorry for herself back then. Bawling and feeling lonely, she had called to cry on Justin's shoulder. No one else though, no one in the old gang, knew about her relationship with Carlo.

But no...it couldn't possibly be Duncan. He would never have called the police and accused her, or let out word about her relationship with Carlo...or put that note on her door. It certainly couldn't be Duncan who murdered Carlo. Why would he do such a thing?

She remembers his embrace again, and shudders anxiously. Suddenly she also remembers other times, certain looks and touches that at the time seemed normal, everyday: putting a warm hand on her arm or back, caressing her hand seemingly by accident when he passed her a book...

"Nooo..." she groans. Could it be...that Duncan was *jealous* with Carlo back in the country? But Carlo had someone else now, Margo. Of course, Annie hadn't been able to hide from Duncan the fact that Carlo's presence—*especially* accompanied by Margo—was a source of pain. Duncan is very astute. *Oh, but it can't be. It just can't. It has to be someone else. Why would he burn down the gallery, then, if all he wanted was to get rid of Carlo? Only a psychopath...and Duncan is no psychopath. I won't believe it.*

Annie sits up in bed and turns on the light. It's two thirty in the morning. *If only Gussie were here,* she thinks, *I wouldn't feel so lonely.* But Gussie is at Duncan's place. *What if Duncan never told the police where I am? What if Duncan is the only one who knows where I am, and who knows about Carlo and me? What if he really is a madman? All killers are madmen. Somebody did kill Carlo. Most likely somebody I know. Why not Duncan?*

Annie is out of bed and getting dressed. She puts on jeans and a T-shirt, reluctantly leaves her beloved flip-flops behind in favor of a pair of sneakers, and pulls on a dark hooded sweatshirt on top. Then she puts her purse and motel key in her backpack and leaves the rest of her stuff in the closet. Before opening the door, she turns out the light in the room. It is pitch dark outside, except for a small light by the door. If only she had her car. But Duncan had insisted on driving her to the motel. That way, if the police checked, he had said, they would find her car still at home and assume that she couldn't be far away. It would also leave her without a way to escape. From him? She looks around, holding her breath, before shutting the door quietly and running across the parking area into the woods. She has no idea where she is going. She can't go home. All she knows is that she can't stay at the motel.

CHAPTER 25

"This was the mos unkindest cut of all."
(from *Julius Caesar*)

Annie runs through the trees down toward the train tracks. She crosses the tracks and finds one of the trails into Dogtown. The moon is up now, and she can see the ground in front of her. She hikes uphill by way of Raccoon Ledges—a great heap of boulders, part of a terminal moraine—to the swamp. At first she plans to go around the western side of Briar Swamp but suddenly remembers that that's where the town line goes. She can't afford to violate any more rules, so instead she takes the trail on the east side. She skirts Pool Hill and the end of Squam Road, and continues through smaller swamps and obstinate catbrier over toward the quarries, where the woods are drier and more open. Annie suddenly knows where she is going: to Josie's house. Josie Mandel believes in her innocence, she even said so, and no one will think of looking for Annie there.

But Josie Mandel is lying in a pool of blood on her kitchen floor with a great, black wound to her head, glassy eyes staring at the ceiling. Annie rushes forward and gets down beside her. She calls Josie's name and feels her hands, which are warm. She tries to feel the old woman's wrist, then her neck, to see if she can find a pulse, but Annie is trembling too violently herself to detect anything. She runs to the phone. *Oh, no!* she thinks. But she knows she has to do it. She dials the police.

"Rockport Police, this call is being recorded," a voice answers.

Annie partly covers the receiver with her hand and tries to disguise her voice.

"We have a very serious emergency, head wound, lots of blood! Please send an ambulance, right away!" she shouts, and shouts again when she gives Josie's name and address. Then she hangs up. She has to leave before they come. *Or else I'll be the prime suspect in Josie's murder, too!* She runs back and kneels beside Josie.

"Josie, Josie, can you hear me?" she cries. Josie moans weakly and Annie squeezes her hand.

"Annie...I need...my son...get him..." Josie whimpers.

Annie is not even aware that Josie has a son, or where he can be found. She tries to envision Josie's biography in her mind, but does not remember anything about children. Maybe the woman is just delirious? Now Annie hears sirens approaching, and flees out the back door. Only when she's deep into the woods does she realize that her backpack is still in Josie's house. On the floor, right next to the telephone.

Eventually, Annie hears the ambulance take off and leave on the dirt road, then continue down the hill toward Granite Street. The sound of the siren weakens after the vehicle crosses Keystone Bridge, and finally disappears as it speeds through town toward the hospital in Gloucester. When complete silence has settled over the woods again, Annie slowly and carefully retraces her steps toward Josie's cottage, to see if she can retrieve her backpack. Maybe they only sent an ambulance crew, and maybe the crew didn't notice her bag? Suddenly she hears voices and the bark of a dog. Of course. The police must have suspected immediately that a violent crime may have been committed, and now they've sent out a search party.

Annie knows these woods as well as anyone, and runs toward one of the quarries. She gets into the water, clothes and all, and swims across a narrow section. Maybe they'll lose the trail that way, and that will delay them. But not for long; it's only a small quarry, and it won't take them more than ten minutes to circle around it, and for the dog to pick up her scent again. Where can she go? Sally's? It's too far. Sally lives in the South End, and she'd never make it through town. Clare's. Clare lives in the Cove. Maybe her guest has left by now.

Running as quickly and as quietly as she can, she makes her way through the woods toward Granite Street. It's downhill all the way, and she nearly falls headlong several times. She jumps across boulders and skids along on soft pine needles. Acorns on a steep trail roll under her feet like well-oiled ball bearings. The sun is just below the horizon now, and soon it will appear and cast its pink light over the coastline. Annie hurries across the street and over toward The Avenues, where Clare lives. Clare rents a small cottage on the lower end of Haven Avenue. "The Avenues" is a section of Pigeon Cove, quiet streets with a mix of quaint, modest gingerbread cottages and larger, ostentatious homes of the seriously affluent, often flanked by great magnolias and impressive topiary. On the seaside, The Avenues are bordered by the Atlantic Path, a walking trail along the rocky shoreline with a grand view of Sandy Bay, downtown Rockport, and the open sea.

Annie hurries along the side of the street with the most trees and shrubs until she comes near Clare's cottage. There she scurries, hunched down, into the yard and over toward the kitchen door. As she passes the window, she notices that the lights are on. Why would Clare be up this early in the morning? Annie peers in. Clare is standing by the stove with her back turned, and Margo is seated at the table with a coffee mug in her hand. *I should have known! Ned said he dropped her off at the corner of Granite and Haven. But why? For God's sake, why, Clare?*

Margo is laughing. Annie can hear the sound of a phone ringing, and watches as Clare walks over and picks up the receiver. She sees Clare's mouth fall open, and when Clare turns to say something to Margo, Annie has to duck to avoid being seen. *Maybe someone is calling to tell Clare about Josie?* Someone in the art gang, maybe, who leaves a scanner on all the time. That still doesn't explain why Clare and Margo are up so early, even before the phone rang.

Annie has no idea where to turn now; she only knows that she has to get out of this yard, immediately. But first she makes a mad dash around the house over to the garage. Clare's little red Mazda is parked there, and Clare usually keeps her cell phone in the glove compartment. *Please, God...*

CHAPTER 26

"But I will wear my heart upon my sleeve
For daws to peck at."
(from *Othello*)

A nnie runs through the avenues and heads for a safe place she remembers from childhood. She hurtles downhill toward the rocks by the bay, and breathes a sigh of relief when she sees it. It's still there! So many old sheds and outbuildings have gotten torn down by new landowners, especially when a water view is involved. She finally makes it safely into her hiding place, an old boat shed on a promontory down in Rowe's Cove, where she and Justin used to hide out long ago. Annie leans against the cold stone wall, trying to catch her breath and calm down. More than a shed, her hideout is a small, square building sturdily built of large, rectangular granite blocks, with a loft for extra storage. The ladder up to the loft has lost a couple of rungs, but Annie manages to get up there and make herself a cozy nook by the window. She checks her watch before dialing Justin's number. They'll probably be still asleep, it's earlier where he lives, but she can't wait any longer.

"Melanie, I'm sorry to wake you up. Is Justin there? What? When? Last night? Yes, I know his cell number." Melanie is

Justin's wife. She never took to New England—those long, cold winters; the crusty, monosyllabic people, the gray little cottages—so she and Justin live in New Mexico, where Melanie is from. And where, Annie presumes, it's hot all the time, and people sit in colorful houses and talk in long sentences.

Annie punches in Justin's cell phone number. When she reaches him he is in a rented car.

"Oh, Juss, I'm so glad I got you. Melanie said you caught a flight last night. Where are you?"

"The plane got delayed, and it took me a while to rent the car, but I'm halfway between Logan and Rockport. But Annie, what in heck's going on there? Why didn't you call? I saw you on TV…you, Carlo, the fire…"

Annie feels tears well up at the sound of her brother's voice. "I didn't do it. Any of it. But Juss, something else has happened—somebody attacked Josie Mandel last night, and now the police are after me for that, too, I'm sure. I'm hiding, Juss, I'm scared…"

"Good Lord, Annie, what have you gotten yourself into? I'm sure you didn't do it, but jeepers. Well, never mind. I'm on the way, we can talk when I get there. Are you safe where you are?"

"I'm fine, I'm in a safe place. Juss, can you meet me at—"

"*Don't* say it," he interrupts vehemently. "I know where to find you, don't I? I know this safe place, right?"

"Yes, but what are you afraid of? We're on a cell phone," she says. Annie, though well versed in computers and any other modern gadgetry that will help her in her searches at the library, has never owned a cell phone, on principle. *What, and be available to anyone at any time of day or night? And spending hours messaging and twittering and sending pictures and playing games? No, thanks.*

"People can listen in. Just do as I say. Are you in the safe place now? Good. Stay there. I'll be in Rockport in half an hour."

People can listen in. Right. Another reason for not owning a cell phone, she thinks.

Annie calls information and asks for Billy Hale's home phone. She doesn't want her voice automatically recorded down at the police station again. She listens to the number given, twice, then calls it immediately before she forgets it.

"Billy? This is Annie Quitnot. I didn't do it, Billy."

"Annie! Where are you?"

"I'm not going to tell you that. Just listen, please, Billy. I didn't do it, didn't kill Carlo, didn't set the fire, and I didn't hit Josie over the head."

"Turn yourself in, Annie, that's the only thing you can do to help yourself."

"No, I'm not going to do that. I'm afraid, Billy. I think somebody's out to get me. Nobody believes me. Everyone thinks I'm guilty. I just want you to know I didn't do it, and tell you that you have to go out there and find out who did. You can't stop looking for who really did it, Billy!"

"But Annie—"

Annie flips the phone closed and slips it into her pocket, wondering whether she should just get rid of it. Just then, the phone rings. Annie looks at it in panic. The number is the one she just dialed. Billy Hale is calling her back. She does not answer, just hopes there is no way for him to trace her here.

CHAPTER 27

"Angels and ministers of grace defend us!"
(from *Hamlet*)

Annie sits on the wooden floor, leaning her back against some old tarps, and looks around in the shed. The sun filters in through the windows, casting dusty rays on the jumble of ropes, anchors, buoys and other marine paraphernalia. She is tempted to wipe the old windowpanes clean but leaves the decades of grime and cobwebs alone. The view is familiar to her anyway, a panorama of ocean and shoreline, including the north side of Bearskin Neck—the side opposite Carlo's. Annie has placed a couple of lobster pots (the old wooden type, flat-topped, not the steam-bent, curved-top ones that they use down Maine) along the edge of the loft, and draped old sails and dry, dusty ropes over them to shield herself from view, just in case anyone should happen to walk in. She picks up a pile of soft old rags to sit on, and with the rags comes a grimy old book, which she brings with her over to the window. When she wipes it clean she finds that it is *The Smugglers of Sandy Bay*. Oh, how she had loved that book! She and Justin read it together, right here by this window, in fact. Ruth Holberg was a local author still alive when Annie was a girl, and Annie had once been with her mother to the author's house, where they were served hot chocolate and cookies. Annie opens the book and sees the inscription: *To Annie. Keep reading! Your friend, Ruth Holberg.* It's her own book. Greedily, she crams it into her sweatshirt pocket.

While she waits for Justin, Annie's thoughts travel in circles. She wants to exonerate Duncan in her mind. Duncan, who for so many years has been a trusted and cherished part of her daily life. But who else could have called the police to suggest that she killed Carlo? Annie has no enemies that she can think of. Unless, of course, she considers Stuart to be one. He would certainly love to see the coveted Reference Desk up for grabs. But what could Stuart have suggested as a motive? He certainly wouldn't have known of any connection between her and Carlo.

The door opens downstairs. Annie hears the soft click of the latch and the scraping of the door against the cement floor. She sits perfectly still until Justin's head suddenly appears over the wall of lobster pots. Then she flops down in a heap on the floor and starts bawling like a child.

Justin gives her a hug before they settle down together on the dirty rags.

"Parked the car off on a side street, not far. Didn't want to leave it too close to here. People might get curious." Justin is still out of breath after running. His jeans are creased, and the short-sleeved denim shirt is damp with sweat. No surprise, he's worn them since yesterday.

Annie hasn't seen her brother for a long time, must be a couple of years now. He has put on a little weight, but looks the same otherwise. The wavy black hair hasn't thinned yet, and his eyes are still piercingly blue. Justin took after their father, while Annie got her Irish looks from their mother, Mairead. After studying Annie for a few moments, Justin opens his backpack and rummages through it. It looks as though he packed it in a hurry; clothes and toiletries are all jumbled inside.

"Well, Sis, here's the paper." He says, pulling out a folded copy.

ROCKPORT KILLER STRIKES AGAIN

Prominent Rockport resident Josie Mandel, earlier murder victim's benefactor, viciously attacked... lies hospitalized in a coma... All Points Bulletin posted for Reference Librarian Annie Quitnot, whose whereabouts are unknown since her flight from a motel room hideout... evidence of Quitnot's presence found near Mandel's body... Valenti widow tells harrowing tale, fears she may be next victim...

There is a picture of Josie on the front page, and the article continues inside the paper, salaciously describing in detail how the victim was discovered in a pool of blood. Justin has a perplexed frown as he reads down the column.

"You never told me Carlo got married. So where are they hiding Margo, I wonder?" Justin says, when they have finished reading.

"At Clare's, on Haven Avenue." Disgust is apparent in Annie's voice.

"How do you know?" he asks with some amazement, and Annie looks up at him. *Is he suspicious of me, too? Well, who'd blame him?*

"I went there, after... Oh, Juss, I *was* at Josie's this morning, I thought she might let me stay there. I went to see her last week, and she said she knew I was innocent. This morning I found her on the floor... just the way it says in the paper.

I was the one that called for the ambulance. Then, stupidly, I left my backpack by the phone. That's the 'evidence' they're talking about. When I realized that, I panicked, and the only friend I could think of was Clare. But before I got to her kitchen door I saw Margo through the window, and that's when I borrowed Clare's phone from her car and came over here."

By now, Justin's eyes are rolling, and he holds up both hands to silence her.

"And this Margo is a friend of Clare's?"

"Apparently."

"Do you think you could just tell me everything without my prompting you? From beginning to end, so I don't have to unravel the story and pull all these surprises out of you like taffy?"

Annie tells him, in as much detail as she can remember, the whole story, including the part about her suspicions about Duncan. When she is finished, Justin puts his head down on his knees for a moment. Then he straightens up.

"So, you are sure you got here without anyone seeing you?"

"I hope so."

"You stay here. Don't even stick your nose out the door. Let's switch phones, so I can charge your battery. Do you still have the phone?"

Annie nods.

"Good. I'll call you. Now, don't move. Promise?"

Annie nods, and Justin gives her a one-armed hug as he crawls by on the way to the ladder. In her anxiety, she forgets to tell him about the phone call to Billy Hale, and the call back that she did not answer.

CHAPTER 28

"When to the sessions of sweet silent thought,
I summon up remembrance of things past,
And with old woes new wail my dear time's waste:
Then can I drown an eye (unused to flow)
For precious friends hid in death's dateless night,
And weep afresh love's long since cancelled woe,
And moan th'expense of many a vanished sight.
Then can I grieve at grievances foregone,
And heavily from woe to woe tell o'er
The sad account of fore-bemoanèd moan,
Which I new pay as if not paid before.
But if the while I think on thee (dear friend)
All losses are restored, and sorrows end."
(30ᵗʰ Sonnet)

The Bard gives her relief and solace, still. Annie, who knows quite a few of Shakespeare's sonnets by heart, lies in the boat shed and stares out the window at a flock of seagulls. They weave and soar on the updraft, sometimes uttering long, plaintive cries that certainly reflect Annie's own mood at the moment. She has begun to mourn. During the years of Carlo's absence, there was always *hope*. Unrealistic, of course, but she knows now that hope was what actually kept her from dealing with the loss of his presence. And now that he will never come back, she owns him again; he is hers to mourn. She grieves in silence, and her friend Shakespeare, as so often before, comes to her aid.

Sometimes her thoughts stray. When they turn to Duncan, she forcefully pushes them away. Duncan has been a pillar, a steadying force during her years at the library. She can't afford, at this fearful and lonely time, to absolutely condemn him to this awful possibility—and yet, she can see no way to free him, either. Therefore she chooses to avoid every thought of him.

Annie's thoughts flit about and light on Clare. She cannot understand Clare at all. *I thought she was my friend.* How could Clare take Margo in? Well…in fairness, it is not surprising. Clare has always taken in strays; she has that soft heart. Annie tries to free herself of jealousy and think of Margo the way others might see her—as a lonely and scared young girl who has just lost the man she loves. No, has just lost her *husband,* she corrects herself. *Clare knows Margo better than I do. They have spent a lot of time together since Carlo brought Margo home with him. Clare has so much empathy. I suppose I should feel ashamed that I can't feel sorry for Margo myself.*

As for friends, there's Sally. Annie trusts that Sally, at least, is still her friend. She knows Sal would be eager to help; however, her husband Matt would probably call the police *immediately*, not because he doesn't like Annie, but because to do anything else would be *illegal,* would be *harboring a criminal,* for Pete's sake. Annie knows numerous other people who she would normally consider friends but who she now realizes are merely acquaintances. And her other colleagues, Marie and Jean, even Maureen—well, they would be embarrassed, even petrified, probably, if she were even to contact them.

For a brief moment her thoughts turn to Stuart, but then she laughs bitterly. She can see him now, taking over her desk. What was that secret, she wonders, that Stuart asked Esa to keep? Nothing sinister, probably. And she has to admit it: as much as she would like to imagine it, she can't quite see Stuart committing murder to get her job. *Then who—dear God, who?* Her mind is going in circles again, and she is getting nowhere.

Annie has put the phone in the sweatshirt's belly pocket, and waits for Justin's call. Finally she feels it vibrate and flips it open. She makes sure the call is from Justin.

"Hello?"

"Did you even check to see that it was me calling?" Justin asks. He knows Annie doesn't like cell phones, and is just baiting her. "Never mind. I'm on the way. Stay where you are."

"Okay."

He brings sandwiches when he comes, and a couple of plastic bags containing drinks, bread, peanut butter, chocolate bars, and apples: a varied and healthful diet. She remembers what Justin grew up on: cereal, macaroni and cheese, pizza, and an occasional hot dog. Now he grabs an apple and a roast beef sandwich, of which he immediately discards half the bread. Apparently, his taste has changed. Or maybe he's trying to lose those extra pounds he's put on.

"I've arranged for legal counsel," he says, biting into the sandwich. Annie turns pale.

"What? You're turning me in?"

"Of course not. Right now, you're to stay here. We'll do this one step at a time. I don't know exactly how it will work, so just keep your cool."

"Are you telling me that somebody else knows where I am?" Annie is getting angry. This is not the kind of help she was counting on. She is beginning to think that she was doing better on her own.

"No. Calm down. Not yet, anyway. I'm your go-between right now. But this is the last you'll see of me in person, in case somebody should begin to follow me."

"Where will you be? And who's this lawyer, anyway?"

"I said you have *legal counsel.* Judge Bradley, that's who."

Annie chokes on her chicken sandwich, and tries to swallow it down with some soda, which only makes matters worse. Justin whacks her on the back, and she finally gets her voice under control. "Good grief, Juss, no! Not Judge Bradley!"

"Shut up, Sis, I know what I'm doing." Justin gives her a firm look. *He looks just like Dad right now,* she thinks. When her Dad had made up his mind about something, nobody could make him change it, and she still remembers that same look and those tightly clenched jaws.

"But Judge Bradley, of all people! Besides, he's been retired for eons…and anyway, I can't afford him, you know that!" Annie tries again, but knows it is futile, and Justin is the only one who can help her now.

"Don't worry about that. I just told him he owes me." Justin looks pleased with himself.

"What? I thought you owe *him*. He's the one who saved your life!"

Justin grins. "That means he owes me. See, you save someone's life, then you're responsible for him." He puts the last of his sandwich in his mouth and chews vigorously.

"You can't be serious," she says, but has to laugh at his nerve.

"Look, you've got to trust me, Sis. Now, give me your phone, and I'll charge it in the car. You take this one, and listen, I'll call you at five minutes before the hour, so you don't have to worry about who's calling. And don't leave this place."

Annie decides not to tell him about the call to Billy Hale. Justin would have her hide. And it's unlikely that Billy will try calling again, since she didn't answer his last try.

CHAPTER 29

"Like one that stands upon a promontory,
And spies a far-off shore where he would tread,
Wishing his foot were equal with his eye."
(from *Henry VI*)

She feels let down after Justin leaves, more alone even than before he came. The sun has come and gone through the window, and even though it's a warm summer day, she feels chilled.

Out on the bay a couple of Star boats, of which there still are a few in Rockport, are doing a slow tango. Their sleek bodies tack together, then turn and continue on, sails adjusted smoothly and effortlessly to catch the wind for a long cheek-to-cheek out to the Sandy Bay breakwater. Annie follows their progress while she waits impatiently for Justin to call. She has already been into the snack bag and helped herself to an apple and a piece of chocolate. At five minutes before every hour, she waits for his call. The afternoon passes, and the sky turns pink and purple. The edge of the clouds hit by the setting sun glimmer golden before turning blue and cold. Could she have missed his call? She takes the phone out of her pocket to make sure she can hear it. Maybe she should call him? She turns on the phone and starts to put in the number, then realizes that she is holding Justin's phone, and would have to call Clare's number. But she can't remember Clare's cell phone number.

Annie hears the church bells strike eight, and checks her watch. Something must have gone wrong; otherwise, why hasn't Justin called? Just then, the phone vibrates.

"Yes? Hello?"

"Get out of there, just get out. I'll meet you at the pit." Justin sounds agitated, breathless.

"Pit" is what people call the smaller water-filled quarries. There are hundreds of them in Dogtown, some just little pools, others larger and swimmable. The smallest quarries of all are called "motions" and, like vernal pools, generally only hold water in the spring. These are shallow, full of sharp granite scraps, and most of them were made by people who only needed some stone for their own use. Over the years, the kids on the island have always gone swimming in the larger quarries and pits. In one of the pits, owned by an artist, boys even were invited to go swimming in the altogether. But that was in the good old days. Now, most of the quarries are privately owned, or owned by an association, and in these days of liability insurance and law suits, the pits are all off limits, well marked with big signs saying "private" or "no trespassing." Without a pass, you can't swim in the quarries. But Justin and Annie, having grown up in freer days, remember the pits fondly—especially Little Parker, where they were always welcome as children. This is the pit where he wants them to meet.

Annie pulls on her sweatshirt, grabs the bag of food—she does not plan to go hungry again—and climbs down the ladder in the dark. Before opening the door, she braids her hair tightly and stuffs it through the neck of her sweatshirt, then pulls up the hood. She puts the plastic grocery bag inside the sweatshirt and pulls the cord tight around her hips. Now she looks like a pregnant gorilla, but that's fine.

Crossing Granite Street is the riskiest moment, but she manages to get across without seeing anyone, and then she picks her way through shrubby backyards rather than going up Rowe Avenue toward the little quarry. She circles the pit and goes to the far end, where she finds Justin in the shrubbery, just where she knew he would be waiting.

"What happened?" she whispers.

"Somebody was following me, might have recognized me. We've got to get you away from here. If they find you hiding out like this, they will certainly think you are guilty, Annie. I think you should consider turning yourself in. At least you'd be safe." They are speaking in hushed voices, but Justin is getting nervous, and is a little impatient with her.

"Yeah, for a long, long time. They've got me, can't you see that? Motive, opportunity, evidence, the whole shebang. I have no alibi for any of these things. Not one. Who the hell did this, Juss? I'm going out of my mind trying to figure it out. And I'm afraid, too. Somebody is after me, I can feel it. Somebody is trying to pin all this on me, can't you see? What would have happened if I had been home the day of the break-in? After all, look what happened to poor Gussie. That really scared me, and that's why Duncan wanted me out of there." But that was when she still trusted Duncan, she remembers.

"I think you're getting paranoid, Sis. Anyway, we'll have to find a safe place for you until we can get you and Judge together."

Annie starts objecting again, loudly. Justin hushes her. A car coming from Steel Derrick, one of the largest quarries, where only shareholders are allowed to swim, drives by on the road that continues past Little Parker. It's a dirt road, and dust billows over to where they sit. It's getting dark, and people are leaving the quarries for the day. As the dust settles on them, Annie covers her face, and Justin tries to stifle a cough.

"I could borrow a kayak down in Gull Cove, and get over to Straitsmouth or one of the other islands and hide out for a while," Annie says, knowing as she speaks that it is a hare-brained scheme.

"Right, and tomorrow somebody would miss the kayak and report it stolen, and the police would probably figure out what happened. And then you *would* have done something illegal."

"I'd only borrow it," she tries, staunchly.

"Like you 'borrowed' Clare's phone?" He raises an eyebrow and looks at her sideways.

"Justin! Come on. Do you have a better idea?"

"As a matter of fact, I do."

Justin gets up and leads her over toward the shrubbery that grows all around the little quarry, flowering branches suspended and mirrored over the water. This is where he has hidden certain aids to a quick getaway. Annie vaguely recognizes the outlines of two bikes and a couple of canvas bags.

"And where are we going on those?"

"To Judge's place."

For once, Annie is speechless. Just then Clare's phone rings. Annie grabs it and checks the number. It's Billy Hale again.

"Who's calling, do you recognize the number?" Justin asks.

"It's Billy Hale. You know, Officer Hale?" She blurts out the tale. The phone stops ringing. Justin stares at her in disbelief.

"Give me the phone," he says, and reaches for it. Annie hands it to him. Justin lobs it into the middle of the quarry, where it instantly disappears from view. Without a word, he drags one of the bikes out of the bushes, stands it up and holds it for her impatiently until she comes over and grabs the handlebars. Then he gets the other one out for himself, hangs one of the canvas bags on each bike, and starts leading the way up the hill and toward the woods, which lie in the opposite direction of Judge's place. Annie follows, shaking her head.

CHAPTER 30

"Then nightly sings the staring owl, Tu-who;
Tu-whit, Tu-who."
(from *Love's Labors Lost*)

"Judge will never agree to it!" Annie says, out of breath already, trying to keep up with Justin's fast-paced biking. It's uphill over rough ground, an old dirt road with pockets of rocks and gravel.

"He won't even know about it," Justin assures her, breathing hard himself. "But that's the last place they'll look."

"And it's all the way over by the Country Club," she protests. "And why are we going this way? Are we going to ride through the woods? I'm not all that good at dirtbiking, in case you can't tell. And it's getting dark already."

Justin stops to give them a quick break.

"Stop worrying. That's why I came prepared. Here, take a look at this." He shows her what's in the bags. Spandex tights and top, and a helmet. Annie looks at him. Has he lost his mind?

"Rented in Gloucester. Tomorrow is the *Round the Cape* bike race. We're joining it. There's a studio up here on the hillside where we can hide out for the night. The owner has gone to Monhegan Island to paint for a couple of weeks. I heard Judge call the guy to tell him about Josie; I guess he's one of her recent protégés. Anyway, we should be safe there overnight. If you can stand owls."

"Owls?"

"The artist's favorite subject, I guess."

They slip up the hill in the dark, past a couple of cottages, and arrive at the studio. The door is locked, but Justin finds the key under a rock by the door. Another trusting soul, Annie thinks. The first thing they see when Justin turns on his flashlight is the painting on the easel: two large, round eyes surrounded by a fringe of feathers. The paintings leaning around the walls are all of owls: screech owls, barn owls, horned owls, saw-whets. Annie sees some she does not even know—and she a reference librarian who deals with schoolchildren! They close the door quietly and spend the night among the owls. Annie dreams of being followed through the library by round-eyed monsters on swooping wings.

In the morning, after returning the studio to the same condition they found it in, they don their athletic gear and goggles. Annie carefully stuffs her red hair under the helmet and picks up her bike, and then they roll down to Granite Street to join the racers just in time. The bikers speed along right through the center of town, waving gaily to the townspeople who line the streets and applaud the racers as they pass. Avery Shattuck stands together with Priscilla Pettengill on the granite step outside the Art Society. Annie waves to them, and they both smile and wave supportively in return, not realizing who she is.

The route goes through Dock Square, where, as always, the largest crowd has gathered, then past Annie's house, which is—not surprisingly—guarded by Officer Hale, and Annie makes sure to turn her face away as she passes him by. People are lining the street even here, as the route continues up South Street. When they get near the Country Club, Justin gets off his bike, pretending to check on his tire. Annie stops too, and hands him the water bottle attached to the frame of her bike. (The bottle is empty, but the gesture looks good, she thinks.) As soon as there is a lull in the ranks of bikers, they pull into a side lane, hide their bikes, and take the phony number-squares off their shirts.

"I can't take the helmet off. My hair!" Annie hisses.

"Here," Justin says, handing her the kerchief he's worn around his neck.

"You think of everything."

"Not quite. I see people horse-riding up the lane. I don't know how we'll get into the stables right now. But we'll think of something," he says confidently.

They are forced to spend the morning in a woodshed until the riders have returned their horses, watered them, wiped them down, curried them, and left. Then they go inside and climb upstairs to a generous hayloft with a view over paddocks, ponds, and streams—and up there on the height, Judge Bradley's comfortably sprawling ranch.

"Okay? You're on your own. Judge is probably wondering what on earth happened to me. Not that I'll tell him—about you being here, I mean. Here, take my phone, I'll see if I can get hold of another one. Also, I'll try getting some food to you. There's plenty of oats around, of course…" Justin says with a grin, and Annie swats at him.

"Go away. I'm not hungry, all I want to do is lie down and sleep. Thanks, Juss," she say, and flops down into the hay.

While Annie sleeps the sleep of the innocent, Justin is being grilled by Judge, who is not particularly satisfied with the answers he's receiving. Judge, a tall, imposing man, is lounging casually in a maroon leather wing chair in his quite impressive library, wearing rumpled chinos and a blue check- ered shirt with the tails out. The curly, gray hair stands out in a bush around his head, Einstein-like, surrounding a broad, weatherbeaten face. Judge listens impatiently to Justin, want- ing to know everything Annie has told him. Naturally, he wants to question Annie in person (perhaps to compare the answers), but that is still to be arranged. Judge is not asking, nor does he want to know at the moment, where Annie is hiding.

"She was in bed, asleep," Justin answers to the question of where Annie was when Carlo was murdered.

"And when the fire was set?" Judge's frequently intent face is neutral.

"Again, asleep in bed. The town alarm woke her up." Justin frowns in concentration, trying to remember the details of what Annie told him.

"And at the time of the attack on Josie?" Judge studies Justin's face while he questions him, and Justin squirms a little under his scrutiny.

"She had been staying in a motel room and had left it to get away. She was afraid of someone—well, she'll have to explain that part to you herself, I don't know what to make of it. I think she's a little paranoid at this point, and who can blame her. But she says that she ran through the woods over to the Cove to see if she could stay with Josie. And found her on the floor. She called the police from there. Tried to disguise her voice. Then she ran."

Judge shakes his head in disbelief. "What the hell was she doing in a motel room? People around here know who she is and would surely have recognized her when she checked in, so what good would that do? And, now that I think of it, the police must have known she was there, since it was reported in the paper. I don't understand it. And why did she leave in the middle of the night?"

"Couldn't really tell you, Judge, you'll just have to ask her. She was afraid, like I said."

"Okay, we'll leave it at that for now. So, after she left Josie's, what then?"

"She heard people in the woods following her. They had a dog; she could hear it barking. She panicked and ran past the quarries over to Haven Avenue to her friend Clare Draper's house; they work together at the library and she thought that maybe she could stay with Clare. Well, there she saw Margo, ah, Valenti, I guess…through the window, so she had to run again."

"Well, well, finally an interesting piece of information. I was wondering where they'd stashed her. So, then what did she do?"

"She borrowed Clare's cell phone out of her car."

"Borrowed?"

"That's what she said, and then she ran and hid in the boathouse. That's where she called me from, and that's where I went to meet her."

"And why didn't she stay in the boathouse?"

"Because I thought I noticed a car following me. And I didn't know when they had first seen me—if they knew I had been to the boathouse. That's when I called her and told her to get out. And then we stayed in the studio overnight, and then—" Justin is hurrying to get the end of his tale, but Judge holds up a hand to slow him down.

"Whoa, don't tell me any more, now," Judge interrupts. "I'll ask you about the rest when I want to know. Okay, except for the details we're up to date. I'm going to need to talk to Annie, of course. Let's try to set up a phone call for later tonight, all right?"

"Sure, Judge. I'll take care of it. I'll go outside and give her a call. Shall we say she calls you at seven o'clock?"

"That'll do fine. And in the meantime, no crazy moves, either of you. Don't answer any questions without checking with me. I don't want you lying to the police."

Justin nods and walks out back to make his 'phone call,' before remembering he doesn't even have a phone. Well, a quick visit to the barn, then.

CHAPTER 31

"Be somewhat scanter of your maiden presence."
(from *Hamlet*)

Moments after Justin returns, officers Elwell and O'Shane pull up in a cruiser, and Judge steps outside. Justin remains in the entry.

"What can I do for you gentlemen today?" Judge asks.

"Would you mind if we had a look around, Judge?" Elwell surreptitiously casts a quick eye around the yard.

"Looking for anything special?"

"Just following up on some calls, sir." Elwell says, looking as businesslike as he can in front of Judge, who is still a somewhat daunting figure.

"Are you perhaps implying I might be hiding something here?" Judge asks with a small, inscrutable smile.

"We're responsible for the safety of our citizens. We'd just like to check, if you don't mind letting us in?"

Judge seems slightly surprised and takes a step back, which just enables him to catch Justin whisper, "What about a warrant?" from where he is standing, right behind the door.

Judge's back stiffens slightly before he steps forward again, effectively blocking the doorway. He smiles affably at the officers.

"I'm sure you've brought a warrant?" Which they haven't. Showing a certain amount of irritation, the officers promise to be back with the required document. Judge smiles benevolently and steps inside, shutting the door behind him. He follows Justin into the living room.

"You imbecile," he hisses, teeth gritted. Then he calmly turns around and starts to walk toward his office.

"I have a job for you. See the trailer out there?" Judge points with his thumb out the window at a well padded cradle holding a sailboat of the Star class. The trailer is hitched to a jeep and ready for transport. "I want you to take that down to the yacht club for me and see to it that it gets in the water. I have a race this weekend, and I'm planning to take her out this afternoon— just had her spar replaced, after the old sitka spruce finally gave out. Enough to make you cry. Anyway, I've got some things to take care of in the office; should take me about ten minutes. Then I'll come out and tell you what you have to do. There are a couple of sail bags out in the boat shed, right next to the barn. While you wait, why don't you stow them below deck for me?" He juts his chin forward and gives Justin a stern stare.

Justin nods. He thinks he understands what he is supposed to do.

While Justin oversees the sailboat getting winched over the side of the wharf (with Annie and the sail bags safely stowed below deck) and dropped into the harbor, Judge Bradley gets another visit from the police.

"Feel free to roam around. I'll just warn you; I have two new horses boarding in the stable. They're down at the end. The one in the last stall, 'Sheik of Araby,' is a bit skittish. You may want to be careful searching down at that end."

This warning, as Judge expects when he issues it, leads to an extra careful search of the lower end of the stables— without result, naturally. Eventually, after having gone through the ranch, the stables, the boat shed, and other outbuildings, and after having driven down the dirt road to the end of the property looking for anything suspicious, the officers give up. As soon as they leave, Judge Bradley makes a few phone calls. When Justin returns with the jeep, Judge orders him to turn right around, and the two drive down to the yacht club together.

"You'll crew for me today. Need to give her a trial run."

"But, Judge...it's been a long time. There's not an awful lot of sailing going on down in New Mexico."

"Bah, you'll do. One of those things; once you know it, you never forget. It'll only be for a short run, anyway."

"Well, I'm not hanging over the side. I've got a wife now. And you're a bit old to rescue me again." Judge makes a loud harrumphing noise. Justin pulls into one of the yacht club parking spaces, and they walk through the gate, where Judge instantly manages to reel in a strong-looking youth to help manhandle spars and sails into a semblance of respectability.

Judge's O.G. Star boat (O.G. stands for Old Greenwich Boat Co.) is one of the early Stars. Built of top grade red cedar (except for the areas that take a lot of stress—the keel plank and ribs, for instance, and the edge around the cockpit, where mahogany is used), it sports the slightly wider bow typical of the particular time and place it was built. One of the hallmarks of the O.G.s was a deck of ship-lapped cedar planks, the gaps filled with Thiokol, with the center deck king plank made out of mahogany. The deck was then bleached before it was varnished, ending up a straw yellow color, and has just been refinished into its Old Glory. The new spar is, like the old one, made of wood. Judge is not in favor of aluminum masts, nor of fiberglass Star boats, even though both are "permissible" these days.

Annie, hiding under a tarp and sundry bags and coils of rope, hears the voices of Judge and Justin, and also recognizes the voice of Brad, one of Sally's boys, who is the helpful youth that Judge has gotten hold of. She lies as still and quiet as a mouse until she feels the boat moving freely, sailing out of the harbor. Then she stretches carefully and shifts position. Once they get beyond the jetty, she senses the pickup of the wind and hears the water cluck against the sides. Peeking through a crack in the tarp, she sees Judge lean back and smile at Justin. There's no sign of Brad, but she still doesn't dare to show herself.

"Josie's coming out of her coma. I didn't think they'd let me see her, but apparently she's asked for me. Going there when we get back." Judge is speaking rather loudly, Annie thinks, even considering wind and waves. Then she understands. Judge "doesn't know" where she is, but wants her to hear what he says. Annie is grateful enough to cry and will make sure that he can honestly say he has not seen her and is uncertain of her whereabouts.

"Did she say she saw her attacker?" Justin asks.

"Don't know yet. They won't tell me anything. But she's still in critical condition, so they're letting her see whomever she asks for. She may not even be lucid, for all I know. But I can see her after seven. They've given her a sedative, so she'll be asleep until then."

Annie feels the boat change course and begin to lean. The swells come in from the stern, and the yacht rises and falls gently, leaning more heavily whenever the wind strengthens. Annie doesn't usually get seasick, but lying prone and stiff and unable to get comfortable, she is beginning to feel queasy. It feels like hours before she is suddenly rolled over onto the opposite side and they sail headfirst into the waves, chop-chop. As soon as they get into the harbor, the water is calm, and they glide smoothly back to the yacht club.

"Well done, Justin. You didn't forget a thing. You can crew for me on Saturday."

"But, Judge! That's the race! I can't possibly. You'll kill me if we lose."

"Lose? Not part of my vocabulary, son. Now, help me with the sails, will you? Nice and tidy, that's my boy. And we can leave this bag down below with the others." He hands Justin a small, zippered sports bag, and Justin tosses it into the hold with a surreptitious wave to Annie. The bag contains a meatloaf sandwich Judge made while he was waiting for Justin, and a couple of cans of soda.

CHAPTER 32

"The big round tears
Cours'd one another down his innocent nose
In piteous chase."
(from *As You Like It*)

Justin is waiting in the living room when Judge Bradley comes back from the hospital. The door slams hard, and Judge disappears into the kitchen. When he appears in the living room, he is carrying a glass containing an ominous amount of whisky.

"God damn," he says. "God damn."

Justin fears the worst: Josie has died, without being able to clear Annie. Or another alternative: Josie has identified Annie as her attacker.

"No, no," Judge clarifies. "Josie was attacked from behind. Never saw who did it."

"What, then?" Has Annie's whereabouts been discovered, or has she suddenly sneaked out and turned herself in? Or, has there been another murder attempt?

"God damn," Judge says again and puts down his whisky with such force that the glass shatters. Then he picks up the lamp from the side table and throws it full force onto the wall.

In the process, the cord gets ripped out of the wall outlet, causing sparks to fly, and the stained glass shade breaks against a frame on the wall. Glass flies in all directions. Justin ducks and hunkers down behind a chair.

"God damn it to hell," Judge says. Then he sits down and covers his face with his plump, coarse hands. His right hand is bleeding, but he seems oblivious.

"What is it, Judge? Anything I can do?" Justin asks, carefully clambering back up from behind his chair.

"Justin, I never before wished I were dead."

This sounds worse than Justin even imagined. Is Annie dead? Has someone killed *her,* now?

"I need to know what's happened, Judge," he says, bracing himself for the worst.

The Judge looks up. "Of course you do, Justin. I'm sorry."

Justin finally sits back down in his chair.

"Is Annie okay?"

"You'd know more about that than I. This is not about Annie." Judge shakes his head sadly.

"What is it, then?"

"It's a long story, Justin. A very long story." Judge Bradley gets up and walks around the room, seemingly surprised when his shoes crunch on the broken glass.

"You see, a long time ago...after Josie became a widow," he continues, "she and I—well, we had an affair, I suppose is what people would say nowadays. I was married then, of course; my wife died just ten years ago. I loved my wife, you know, just like Josie loved her Grant until he died. But Josie and I...well, never mind. Another time, maybe. Then one day, Josie said she wanted to break it off. Had enough of just being somebody's mistress, I guessed then; she's never been a shrinking violet. She packed up and went to Italy to study art, which she always said she wanted to do. She stayed for almost two years. When she came back, she was determined that we shouldn't see each other, except as we met by accident around town or so. Some years later she inherited all that money and started throwing parties and helping artists—like Carlo, for instance." Here, Judge falls silent again.

"I see," Justin says, although he really doesn't. He is just hoping to encourage Judge Bradley into continuing. Judge completes another circuit of the room, shaking his head, making his hands into fists and pushing them into the pockets of his pants. He stops by the door and turns to Justin.

"Carlo was my son. He was *my* boy," Judge says, and leaves the room. Justin does not follow him, just remains standing in mute amazement, and hears the clink of glass again in the kitchen. When Judge comes back he has a new glass, with a somewhat less intimidating amount of whisky.

"You see, Josie knew I would never divorce my wife. My son George was about to get married, and…well, I had my position to think of. And if Josie had gone on to have an out of wedlock baby *here,* she was certain that good old Uncle Brent would have cut her out of his will. As soon as she knew she was pregnant, she knew her plans had to include that money. She was determined that one day, somehow, she would use it to help her baby. So she found a good family in Turin, and they adopted the boy. She kept in touch with one of Carlo's 'aunts' all the years of his growing up, and then, one day, he came here. Of course, Josie and the aunt had arranged this between them. Josie had helped support Carlo all during his childhood, and now she financed his projects just like she had done before for so many other artists. No one was the wiser, not even Carlo. He never knew she was his mother—until this year, when he came back from Rome. I guess he got a little frisky one day when Josie started berating him for bringing Margo with him, and then she let the cat out of the bag." Judge bows his head. "I don't think she ever told Carlo who his father was, though."

Justin can see that this pains him more than anything, even more than the fact that Judge himself hadn't known. Judge Bradley turns away to hide the tears he can no longer hold back.

"I'm going to bed now, Justin. Tomorrow we have some work to do."

CHAPTER 33

"The worst is not,
So long as we can say, 'This is the worst.'"
(from *King Lear*)

Annie twists and turns in the dark cabin of the Star boat, trying to go to sleep. She wants to fall asleep early, so that she'll be awake in the morning and not be taken unawares by some early rising sailor.

But sleep won't come. It is past midnight, and the town is quiet, all traffic having died down. Music from a party in one of the homes further out in the harbor wafts by. A fog lies out over the sea, and long, sheer tendrils from it slip into the harbor and swirl around the masts. Annie lies, stiff and uncomfortable, and listens to the soft music, the jangling and tinkling and snapping of ropes and bells and buoys, and the soft clucking against the hull of the boat. Finally she sits up and peers out over the cockpit. She turns her head a little, toward the innermost shore of the harbor. There, straight ahead, lies her house...so close, so tempting. It would be so easy to swim over there, it's no more than fifty yards, and then scale the rocks, climb the fence and she would be right at her kitchen door. She could sleep in her own bed. But she doesn't have a key with her, and the door is, for once, locked. However, as she well knows, one of the windows on the ground floor has a broken lock, and could be pushed up to let her in. Ned Mazzarini just shook his head when he was there last, and said, *"Now Annie, deah, whacha waitin' foah? A buhglah could get in heah without so much as a how-dyee-do."* Well, even if she did get in that way, what if they've rigged up some sort of alarm to catch her? Dispirited, she goes back down into the cabin and tries again to go to sleep. After a while, the music stops. The party must be over. There is no wind, and she can hardly feel any movement of the boat. Even the tide is at a standstill. Maybe she can sleep now.

A little later she rolls off the berth and starts to crawl back up the steps. She's made a decision—she can't stand being cooped up any longer. She intends to slip over the side quietly and go home, at least for a couple of hours. The fog has thinned, only a slight mist remains, and the moon casts a diffuse light over the water. Just as she puts her hand over the edge to pull herself up, she hears a strange, muffled sound. A soughing, sighing, muted sound. She sticks her head up. Then she screams.

"No! Get out of there!" she shouts, and a shadow disappears out of her yard, where a small fire is burning against the side of the house. It is licking its way up toward the roof; she can hear it crackling now. She climbs out of the cockpit and jumps down onto the float, no longer worrying about making a racket, and clambers up the ladder to the yacht club deck. From there she runs out on T Wharf and over toward her house. The fire is spreading rapidly, the wall of her living room and the upstairs bedroom is already covered in flames as she nears the end of the wharf. After that, the house is out of her sight. She bangs on doors and windows at every house as she passes by, screaming, "Fire, fire!" When she gets to her house she rushes down the narrow alley into the back yard, where Officer Hale steps in front of her and stops her from approaching the burning building.

"My house, Billy, my house is burning!" she screams, wild eyed. She can smell acrid smoke, and wood burning, and another smell, gasoline. Through the windows she sees that the fire is starting to burn even inside the house.

"Billy! Help me put the fire out! Call the fire department! Oh, come on, help me, Billy! Let me get by!" Hale has a firm hold on her wrists.

"Step back, Annie. Fire engine's on the way. And so are we, I'm afraid," he says with a sigh, pulling her away from the fire, dragging her out of the yard, and pushing her into the cruiser. She hears the town horn blaring and sirens of fire engines, and as the cruiser pulls onto Broadway, she sees a fire engine careening down the street, going full speed. The cruiser she is in is going in the opposite direction, toward the police station.

CHAPTER 34

"Truth is truth
To the end of reckoning."
(from *Measure for Measure*)

"Well, Annie, what have you got to say for yourself," Judge Bradley asks. Last night when she was brought in, she was allowed one call, and had called Judge's number, since Justin no longer has a phone. By sheer good luck Justin had answered and promised to inform Judge and see what could be done. After that, Annie slept—well, spent the night, anyway—on a bunk in the holding cell (unisex, the luxury of separate cells for males and females will be enjoyed at the new site), and Judge has arrived early, before she has even been questioned. Annie assumes this is Judge's doing, if indeed he has agreed to act as her counsel.

"Is Josie okay? Did you go and see her last night?" is the first thing Annie wants to know.

"Josie will recover, according to the doctor. Now, what can you tell me about last night?" First things first. Judge is all business.

"Someone tried to set fire to my house," Annie says, somewhat truculently.

"The police say they caught you there, which suggested to them that it was you who set the fire." Judge is good at just this sort of thing. Attack, and see what nerve you may strike.

"Sure, and why would I set fire to my own house?" Annie has had about as much as she can take now, but she realizes that she both needs and intends to accept Judge's help, and for that reason, she must stop being a smart-aleck and settle down.

"To cast yourself as a victim."

"Do you really believe that, Judge?" She looks him in the eye to try to read his mind.

"What would you like me to believe?"

Annie tries to explain. "I saw someone in the yard when the fire started."

"Who did you see?" He leans forward intently.

"How could I tell who?"

Judge looks skeptical, and Annie tries to remember exactly what she saw.

"It was pitch dark. I was still out in the boat. All I saw was a shadow. I got out of the boat and ran home. That's when Billy Hale caught me. The fire was already going full blast, then."

Judge decides to switch tack.

"Annie, why did you go to visit Josie? Not the night she was attacked—the time before. And what did she tell you at that time?"

"I was out for a walk in the woods, and when I passed her house she was sitting in the yard. She waved at me to come over. We talked. She said she knew I didn't kill Carlo."

"Anything else?"

"She said a lot of things."

"Anything that surprised you?"

"She said…she said Carlo was still fond of me."

"Really. Anything else?"

"Nothing I can think of. At least nothing that seems important. She mentioned there was something she wanted to show me, something she wanted to talk about. I said I'd come back. I couldn't stand talking about Carlo just then."

"Okay. Another thing I was wondering: why did you move into the motel?"

"Because I'd had an intruder at my house."

"Anyone know you went there?"

Annie looks at Judge. What is he trying to find out? Should she tell him about Duncan? And how much should she tell? That he offered to help her? That she doesn't trust him?

"A friend rented the room so nobody would know it was for me."

"A friend?"

"Yes."

"Could you elaborate on that?"

Annie sighs in defeat. "The director of the library. Duncan Langmuir."

"Aha. Now, I wonder why I had to drag that out of you. Are you trying to protect him? Or…are you afraid or unsure of him?"

Annie closes her eyes and bends her head down. "I am afraid of everyone, Judge. Everyone. I can't trust anybody."

He waits for her to sit back up. "Are you afraid of me?"

She shakes her head. "No. Not you, and not Justin. Everyone else. No, not Josie, of course. And not Sally Babson." Annie looks a little calmer now, and leans back in her chair.

"Okay, that's a good start. Now, we're going to see how hard it will be to get you out of here. I will do all I can. So, you sit tight, and stop worrying. You have four friends, at least. Right?" He puts his hand on her shoulder and gives a squeeze. It reminds her of Duncan's squeeze, but this one doesn't frighten her.

"Right, Judge. Oh, did my house burn down?" she asks, as if it really doesn't matter much any more.

"No, Annie. There was some damage to the wall and roof next to the patio, but the fire department got there in time. They're good, those guys. They sleep with one eye open."

"Lucky ducks." Annie can't even close *one* eye. "Oh, I don't mean that. I'm very grateful to all those guys. Oh, Judge, will I ever be back in my house?"

"Sure you will. But not until this is over. Someone tried to douse the wall around your bedroom and the kitchen entrance with gasoline. Looks like they really meant to get you this time. Of course, the police will say this can be interpreted in more than one way."

"Right. First I kill someone I love, then I burn his house down, then I'm an intruder in my own house and nearly kill my own beloved Gussie, then I go and try to kill an old woman who was good to the man I loved, then I decide to burn my own house down. I must be a pretty screwed up person, Judge."

Judge chuckles. "Well, Annie, somebody around here sure is."

CHAPTER 35

"But now I'm cabin'd, cribb'd, confined, bound in
To saucy doubts and fears."
(from *Macbeth*)

*L*IBRARIAN ARRESTED; FREED ON BAIL
Did Quitnot set her own house on fire?...caught in yard by po-
lice...latest victim Mandel out of coma, unable to identify attacker...
no other suspects yet named...Library Trustees consider Quitnot termi-
nation...

The afternoon edition carries the news, but Judge keeps it
away from Annie. Judge still carries a lot of weight, apparently,
as he manages to get Annie out on bail. He convinced the chief
that Annie had not skipped town, only tried to stay hidden
from someone she firmly believes is out to harm her. He mentioned to the chief that Annie had voluntarily called Officer
Hale from her place of safety. But still, there must have been
more to it, Annie thinks. Judge must surely have put his own
reputation on the line by vouching for her,

Judge Bradley tells Justin not to let Annie use the phone,
watch TV, listen to the radio, or read the papers, and he does
not want Justin to talk to her about any news or rumors he
hears. If Annie wants to talk and unburden herself, she may do

so, but he does not want her "contaminated." He wants to get every detail out of her first, and if he is to get at the truth, he doesn't need media speculators or town gossips to influence or scare her. And he has asked Justin not to tell Annie of Josie's confession about Carlo's parentage—yet.

Justin takes Annie out for a walk in the South Woods to get her mind off things. He takes his phone back, saying she doesn't need one right now anyway, and Annie is relieved to be rid of it. She is excited when she finds coyote tracks; she often hears coyotes in Dogtown and has seen a young male a couple of times over near Folly Cove, but never here in the South Woods. Of course, with the ever-increasing number of wild turkeys around here—they even come out and attack mailmen, and hamper traffic on South Street and Nugent's Stretch, looking around lazily, unwilling to get out of the road—the coyotes have a ready larder. Last year someone shot a coyote in Pigeon Cove, which caused a furor among the Green people. Apparently the coyote had been pilfering pets in the Cove, and someone decided to take the law into his own hands. *Could just as well have been a hawk that got the pets,* Annie thinks when a red-tailed hawk swoops down and comes back up with a small, squirming creature in its beak. The hawk flies off to the edge of the woods and lights halfway up a tree, where it goes on to enjoy its noonday meal.

Justin and Annie walk along the paddocks, and Annie picks a small bouquet of chamomile and harebells that grow along the rail fence, and later adds a few slender gerardias that sway back and forth in the little wavelets at the edge of a small pond. They sit down on a sunny, grass-covered ledge along the lane and eat wild strawberries. Annie leans back against the banking, where the pink sheep laurel has long since finished blooming and spiky seed clusters are forming, and closes her eyes. Her hair spreads out like a red chenille pillow around her head. She hasn't bothered to braid or gather it; her librarian image doesn't matter just now. The jeans and T-shirt are grimy from days of sleeping in haylofts, on the boat, and in jail, but she has too many other worries. She had wanted to go to her own house and take a shower, but there's still a large opening in the wall on the back side of the house, and besides, the place is yellow-taped, and the police are still checking around for "evidence." Annie has already called Ned Mazzarini to come and do the repairs that are going to be needed, which he promised to start on as soon as the police are through.

"Juss, who paid my bail?" Annie sits up and squints at him.

"I don't know, Annie."

"I don't believe you."

"Fine. Okay, I wouldn't tell you even if I knew, how's that? Somebody who trusts that you won't run." He stands turned away, with his hands in his pockets, chewing on a piece of grass.

"And who has a lot of money, I suppose. After all I've been accused of, and having 'run' before. Right?"

"Wouldn't know, kid. Could we change the subject? This is spoiling a perfectly good outing."

"You're right. Juss. Hey, could you do me a favor? Could you call Sally Babson and tell her I'm okay, and that I'm sorry I haven't called?" This whole thing is not going to sit really well with Matt. He will probably never let Sally see her again.

"Sure. Anybody else?"

"Not unless you could get word to Josie and tell her I hope she feels better. Oh," she adds, "I almost forgot. She was sort of delirious, I guess, but when she lay there on the floor, she said something like 'I need my son.' I never heard anything about her having a son, did you? Annie shakes her head, remembering Josie lying on the floor in that pool of blood. "Oh, Juss, she was so upset about Carlo. Carlo was her favorite, you know, of all the artists that she's ever supported."

Justin has to be careful here. "I guess he was. I'll see what I can do. Judge is going back to see her tonight, I think. I can send word with him."

"Another thing. Could you go to the library? Just go in, walk about, see what they say? The librarians, I mean, not the townspeople. Not rumors; I want to know what they think about what's going on…about me. Or, maybe you can pick up any bits of fact that we may have missed…oh, I don't know what I mean. Just if there's anything, you know, see if you can get a feeling about anything or anyone there."

"Does that include Clare? And Duncan?"

"Nobody specific, Juss," she says, but Justin gets the feeling that Clare and Duncan are definitely included.

CHAPTER 36

"Give thy thoughts no tongue."
(from *Hamlet*)

When Justin calls Sally, she asks if Annie can come over for dinner.

"I'll send Matt and the boys up the line. They can go to Mickey D's or wherever they want. And to the computer store. They need some burnable CDs and ink for the printer. They've got at least a couple of hours' worth of stuff to do, so Annie and I have some time to visit. Tell her I miss her!"

Judge says she can go if Justin comes along. By that he means Justin has to keep the conversation on track. No chatting about "what people say." No opening her heart, no giving out any information. No discussion about anything to do with the murder, the fires, the attack—none of it. That won't be easy, at Sally's, but that's the condition. Just a nice, social, friendly evening. *Okay?* Well, okay.

When Justin gets back from his visit to the library, they borrow the jeep and go over to Sally's. Sally lives just a few streets away from the Bradley homestead, and Annie doesn't have time on the way over to ask him what, if anything, he heard at the library.

Sally and Matt live in an old cape on Eden Road, in the southern part of Rockport called Land's End, named after that other Land's End in the south of England. Other names in this area were also borrowed from the English counterpart: Penzance, Camborne, Tregony. The rocky coastline between the beaches even bears a slight resemblance to the Cornwall coast. Well, very slight, perhaps.

Through the picture window in the living room, Sally and her family have a view of the sea and of Thacher Island, with the famous Twin Lights. The island was named after Anthony Thacher, who was shipwrecked there in 1635—the earliest known shipwreck on the New England coast.

A five-minute walk from the Babson's house lies Loblolly Cove, and if you walk a little further, you get to three lovely Rockport beaches all in a row: Pebble Beach, Cape Hedge Beach with its great hump of softly rounded pebbles, and the sandy stretch of Long Beach, which ends at the Gloucester border.

Matt and the boys are gone, and Sally is waiting eagerly. She opens the door and leads Annie and Justin inside, hurrying them into the living room. She is spilling over with news and burning with curiosity, but Justin quickly sets her straight.

"Annie promised. She can't discuss any of it, Sally."

Grudgingly, Sally understands and agrees to follow the rules. But what is left to talk about, then?

"Brad said he helped Judge Bradley with the boat yesterday," she says, brightly.

"And a good job he did, too. Nice boy. Judge told him that any time he wants to go out, he'll teach him how to sail a Star," Justin says.

Sally beams. That would mean a huge deal to her boy—and keep him away from brother Ben for a while.

"Annie, how would you like to come with me tomorrow morning?" she asks. "I volunteered to help set up for the concert at the Art Society. You know, place out folding chairs, set up tables, collect napkins and tablecloths and stuff that people are supposed to bring by. It would just be the two of us at that time, the others won't come until Friday morning because the concert isn't until Friday night."

Annie looks at Justin, who shrugs.

"You'd have to ask Judge first."

Annie nods. "If he says okay, I'd love to. As long as Avery won't be there. And as long as that Mrs. Ridley isn't going to be working with us. She'd call the police, I'm sure. Boy, I'm beginning to *feel* like a criminal, always running and hiding. And I *am* free to move around, really, as long as I don't 'leave town.' If Justin can drop us off by the side door and pick us up after, maybe Judge will let me."

They fish around for safe topics to discuss for a while, and then, suddenly, they hear Matt's car. Matt looks like a storm cloud walking in but controls himself at the sight of Justin.

"It's okay Matt. She's legal. And we're leaving, so you don't need to make a scene in front of the boys," Justin says calmly. Matt buttons his mouth, and Annie gives Sally a warm hug on the way out.

CHAPTER 37

"Speak less than thou knowest."
(from *King Lear*)

When they get back to Judge Bradley's house, where Annie has been promised she could stay until Ned Mazzarini has fixed her house so that it is livable, Judge tells Annie that Duncan has called.

"He said to tell you they're not having the weekly get-together tomorrow, and sends his regards."

"Is that all he said?" she asks warily.

"He asked how you were." Judge doesn't mention whether Duncan had sounded anxious or just curious.

"What did you tell him?" The roles are reversed, now, with Annie trying to pump Judge for information.

"I said, 'As well as can be expected under the circumstances.' He can take that any way he wants."

"And?" Talk about pulling taffy, she thinks.

"That's pretty much it."

"Pretty much?" Annie is getting frustrated.

"He'd like to see you." Judge looks noncommittal.

"He said that?" Annie doesn't know whether to feel anxious or grateful about Duncan's wish to see her. In broad daylight and in the safety of Judge's home, it seems difficult for her to imagine Duncan as a murderer.

"Yes. I said he could give me a message and I'd pass it on, but I guess that wasn't what he had in mind. So I said it would have to wait."

"Oh, Judge. Duncan didn't happen to say anything about my dog? He's taken care of Gussie for me since he brought me to the motel." Pangs of guilt strike her. She has hardly even thought of Poor Gussie, with disaster after disaster taking the front seat.

"As a matter of fact, he did mention the dog. He said to tell you Gussie is mending fine."

"Thank God." *That must be a good sign,* she thinks.

She wonders why the librarians are skipping the Thursday evening coffee, and then remembers that it would have been Clare's turn. And Clare presumably still has a 'houseguest.' Well, well.

Annie asks about helping Sally tomorrow, but Judge is not keen on the idea.

"Nobody is going to come after me in broad daylight, out in public, in the middle of town!" Annie says.

After some deliberation, Judge smiles craftily. "Maybe you can use another pair of hands. Like Justin's, for instance?"

Annie groans, and Justin makes a face.

"You know, I went through this all the time when I was a kid. Justin always had to stay with me and make sure I was okay," Annie says. She looks at Justin and they both laugh.

"That's the condition. Take it or leave it."

"Well, okay then. I guess it's a good idea. I know you don't want me to talk about or hear about anything to do with any of what's going on. Sally would certainly try to grill me if we were on our own, and maybe right now I'm no match for her third degree," Annie admits ruefully.

"Fine. I'll leave you two alone for a while then. Got some reading and notes to catch up on. You can shut the place down when you're ready to retire." Judge rises from his favorite chair and brushes some crumbs of the front of his shirt. Seated, he looked somehow small and sad, standing up he is tall again, broad-chested and strong looking. When he turns to them, his eyes are still sad. "Goodnight, children."

"Goodnight, Judge," they say in unison.

Once Judge Bradley has retired to his bedroom, Annie asks Justin about his afternoon at the library. Justin sits back in his chair.

"Well, you know I'm not really supposed to talk to you about this, but I'll tell you what I can," he says quietly. "Unfortunately, they all recognized me. Except Stuart, of course. What a twit. He tried to tell a kid how to do a search on the Internet. You'd think he was sharing the secret of the holy grail. Made it twice as hard for the poor kid by giving him so much information that the kid's eyes bugged out. As soon as Stuart turned his back, the kid slipped away. Then Stuart asked *me* if I needed some guidance, and I said, 'No, just looking,' and he said, 'Right, and when you want to find whatever it is you're looking for, I'll be right over here.' I see what you mean about this guy."

"Did you see Duncan at all?"

"He saw me. Looked disturbed and hightailed it into his office. I was about to follow him when Clare stepped out into the corridor. When she saw me, she almost went back in to her office too. Then she put on a big, phony smile and became very friendly, and said how glad she was to see me, and asked how you were, and said how they all miss you. And I said, 'How's your houseguest?' and she turned beet red and started stammering about how sorry she was to have turned you away, and were you still staying at the motel? Then she was suddenly 'in a hurry' and had to run off."

"Not much, then. Was Jean at my desk?"

"Yes, looking a little flustered, trying to help a very cranky customer find something."

Annie tries not to smile.

"And then Dot came in to pick up an envelope you had set aside for her, and Jean found it and gave it to her," Justin continues.

Annie hopes this doesn't mean that Jean has managed to rearrange her files already.

"Marie looked away when she saw me," Justin continues.

"Was Esa around?"

"Who's that again? Oh yes, the janitor, you said. Yes, actually I felt he was following me around for a while. When I decided that maybe it was time to go, he was up in the children's room talking to Stuart. Stuart seemed angry at him and kept shaking his head, and the poor boy looked upset."

"He's not really a boy, you know," Annie tells him. "I know he looks like one, but he's actually in his late thirties. He likes me. You know, like a little boy likes his teacher, that kind of thing."

"That explains it."

"Explains what?"

"Well, when I first saw him, he was putting some flowers on your desk, while Jean was around the corner with her cranky customer. I didn't see flowers anywhere else. Maybe they were for you, then?"

"What kind were they?" The answer will tell her.

"Oh, I don't know, something pink and yellow. Peonies and sunflowers, maybe?"

Annie laughs. "That sounds right. The sweet boy."

"I thought you said he wasn't a boy," Justin teases.

Annie turns on the radio for some music, but Justin turns it off when the news comes on. Annie tries in vain to find a book among Judges bookshelves, and ends up with an old magazine instead. She can't concentrate on reading anyway, and her mind starts churning on what Justin told her. So, Clare tried to find out where Annie was staying. And she hadn't told Justin whether Margo was still her houseguest. Oh, dear. Poor Margo. Lost both her husband and her home.

"Time for bed, Sis. I'm beat. How about you?"

CHAPTER 38

"The weight of this sad time we must obey;
Speak what we feel, not what we ought to say.
The oldest hath borne most: we that are young,
Shall never see so much, nor live so long."
(from *King Lear*)

VALENTI FUNERAL POSTPONED
...according to police sources, parents of victim have requested delay... arrangements being made for trip from Turin, Italy... widow reportedly anxious to have services go forward... still fearful, wishes to leave area, with suspect free on bail...

Judge grabs the paper from the mailbox early in the morning, and makes sure to hide it before Annie has a chance to see it. What is missing in the news article is that the parents who requested the delay are Josie and Judge. Not officially, of course. Judge Bradley made a phone call to the Valentis, explaining—as briefly as possible, but in full—what has happened. He gave them the whole story, parentage and all, and it was a tortured half-hour on both sides of the Atlantic. The Valentis at first requested that the body be flown home to Italy immediately, but in the end agreed to wait. Once the Valentis sensed that the emotional turmoil was equal on both sides, they asked Judge to do whatever he felt was best, and to keep in touch and let them know what was happening. They expressed a wish to be present at the funeral, whenever it was to take place. Judge promised to call them again, once they'd had some time to think about everything, and said he would keep them informed. Then he called the funeral home and said that the parents—without specifying—had requested the delay.

Unofficially, Judge Bradley is also going along with a police request for a delay of the funeral. Additional forensic tests may need to be performed. Furthermore, they need the body to be available for "viewing" for some additional time. By whom? Judge ponders. The parents? The suspect?

Judge knows he will have to tell Annie about the funeral, but it can wait until later in the day.

⚜

Justin and Annie arrive a few minutes before Sally, and sit in the car in the bank lot waiting. The bank sometimes allows Art Society members to park there, and for special events, like the concerts, that take place after banking hours, they also give permission for guests to park there. The bank lot sits on a ledge above the lane that goes by the back of the library, so Annie keeps a low profile.

"There's Duncan, I think," says Justin, who is keeping an eye in the rearview mirror. Annie peeks over the lower edge of the passenger window. Duncan is standing by the back entrance talking to Clare, who has her back turned. He looks angry, making sweeping, agitated gestures with his hands. Clare bows her head, takes a tissue out of her pocket, and lifts it to her face. Duncan turns and stomps into the building, and Clare runs over to her car, gets in behind the wheel, and sits there, hunched down. What made Duncan angry with Clare? *Is he trying to find me? Was he asking her Clare if she knows where I am?* Annie wonders, suddenly anxious again.

Sally is knocking on Justin's window, smiling.

"Sorry I'm late! Had to stop for gas," she says. Annie takes a last look over at Clare before getting out of the car. Clare is still sitting there, hunched over the wheel.

The Art Society is situated on Main Street, just above Dock Square, in a building that formerly served as *The Old Tavern*; one of many watering holes before the town went dry. The large exhibition hall in back of the original building was added some years later. This month it is hung with a member's show, which will be left up during the music festival. All the sculptures have been moved to the rear to allow chairs to be set up for the concert. Stacks of chairs and tables crowd the little back room, where refreshments will be served after the program. Justin's presence turns out to be a great boon, of course, as he starts carting the heavier pieces around. Once all the chairs are arranged around the stage, auditorium fashion, the three begin setting up tables in the back room. Now and then people stop in and drop off bags of paper goods and soda, which Sally stows under the tables. She leaves the laying on of tablecloths and napkins for the next crew.

When they are finished, they walk around the great room and study the art works. Sally opens a quart of soda and rummages through the bags for paper cups.

"We should go to one of the concerts, Annie. If you want to come with me and help pour the punch, we don't even have to pay our way! And they're going to have a special show in the back room, too, which will be hung this afternoon. All those paintings that are stacked up over there, see? Don't know how they're going to fit them all into this little space. How about it, wanna come?"

"I don't know, Sal. I'd love to, I guess, but I don't want to cause any embarrassment to the society. You know, if Avery shows up, he'd probably be apoplectic. Or Mrs. Ridley—if she were to come, I'd be turned into a pillar of salt the minute she saw me. Besides, I'm sure Judge won't let me."

"Well, let's wait and see," Sally says with purposeful cheerfulness. "There's still a couple of weeks left of performances." They toss their paper cups and napkins in the trash and look around to make sure all is neat. Justin stays in the main exhibition hall and adjusts the chairs into perfect rows.

"You know what I heard?" Sally has lowered her voice.

"What?"

"Freddie Smith, pardon me, *Smythe,* was at the coffee shop this morning, and he was blabbering about how he's been talking to Margo. He's made her an offer for Carlo's place—oops, here's Justin," she whispers. There are no more opportunities for them to talk alone. They leave together, and Annie promises to call.

Justin drives slowly past Annie's house on the way back to Judge's, and Annie suddenly hollers at him to stop the car.

"Why? What's the matter?" Justin says, trying to pull over and ending up alongside a fire hydrant.

"That dog! I think it's Leo!" she says, climbing out of the car before it has come to a full stop. She runs across the street and into her back yard, where she saw the black shadow disappear.

"Leo!" she calls. Justin hears a dog barking, and in a moment Annie appears around the corner. She leaves the yard again through the blue gate, followed by a bounding black lab. She lets the dog into the back seat, climbs in herself, and slams the door.

"Hurry up, Juss! Get out of here!" she hisses.

"Now what? What are we going to do with this dog? We can't bring it back with us!"

"Of course we can. Judge loves dogs," Annie says confidently.

CHAPTER 39

"...We are such stuff
as dreams are made on, and our little life
is rounded with a sleep."
(from *The Tempest*)

Judge does love dogs, especially black labs, and instantly takes to Leo.

"So, this is Carlo's dog, eh?" he says, giving Leo a good ear scratching. "If he's been loose this whole time, it's lucky he hasn't been picked up and taken to the pound. No collar! But he doesn't look like he's starved. Hope he's not a trash dog! If he's going to be living here, he's got to have manners."

But Annie has a different plan. "Why can't I take Leo with me and move back home? I'm sure he and Gussie will get along, as soon as I can get him back from Duncan. Justin can stay with me, too," she adds, ever so graciously. "I noticed that Ned already has closed the hole at the back of the house for me. Nothing illegal about my living in my own home, is there?"

Judge looks crestfallen for a moment and glances at Justin. Justin thinks he understands: the dog is a link to the son Judge never knew he had, but Annie knows nothing of that yet. To her, Leo is a simply a link between her and Carlo.

"I don't know, Annie," Judge Bradley says. "I suppose it would be okay. There haven't been any attempts on anyone lately. We can try for an overnight and see how it goes." He gives Leo another rough-and-tumble before wiping his own nose surreptitiously with the back of his hand.

Annie spends the night tossing and turning in her bed upstairs. *Home at last!* All that's missing now is Gussie. She misses the scritch-scratch of his paws on the floor, and the looks he gives her that can express more than words. Justin is sleeping downstairs in the alcove, which Annie straightened out as soon as they got there, eager to remove any reminders of intruders and other unpleasantness. It still smells slightly skunky from the gasoline the arsonist poured onto the outside of the house, and there is a strong, acrid smell from the charred timbers outside her window, but that will fade away in time.

The charred smell also reminds Annie of the fire at Carlo's, and of Freddie Smythe's offer to Margo. Now maybe Smythe will get Carlo's place after all, and then he will be able to combine Carlo's property and the neighboring lot with the fish shacks that he's already bought, which will then allow him to build a pretty substantial edifice—maybe even a McMansion. *How shady is Freddie Smythe? Could he have set the fire? Or worse…* Annie untwists herself from the stranglehold of the sheet. She has got to stop suspecting everyone. She's getting paranoid, just as her brother said.

Memories hang like dewy cobwebs in the upstairs bedroom. Up here, Carlo is back in her life again, alive, and she gives in to him, allows every thought full freedom. At the end of a long night she accepts the truth: her love for Carlo never diminished. She knows now that on the day he died, she had felt his pull as strongly as she had back in the day when they were together. In fact, she thinks, *this* was the real reason she had become so afraid of Duncan. Duncan's tiny little overture to a closer, more intimate relationship—and maybe it had only been a misperception on her part—had scared the daylights out of her. Her mind had hooked onto it and twisted it into something else, something more—something sinister, in fact. It was surely her imagination that had turned Duncan into a killer. It had prevented her from seeing the truth, which was that she just hadn't been ready to give up her love for Carlo yet. Even the slightest spark of temptation to enter into a new relationship had been enough to awaken her fear of losing Carlo completely.

Now she allows herself to hear Carlo's voice, enjoys the gently accented words that seem to drift into her ear from the pillow beside her, feels his presence and his warmth.

"Lean close thy cheek..."

She is reading Heine to him, and he responds with Shakespeare.

"See! how she leans her cheek upon her hand:
O! that I were a glove upon that hand,
That I might touch that cheek."

She feels a thrill at being able to accept still loving Carlo—stretches her arm out toward him, exuberant in her love—before she remembers that he is dead. Then her dear and ever loyal friend Willie comes to turn the dagger...

My grief is onward and my joy behind...

Annie vows to stay away from the Sonnets for the time being. Too much grieving there. She feels a need to celebrate instead, to revel in her love, before she has to give it up, forever.

CHAPTER 40

"The undiscover'd country from whose bourn
No traveler returns."
(from *Hamlet*)

"*I'm going.* I'll sit in the back. I don't care what people say."
Annie stands defiantly on a rock at the Headlands, the breeze catching her hair and fanning it into a great red aureole in the sunrise. Leo, restrained by Justin with a brand new collar and leash, looks at her adoringly. They have risen early, Annie, Justin and Leo, to take a walk and clear the stench of smoke and gasoline out of their nostrils. Judge had called early in the morning to ask how things were going, and to tell her that the funeral was being arranged.

"I don't know, Annie. You don't want to create a scene at the funeral...." Justin shakes his head and throws his hands up in the air, and almost loses hold on Leo's leash.

"*I* won't create a scene. If anyone else wants to, that their problem." Annie juts out a stubborn chin. Justin remembers that chin well. Better tread carefully.

"You might still be the cause of it, you know," he says, modulating his voice to sound calm and reasonable. He sits down one of the stone benches that look out over the bay, and pats the seat next to him for Annie to join him. She sits down, a little huffily, her chin still sticking out contemptuously.

"You mean the grieving widow might object to my presence? I'm sure nobody else would. Margo is paranoid. If someone is out to harm her, it certainly isn't me. And why isn't she waiting for the Valentis to come? I can't believe she won't wait for his parents!" Annie is incensed. "How insensitive can she get? Does she have more of a claim on him than his own parents?"

"Apparently Margo has convinced people that she is in immediate mortal danger as long as she has to remain here. She's had a threatening note, I understand. After the funeral, she will go to some other 'undisclosed location,' where I assume she will wait for whatever inheritance she is to get. I can't imagine there's much there, with the building burned down and the art works gone."

Annie turns toward him, looking stunned.

"Oh, Juss, I never thought of that. An inheritance, I mean."

"One more reason that she might be hostile toward you—if she thinks you caused her inheritance to go up in flames."

"Good grief. I've felt so bad about that, for his sake, I mean, all those paintings of his gone. Years of work. I know he was preparing for a big retrospective and had borrowed paintings back from a lot of collectors. I suppose there might be some insurance to cover the losses..." But that would never make up for the loss of his paintings.

"Anyway, are you sure you want to risk that? Turning his funeral into a circus?"

"I'll wait until everyone is inside, and then slip in afterwards and sit in the last pew. I'm going, and that's final, Justin. I loved Carlo. Until the day he died. I'm not letting him go anywhere without me being there." Annie clenches her fists and bites her lips together, but cannot hold back the bitter tears. She hides her face in her lap.

"Oh, Annie, come on now." Justin gives his sister a rough squeeze. "Let's go home. We'll have to tell Judge."

Annie nods gratefully, and Justin puts his arm around her back. Then, with a sharp whistle, he tells Leo to hop to it.

"I doubt if Judge will be easily convinced to let you go, Sis, but if he does, I'll be right there with you, never fear."

"I wish you lived around here, Juss. Can't you convince Melanie to give it a try? Maybe if she came here during the summer, or any other time than winter, she might grow to like it?"

CHAPTER 41

"Come away, come away, death
And in sad cypress let me be laid
Fly away, fly away, breath,
I am slain by a fair cruel maid."
(from *Twelfth Night*)

The funeral is held two days later. Despite her fears, Judge has given the green light for Annie to attend. He knows, of course, that nothing would stop her. Justin drives her to the church in Judges jeep. As promised, Annie stays hunched down in the back seat of the jeep while the mourners enter the church. Quite a crowd has turned up; there is a line up the steps. Apart from parishioners, who go to every funeral, and the curious who wouldn't miss any part of this particular show, the art community is, of course, well represented. Then there are the selectmen and other prominent town politicians who can't pass up the opportunity to be seen here—and maybe even appear on TV. The media vans are parked farther down the street.

Judge disappeared early in the morning in his Buick, and Annie doesn't know. whether he plans to come. He was agitated last night when she told him of her decision to go, but he didn't try too hard to talk her out of it. In the evening, he asked

Annie and Dot if they wanted to accompany Josie and him to say a final good-bye to Carlo at the funeral parlor. Dot said no with a shudder, and Judge shrugged. "Dottie, you're such a sensitive little thing," he said, with something that came pretty close to tenderness. Annie also said no to going. She would remember Carlo alive.

Justin sits in the driver's seat and waits with her, watching as the parade of dignitaries and curiosity seekers, friends and admirers, enters the church. Duncan arrives, representing the library, Annie supposes. Carlo had been a long-time patron. Duncan is looking around. Is he looking for her? Annie wishes she could go over and ask him if she can have Gussie back. Priscilla Pettengill arrives, but not Avery Shattuck. Well, no surprise—it might have seemed a bit hypocritical for him to show up. Like gloating, even.

Judge's old Buick suddenly turns up, and he lets some passengers off by the church entrance before going down the street in search of a parking space. Broadway is always made one way when anything is going on at the church, like a wedding or a funeral, and every Sunday for Mass. Cars are parked on both sides of the street for the length of the block. The passengers, who turn out to be Josie accompanied by Dot and two other older people Annie does not recognize, slowly make their way up the stairs. Josie looks pale but composed. Dot supports her stiffly. Judge Bradley comes running just as they reach the top step, and they wait for him and all go in together.

Another car pulls up to the church, and Clare and Margo step out. Margo is dressed in black and wearing large, dark sunglasses. No veil—but that wouldn't be her style, now, would it? Clare takes Margo by the arm and leads her up the steps and into the church. Margo is to be the last to arrive, of course, being the widow. Annie gathers courage and steps out of the car, followed by Justin.

"Are you sure, now?" he asks.

"Yes. Hurry up, before they close the door."

They make it inside, and find seats in the last pew, just barely. The church is filled to capacity, and any other latecomers will have to stand at the back.

The service begins without incident. When the coffin (which is empty, presumably since the body is still needed in the police investigation) is wheeled up the aisle, Annie starts crying softly, wishing she had thought of wearing a pair of big sunglasses herself. Under the flimsy gray raincoat she is wearing a blue and purple silk dress—the only item, other than her kimono, left in her wardrobe from Carlo's days. A year after he left she went through and tossed things out, but of course that hadn't helped. Everything around her still reminded her of Carlo—every book he had read from, every room in the house where she could still hear his voice, even the sky and the trees.... She wouldn't be able to get rid of him, no matter where she moved. And she had jealously kept the tapes of his voice, although for a long time she hadn't been able to listen to them.

Annie's face is partially covered by a gray scarf, which she also uses to dab her tears until Justin passes her a crumpled paper napkin. Annie tries to focus on the stained glass windows, but her eyes are drawn to Margo and Clare up in the first pew. On the other side of the aisle, Judge, Dot, and Josie and her elderly companions are seated. Margo looks straight ahead during the whole service, standing and sitting whenever Clare's arm guides her to do so. Annie can't see Duncan from where she sits, and finally stops looking, drawing the scarf tighter around her face. The service drones on. Annie cannot concentrate on the interchanges between priest and congregation. The responses and amens, the readings, the words to family and friends all go unheard. When the incense thickens, she becomes aware again.

The coffin goes by, on its way out of church this time, and behind it Margo, staring straight ahead, bravely steadied by a stony-faced Clare. Right behind Margo come a tight-knit group made up of the elderly couple and Judge, who is supporting Josie on one arm and Dot on the other. Josie still has a small bandage showing, and is walking proudly erect but with red-rimmed eyes. Dot is white-faced and leaning heavily on her grandfather. Instead of the usual baseball cap, Dot is wearing an unflattering black hat with a rather too wide brim decorated with black silk roses. Her pallor accentuates the pink splotches of acne on her cheeks and a faint blue shadow under her eyes. An old-fashioned black dress, which might once have belonged to her grandmother, does not hide the fact that Dot has gotten even pudgier lately.

Clare catches sight of Annie, and her eyes saucer. She tries to engage Margo's attention in order to prevent her from seeing Annie, but it has the opposite effect, as Margo comes alive and begins to look around. Suddenly Margo stiffens. She lets go of Clare's arm and runs, past the coffin and out of the church, onto the stairs, where she screams hysterically.

"Help, she's after me!"

Justin grabs Annie by the arm, and they manage to fall in with the throng and make it out to the crowded vestibule, where Justin shoves Annie through a door and they disappear down into the basement. They stand silent in the dark, waiting for police sirens or some other calamitous noise, but the hubbub outside finally abates, and they hear the cars leave. There is to be no reception; and by an early telephone agreement between the Valentis and Josie and Judge, the burial will eventually take place in the Valenti family cemetery in Italy.

Justin steals upstairs and calls softly to Annie that the coast is clear, but on opening the church door a crack, he sees the cruiser across the street.

"We've got to get out the side door," he whispers.

They walk quietly up through the church and manage to slip away by the side door, around the back of the church and through hedges and back yards over to Main Street.

"Wait here while I get the car," Justin says. Annie nods, drawing the raincoat tightly around her.

In the jeep, as they get within sight of Annie's house, Justin notices that the place is guarded, and continues without stopping.

"Where are we going?"

"Up to Judge's. Someone's on watch at your house."

"Ah. Is it me they're guarding, or her, I wonder?" Annie asks rhetorically. "And what about Leo? We can't just leave him there!"

"I'll go and get him as soon as I drop you off, if Judge says okay."

Judge Bradley isn't back yet, but Justin has the key and lets them in. They go and sit in the living room, where Annie leans back in an easy chair and closes her eyes. Justin says he'll go and fix himself a drink, and leaves her alone to collect herself.

It was an ordeal, but she was present. She has no tears left now, just dry sobs, and soon the sobs run out, too. Even after the incident with Margo she does not regret going. Annie feels certain that she has a larger claim on Carlo than Margo does, despite the fact that it was Margo he married. To anyone else this might seem unreasonable, but Annie brushes it off as simply beyond understanding, She sits up, somewhat calmer now, when Justin comes back into the room.

"Well. Are you satisfied?" Justin asks, stirring her feelings back up again.

"What do you mean? Of course I'm not satisfied. But *she's* the one who ruined it. I had as much a right to be there as she did," Annie insists stubbornly.

"Being his wife, she might not think so." Justin takes a sip of his drink, which looks like a pretty stiff shot of whisky on ice.

Annie shuts up. Justin doesn't understand how important it was for her to be there. And now, as much as she wants to hold on to Carlo, she knows she must begin a different process, and the funeral was the beginning of that process. Everything else is unimportant at this moment.

CHAPTER 42

"Neither maid, widow, nor wife."
(from *Measure for Measure*)

After a while they hear Judge Bradley's car drive up. He opens the door and people shuffle in: Dot, Josie, and the elderly couple they had seen with her at the church.

"Ah, there you are," Judge says when he sees them. "I want you to meet Mr. and Mrs. Valenti, Carlo's parents. They flew in just this morning, after I called and told them the funeral was going to take place right away, after all."

Annie, shaken, takes Mrs. Valenti's hand, but the woman pulls her into a warm embrace.

"Annie. I so wanted meet you. Carlo tell us so much about you. Aah..." she wails, and begins to sob.

"Let's go in and sit down," Judge says, herding everyone along. "Justin, come and help me get some drinks and glasses. Dottie, you come and help, too, please. Fix us some coffee. It's been a damn long day for everyone."

They disappear out to the kitchen, and Josie takes Annie by the hand and leads everyone into the living room. Annie walks in a trance. The Valentis know who she is, but they don't seem to think she killed their son. Of course, they've been talking to

219

Judge. But where is Margo? Why are they not with their son's widow?

Judge and Justin show up with trays and pour liberal amounts of amber liquid into cut crystal snifters. Dot has started the coffee machine and begs off for the rest of the evening. She is still pale, emphasized by the black dress.

"Bye, all," she says in the doorway. "Grandpa says he'll bring you home, Josie. I'm really tired, and I have to be at work early tomorrow." Her face turns weepy, and she goes up to her grandfather and puts her cheek against his chest, as if she were still a small child looking for a reassuring hug. Judge, never one to encourage weeping and gnashing of teeth, refuses to encourage her by showing any sign of sympathy or affection this time, and just waves at her to run along.

They drink without raising their glasses—perhaps that would be unseemly. There is a small, uneasy silence before Mr. Valenti finally hoists his glass, angrily, as though he's defying the God that stole his son away in such a barbaric fashion. Mr. Valenti is a short, wiry Italian with curly white hair, balding on top. His wife is likewise short, but rounder and gentler, and with black and shiny hair gathered in a curled braid on the crown of her head. She is dressed in a loose garment that disguises her form, but you can tell that she is of rather generous proportions. There is certainly no likeness to Carlo in either of them.

"To Carlo," Valenti says, and they all echo, "To Carlo." Annie takes a gulp, makes a peculiar, gurgly noise, and begins to cough. Her face turns red, and her eyes fill up while she tries to control her coughing. Then tears begin to roll, real tears, salty tears of unbearable grief, and she runs out of the room.

Mrs. Valenti follows her, and puts a large, soft arm around Annie's shoulder.

"Annie...*cara*...Annie love Carlo, yes?" she asks quietly. Annie nods. "Carlo love you much also. We expect *you* be his *moglie*...wife, you see? He will ask you, he say. You see? This Margo, she no can be his wife, no. Come, we tell you." Mrs. Valenti leads Annie back into the living room.

First they all take turns to tell her about Carlo's true parentage. It is a long and difficult tale, with emotions running deep on all sides. In the end the four grieving parents embrace and cry bitterly together. Annie is shocked and totally unprepared for the unraveling story, but it doesn't take her long to see how it all falls into place. Now she also understands why Josie and Judge had become so involved when it came to Carlo's murder. And she understands something else: with a combination of American genes (and Josie and Judge had surely provided some particularly strong and interesting ones) and Italian culture and nurture, no wonder Carlo had presented such a strange and multifaceted personality, European and American at turns. And as a son of Judge, some of Carlo's local controversies now seemed laughably logical.

"Was this what you wanted to tell me, that day when I visited you?" Annie asks Josie.

"No, dear. We'll come to that in a while," Josie says.

When Annie has absorbed the facts concerning the relationship between *them* and Carlo, they turn to the relationship between *her* and Carlo. But they begin with the story of Margo.

"No is *possibile* Margo Carlo's wife," Mrs. Valenti says.

"What do you mean?" Judge asks.

"Margo is already married before. *È stato sposata...*to Signor Paolo Buonarotti, in Firenze...in Florence. *Due anni fa...*two year ago."

"You mean...she is divorced?" Annie asks, startled.

"No, not *divorziato*. Still married. *È catolico,* Signor Buonarotti. DeVoe is Margo virgin name," Mr. Valenti says.

"Virgin?"

"Maid name? Maid same as virgin, no?"

Annie can't help laughing. "Oh, yes of course, I see. But I still don't understand. How could she marry Carlo then?"

"Non comprendo—I do not understand this also, Anna. Signor Buonarotti say Margo no is good housekeeper, but this okay, fine. But Margo also no is educated, she know nothing of Italian *arte, letteratura, no Dante.* He send her to Roma, give allowance, want her learn Italian *coltura.* But she want have fun. She meet American artists, begin study with Carlo. Carlo feel sorry for her; she have such old, boring husband. She say she *venti-tre...*twenty-three, but really she is...*trenta-sette...*thirty-seven, yes? Carlo no know this. He want help her get back United States. So, she come here with him, Anna." Valenti shakes his head wearily. "And please, Anna, my name Antonio. Name *della moglie...*my wife name Gianna," he adds, and Mrs. Valenti nods.

"We'll have to look into the marriage. There's no sense in speculating," Judge says.

"Anyway, Carlo no love Margo, *mai,* never. She only his *studente,* want to go America, study art. Carlo say he help. He bring her, maybe find sponsor, he say," Gianna continues explaining.

"Yes, Annie, and this is *part* of what I wanted to tell you," Josie cuts in. "You see, Carlo told me shortly after he returned that he was finally going to ask you to marry him. But then when he saw you, something went wrong, he said. I told him, 'Of course, what do you think? You come back after five years with that Margo and let her move in with you, what do you expect? Did you bother to explain?' At first he was angry and said that he had tried, but you hadn't let him finish, and then he said I had no right to tell him how to live his life. Then *I* got mad, and I said, 'Yes, I do! I'm your mother!' And then of course I had to explain the whole thing to him. And," she says, turning to Judge, "I also told him who his father was."

Judge bows his head in silence, and when he looks up he reaches over and squeezes Josie's hand. *So, Carlo had known after all.* Then, still speechless, he nods to her to continue.

Josie tries to pick up the thread. "Well, after Carlo recovered from the shock, he promised he was going to get Margo out of there, and then he was going to prove to you, Annie, that he loved you and had never been able to forget you. And then he was going to get to know Judge. You know, Gianna and Antonio, that Judge and I would never replace you in Carlo's heart. In fact, he was eager to have us meet each other. But apparently, getting rid of Margo was harder than he thought. I guess maybe he had counted on me to sponsor her, but as you all know, I didn't like her *or* her art work."

Judge has recovered his speech, and nods. "Josie called to ask my advice about the sponsorship, and I agreed with her. Margo seemed like a user. Wish to God I had been more helpful," Judge says ruefully.

"Anyway, one day Carlo gave me a sealed envelope," Josie says, "saying he would like me to keep it in a safe place. After the news I had given him, he had made some corrections in his papers, he said, and asked me to keep them in my safe. I passed them on to Judge, of course, who also happens to be my lawyer," she adds, with a nod toward Judge Bradley.

Judge pulls an envelope, still sealed, out of his pocket. He slits the envelope with a penknife, unfolds the paper, scans the contents, and looks up at them.

"I guess the time has come to read this. Then we'll see who will handle things from here on," he says, and starts to read the text out loud.

"*I, Carlo Valenti, being of sound mind and body, hereby give and bequeath my entire estate to Annie Quitnot...*" Judge Bradley doesn't get any further. Annie wails shrilly and starts sobbing, and pleadingly holds up her hands to make him stop. Gianna goes over to embrace her, shushing Judge.

"It will wait *un momento,* no?" she says, and Judge Bradley nods.

CHAPTER 43

"The glowworm shows the matin to be near
And 'gins to pale his ineffectual fire."
(from *Hamlet*)

It is late at night before they leave Judge's place. Annie's car is still at home in her garage (the door won't budge, and now the car is well and truly stuck inside), but rather than borrow the jeep again, they decide to walk. It's a balmy night, and the air is heavy with the fragrance of flowers and blooming shrubs. The cloyingly heady odor—from a distance still pleasant—of night-scented stock wafts over from a nearby garden, and the moon makes the white flowers appear luminous. They walk downhill along South Street toward the harbor and Annie's house. The harbor is quiet, the water so still it mirrors not only the moon but even the stars. Their steps echo in the deserted street, as though they are walking on a stage. Maybe the whole evening was just a play?

No one appears to be guarding Annie's house now, except Leo, who gives up a short bark followed by a prolonged, miserable whine when they enter the yard.

"Oh, dear, poor Leo! We forgot about him! He didn't get supper, even," Annie says, quickening her step to get inside to rectify her neglect.

The Valentis and Josie and Judge have told her so many things, all equally surprising and heartrending, that she is sure she'll lie awake all night, fretting, second-guessing everyone's actions, wondering if things would have gone differently, *if only…*

Annie tells Justin to go to bed; then she goes out to the bindery. She lifts the sheet off the worktable. The calfskin is lying flat, waiting to be cut. Despite being exhausted, Annie makes up her mind to go ahead, and mixes the flour-and-water paste. She wraps the book in brown paper and creases the paper around the boards of the book to make a template. Then, with hands steady, she cuts the leather.

Much later, with the freshly covered book sitting with its boards bent backward and held in the open position while they dry, Annie finally crawls into bed. Tomorrow she'll put the book in the press, to correct any warping that has occurred.

She hardly puts her head on the pillow before she gets up again and goes down to the kitchen. There she whips together a carefully separated egg white and some vinegar with a fork, and lets it stand in the cup.

When she goes back to bed, she lies for a long time trying to remember everything said during the evening, and to make order out of it. Annie knows that she is desperately trying to find proof that Margo is the murderer. If only she didn't have an alibi. And what motive would she have, if she hadn't known of any inheritance? Annie will have to make sense of things in the morning.

CHAPTER 44

"How oft the sight of means to do ill deeds
Makes ill deeds done!"
(from *King John*)

Annie gets up and pulls her kimono on over her pajamas. The phone rings insistently, and she goes to answer. The voice on the other end of the line is one she does not expect.

"Hi, Annie, it's Clare." Annie squeezes her eyes shut in anger. Most of all, she'd like to just hang up, but she doesn't. After a few momentary pause, she responds.

"Oh. Hi Clare." She tries to keep her voice calm and even.

"I need to talk to you, Annie. Can you come over?" Clare sounds hoarse, as though she hasn't slept well.

"And meet Margo? No thanks." Annie can't help sounding short.

"I'm alone, Annie. Margo's moved on. I don't even know where she's staying. She has to be protected from you, she said, and I guess my place isn't safe enough. So, will you come over for coffee?"

Annie sighs. She can't help feeling curious, now. "I would, Clare, but my car is stuck in the garage. Literally. The door won't open. Why don't you come over here? Justin's here, but I'll send him out for a while so we can talk, if you want."

"Okay. I'll be there in a few minutes."

Annie sends Justin off for a walk with Leo. "Stay away for an hour, so I can have a chat with Clare. Then come back and join us."

After Justin leaves, Annie throws on a clean pair of jeans and a T-shirt and hurries back down to the kitchen. She starts the coffee and thaws a couple of muffins she bought at the Strudel Shop last week, in what suddenly seems like a previous lifetime.

Back in the day when she had her shop on the Neck, she would stop in at the Strudel Shop for coffee and a cranberry muffin early in the morning, and sit and enjoy the quiet out on the deck overlooking the harbor. In the off season the Strudel Shop would often be left unattended with freshly brewed coffee and a basket of strudel, croissants, or muffins on the counter. There would be a box to put the money in. ("Help yourself, make your own change," the sign said.) Small towns are nice that way. And before the town put in the new restrooms on T Wharf, tourists looking for relief in the downtown area could only find it at the Strudel Shop (or at the library, of course, but not many think of it) without actually shelling out for a meal.

From the Strudel Shop deck you can see as far as Star Island Park on the other side of the harbor, and after that the houses, including the Hannah Jumper House, are hidden from view by the Yacht Club building. The Sandy Bay Yacht Club takes up half of the "cross" of T Wharf. The view from the deck also includes the back side of Motif #1, as well as the tour boat floats. In the summertime you can sit and watch as the schooner

Appledore takes off from Tuna Wharf, loaded with a bunch of camera-toting tourists. The skipper motors the schooner out of the harbor before putting up sails. (The tourists are allowed to help with raising sail, and there is a lot less risk of mishap or embarrassment once the schooner is out on the bay.) On the way back from the trip, the captain will make a foray deep into Sandy Bay and shoot the cannon, scaring the seagulls into the air, where they will swoop and screech in vexed agitation for a while.

Seals often gather in large numbers out on the Salvages and sometimes venture into the Rockport Harbor. One year one of them picked a favorite rock in the water directly outside the Strudel Shop, where it would lie and take some sun. Sometimes it would slap its flippers together as though applauding the scenery or simply expressing the joy of the day. Annie had loved to sit out on the coffee deck and watch the harbor come alive before she went to open her shop. Many times she'd been late opening up, too engrossed in watching lobster boats chugging slowly out of the harbor, early-bird sailors being brought to their boats in the yacht club launch, or cormorants diving, sylph-like, for fish. When full, the sleek-necked birds—so graceful in the water—would pose like awkward statues on the rocks while drying their surprisingly large, vulture-like wings.

The smell of cranberry muffins warming reminds her of those days, and of Carlo. Clare knocks on the kitchen door before walking in. She gives Annie a vague and impersonal hug. Her face is swollen and her nose is red, as though she has a bad cold. Has she been crying?

"Come in, Clare, sit down. Or should we sit on the patio?"

"I'd just as soon sit inside. Then I won't feel quite so inhibited. I'm embarrassed about some of the things I've done recently, Annie, and I'd just as soon get it over with. We can always go outside later."

"Fine with me, Clare. Here, have some coffee and a muffin." Annie indicates the spread on the table. "Before you start, there's one thing I'd like to ask you: What do you know of Margo's and Carlo's marriage, Clare? Were you at their wedding?"

There is a long pause, during which Clare sits with her head down. Finally she looks up at Annie—looks her straight in the eye, and shakes her head a little before speaking.

"Annie, I called Judge Bradley just before I came here. He's the one who encouraged me to call you. You see...oh, I hate to admit it. Margo tricked me. I'm pretty gullible, you know that already, and I know that myself, but Annie, she was absolutely distraught. She came to my house. You know how she found Carlo, I mean...dead and all that—and then the police wouldn't let her into the place. She said she had nowhere else to go, no one in the world left to turn to. You know me, I'm a sucker for a sad tale. Then she said—between all these hacking sobs—that she and Carlo were supposed to have gotten married that very day, and now she had not only lost *him,* she was left with nothing, not even a penny. If this had happened a day later, she said, at least she would have had something...well, you get the drift. So, I broke all the rules and made out a marriage certificate, dating it the day before his death. I thought, *Who will it hurt?* This horrible thing had already happened, there was no turning the time back, and there was only this small window of time to help the poor kid. It seemed sort of preordained that I was there to help her. God forgive me. I am going to resign as justice of the peace, of course, in case you should ask. I never actually filed the marriage certificate, though, because before I had a chance to, all these things started happening that made me upset...like you getting accused." Clare takes a break and blows her nose. Annie decides that Clare's nose is obviously red because she's been crying.

"Oh, Clare. If only you knew. If only I had known," Annie says. She is shocked, and sad—and yet, somehow, triumphant. *Carlo did not marry Margo.*

"I'm so sorry, Annie. I can't tell you how sorry I am," Clare says. "I'm probably out of my job at the library, too. I told Duncan that Margo had been staying with me, and he hit the roof."

Score one point for Duncan. Annie shakes her head, trying to put everything together. She is feeling hot, and needs fresh air.

"Let's go sit out on the patio for a while, Clare."

Annie loads up a tray with the coffee and muffins, and Clare carries the mugs. They sit quietly for a few minutes, sipping coffee and watching a sailboat put in at the yacht club, sails luffing gently. Annie pushes the muffins toward Clare, who shakes her head.

"Well, Clare, I can't blame you for everything that has happened. You were only acting true to form, taking Margo in. I don't know what can be done about the marriage certificate, but I know you well enough to know that you didn't do it for gain. I honestly hope you can work it out. But in what way do you think she tricked you? I mean, do you or do you not believe that they were actually about to get married?" Annie is careful not to sound overly accusatory, even though she is not exactly in a forgiving mood.

"I don't know any more, Annie, that's just it. I certainly did at first. I agreed to do it, and when I went to make it out, she had all the papers for me. Birth certificates, medical forms, passports, the lot, enough so that it seemed to corroborate her story. Maybe some of it was fake—a lot of forms can be downloaded online now, and she had been using my computer for hours, to e-mail friends, she said. Anyway…after I finished the certificate, I thought she changed. She didn't seem at all like a grieving widow. Actually, she became pretty lively, even sort of jolly. I was kind of taken aback." Clare actually looks as if she is about ready to cry, but steels herself.

"So you began to think that she was just interested in the inheritance?" Annie goes on, relentlessly.

"Well, I don't know…. I mean, it's true that *before* the fire there was the gallery and the art works, and whatever else Carlo might have had of value. I doubt if he had a big bank account—I mean, Josie was still helping him, I'm sure. Then after the fire, there was nothing much left to inherit anyway, I thought—unless there was some kind of insurance policy—but people don't generally take care of those until *after* they're married. In a way, maybe she's worse off now than before, because now she'll be responsible for the funeral and all kinds of bills, you know. So it's not like she's gotten a lot out of the whole deal one way or the other, is there? Married or not, I mean." Clare is shaking her head, looking a little confused.

"But she *is* married, Clare," Annie asserts.

"What do you mean? I just told you, I didn't file—"

"No, no, what I'm trying to say is, she was already married *before* she met Carlo. This would have been bigamy, if it had gone through. She's married to an Italian. She just kept her maiden name." Annie bores her eyes into Clare's, and Clare wilts in shock.

"Oh my God. Why didn't Judge tell me all this?"

"Carlo's parents only told us about her marriage last night. They were at the funeral, did you know?" Clare looks thunderstruck.

"I had no idea. I wouldn't recognize them, of course, but Margo would. Maybe she just didn't notice them at the church?"

"Well, they noticed her. Anyway, as you see, presumably she *does* have someone somewhere in the world to turn to. You were duped, all right. Carlo was murdered, and she saw her chance and took advantage of it—and of you. But you know, none of this really matters. We still don't know who killed Carlo, do we?" This is what Annie needs to know, more than anything else. Whatever she can draw out of Clare, no matter how much pain it causes, she will work for.

"Well, I certainly never thought you did it."

Annie doesn't believe her. "Never?"

Clare looks up at Annie with her innocent, blue eyes. She has such a childlike, pretty face: pale skin that blushes so easily, surrounded by a short cap of wavy blond hair, and then those big, blue eyes.

"Never. It's true that Margo duped me, I guess—and she did actually try to convince me that you killed Carlo out of jealousy—but, no, I never really did think that you could have done it. Of course, before she told me, I didn't know anything about you and Carlo having been lovers, so that was a bit confusing. Who knew that? Nobody. You two really kept it secret." Clare looks down at her hands.

A dog barks, and Leo appears around the corner, followed by Justin. Clare gets out of her chair, open-mouthed.

"You're early, Juss," Annie says, sounding a little annoyed.

"Sorry, Sis, Leo had a bit of a tussle with a friendly mutt, and got a scratch on his nose. I thought I'd better take care of it." Justin says, and he and the dog take off for the medicine cabinet.

"*You* have the dog? How did you get him?" Clare asks.

"I didn't *get* him, he came here of his own volition. Why, was he with Margo, too?"

"Well, he was at first, but he didn't get along with my menagerie. So Stuart took him over. But then I don't know what happened; somehow he got out, I guess, and went missing." *Well, another little morsel of truth comes out.*

"Stuart? I don't believe it." *So, Stuart is involved in this tangled web, too. I knew it.*

"Now, wait. I know you don't like Stuart, Annie, but he's been very kind to Margo the whole time. And very decent to me, too…said he would support me any way he could. I mean, he knows about the marriage certificate—Margo told him, unfortunately—and I told Stuart how mad Duncan got just over Margo staying with me. So Stuart said he'd explain to the trustees, and to Duncan, things like that, if it became necessary. Duncan isn't speaking to me at the moment. And he doesn't even know anything about my involvement in the marriage! All he knows is I took Margo in. Said library staff should really try to keep out of these scandals, anything that could hurt the library. Pooh, he's more worried about the image of the library than about people who've been seriously traumatized…well, at least I *thought* she was traumatized…. Oh, Annie, I just don't seem to know anything anymore!"

Justin joins them on the patio, and Annie plays with Leo, fondling his ears. Leo licks her hand and makes happy, whiny noises.

Shortly after Justin's arrival, Clare leaves. Justin says he'll do the supper tonight, and Annie happily goes out to the bindery. The book is ready for endpapers. She cuts the marbled papers to size, selecting the best area of each sheet to use, then pastes them in. The leather at the edge of the book is thin and fine, and there are no bumps or ridges showing. Later, she will tackle the gold tooling.

Annie has mixed feelings about Clare's visit. On the one hand, she is bristling with anger over all the trouble Clare has caused with her Pollyanna, do-good schemes. On the other hand, she knows that Clare never meant any real harm. But how does that help now? And why didn't Clare feel loyal to Annie, instead of this…ooh, she can't think of a name for Margo that she would even be willing to pronounce. As things stand, Annie is still the only suspect in Carlo's murder, and nothing Clare has told her can change that fact. But in Annie's book, things are changing. So, there was no marriage. Had Carlo actually ditched Margo? Is that why she had gone to Boston? And then come back to face Carlo, and killed him in anger? But he had been dead long before her train pulled into town.

CHAPTER 45

"A parlous boy."
(from *Richard III*)

Annie is walking Leo the following morning when she runs into Esa, who stares in surprise from Annie to the dog and then back again.

"Miss Annie! You found him!" Esa shouts, and starts jumping up and down.

"What do you mean, Esa?"

"Well, you see, Mr. Swell let me walk the dog, and then one day he got loose, and Mr. Swell got very mad at me and wouldn't pay me any more money to walk the dog, Of course, he didn't have a dog anymore," Esa says, trying to get everything straight.

"That's right, Esa. He's my dog now, you see."

"That's great, Miss Annie. I'm sure he loves to live with you."

"So was that the secret that you had with Mr. Cogswell?"

"No...well, I don't think I'm supposed to tell you. But maybe I will anyway, because you won't tell anyone, will you?" Annie shakes her head. "Well, the secret was that I saw Mr. Swell give Miss Margo a ride. She's so pretty, Miss Margo, don't you think? I think it was real nice of Mr. Swell to help her. But when I told him how nice I thought it was, he got very mad at first and then he got nice again and said that it should be our little secret, and he gave me five dollars. And then he said if I kept the secret real good, he would let me walk the dog, and he would pay me a dollar every time. And he did that, until I lost the dog. But it wasn't my fault, Miss Annie, 'cause the collar was too loose, you see, and it just slipped off," Esa says, looking anxious even at the memory.

"I'm sure it wasn't your fault, Esa. When was it that you saw Mr. Cogswell give Margo a ride, do you remember?" Annie asks.

"Yes, I remember. Because that's the day that I saw Miss Margo come off the train from Boston. I was getting a donut up at the station, and then I went to see the train come in. I always like to watch the train come in, you know. It's fun. I'd love to go on the train some time. To Boston, maybe," Esa says. *So, it was Esa that provided Margo's alibi.*

"Okay, and when did you tell the police that you saw her get off the train?" *It is fortunate that Esa is fond of me, and doesn't mind getting questioned this way. With anybody else he would have the jitters by now,* Annie thinks.

"Well, actually I told Mr. Swell that I had seen her, and he got real excited and called the police, and then he told me that I had to tell them I saw her so Miss Margo wouldn't be in trouble, and he said otherwise I might be in trouble, too, so I told them, when they came to the library to talk to me." Esa looks quite proud to be able to report all this to Annie.

"I see. And was that when Mr. Cogswell picked her up? From the train, in the morning, I mean?" Annie smiles encouragingly.

"Nope. It was later. A-a-a-t…uh, at lunchtime. After the police talked to me. I was eating my sandwich out on the bench in the reading garden. That's when Miss Margo came walking up the lane, and Mr. Swell drove by, and she stepped to the side. And then he stopped, and they talked, and then she got into his car and they left. And then I went back inside to clean the toilets." Esa nods with satisfaction.

Annie tries to understand what this might mean, but she can't quite see how it has any bearing on anything. So, why the big secret, then? After all, by the time Stuart picked Margo up Carlo was dead already, lying in the morgue. She shudders.

"Are you okay, Miss Annie?" Esa looks concerned.

Annie smiles to reassure him. "Yes, Esa, I'm fine. And thank you for taking good care of my dog."

"Is he your dog then, Miss Annie?" Esa lights up at this idea.

"Yes, he is now. Well, I'd better run along," Annie says.

"Don't forget, Miss Annie, don't tell Mr. Swell that I told you about the secret," Esa says, still a bit anxious.

"Don't worry, Esa. I won't tell anyone without checking with you first," she says, and waves as Esa hurries up the street toward the library.

Annie is left standing in the street biting her lip, pondering if Esa's information, added to what she already knows, changes anything. She turns around and walks back to the house, even though Leo balks and tugs at the leash, disappointed at such a short walk.

Once inside, Annie zaps a cup of coffee in the microwave, pulls her favorite ratty chair over to the window and tries to create a timeline of all she can remember. *Let's see. Carlo's murder takes place on Wednesday. A week and a half a go. It seems more like a year. The first event after the murder—that I know of, at least—is Margo stepping off the Boston train, where she is seen by Esa, who later, at Stuarts prompting, reports this to the police. Margo walks from the train down to the gallery, where she discovers Carlo's dead body on the rocks. The police investigate, do not believe burglary was involved, as they have no evidence that anything is missing.*

What happens next? *Oh, yes, around lunchtime, Stuart picks Margo up outside the library and drives her somewhere. In the afternoon the police question me after two people come forward and name me as a suspect. The day after...I think...Sally sees Margo on the Neck, trying to get into the gallery to pick up "her stuff," but the police won't let her inside, as it's still considered a crime scene. Ned Mazzarini picks Margo up from there because "powah Mahgo," as he calls her, still has no transportation. Then Ned drops her off near Clare's, although he doesn't know that's where she's going. Well, Ned's a gentleman, I'm sure there's nothing sinister there.*

Annie stops working on the time line for a moment. Something is bothering her, there is something she is missing. *The Scout? Where can the Scout be hiding? Margo tells Ned that Carlo must have parked it somewhere else. Margo reports it missing to the police. Billy Hale tells me that it might be stolen. Those are slightly different takes. Obviously, Margo hasn't been able to find it, since she has to catch rides with people. Where did Stuart drive her, I wonder? Well, could the two people who came forward to the police be Margo and Stuart? Is there something going on there? Why is he so anxious to be helpful to Margo? And why so secretive, bribing Esa to promise not to tell?* Annie can make no sense of this connection, and decides to leave it alone for the moment.

Well, then. During the time that Margo is staying at Clare's, she wangles the marriage certificate out of Clare, presumably in order to end up owning the gallery and Carlo's paintings. Someone breaks into my house and attacks Gussie, wrecks my computer, and tosses my books around. In search of something? What? I have nothing of particular value, no paintings or jewelry anything else with any connection to Carlo, and assuming that all these things are tied together, the break-in must be something to do with Carlo, but what?

What follows next? *The fire at Carlo's gallery, where it seems Margo loses whatever she gained by the marriage certificate. And then, after Clare turns me down as a houseguest, Duncan brings me to the motel. I watch the newsreels on TV, where the grieving widow claims to be afraid for her life, and I am pictured as the suspect in the murder. Then I get scared of Duncan, and run, and find Josie viciously attacked. Then, thank goodness, Justin arrives, and lines up Judge to help me.*

"I must be brain-dead," she says to herself. "I know I must be missing something, but what? Time for a break."

CHAPTER 46

"Who calls me villain? Breaks my pate across?"
(from *Hamlet*)

Annie stops in the kitchen to pick up the egg-vinegar mix before going out to the bindery. The book comes out of the press, and she gathers the rest of the equipment for gold tooling: electric writing pen, pallet, foundry type, cotton batting, and the pumiced cushion for the gold leaf. When all is ready, she strains the egg and vinegar into a clean jar. The *glair* will make the gold leaf adhere to the leather. She places the leaf over the dried glair, which she has rubbed with a little Vaseline to make the gold stick, and breathes gently on it to flatten it before adding another piece on top. She chooses the foundry type for the title—all caps in a Roman style—sets them in the pallet, and puts the pallet on the finishing stove to heat slowly. She has marked with a little tick on the gold leaf the point where the line is to start, and when the pallet is the correct temperature, she applies it. Afterwards she tapes down a rough sketch on thin paper over the gold leaf, and works freehand with the electric pen on the decorative vines and tiny flowers that will surround the single word of the title:

CARLO

When Annie leaves the bindery, she is overcome with gloom and cannot stay in the house. She puts Leo in the back of the Chevy, but he quickly jumps into the front passenger seat. He circles the seat a couple of times before he lies down and gives her a long, smoldering look. Annie smiles at him.

"Okay, loverboy. You win," she says and starts the engine.

Justin spent a couple of hours earlier in the day getting the garage door to go up, and then nailed a board on each side to keep it from coming down. She'll have to call Ned one of these days for a more permanent fix…and to do the windows, she thinks. If she doesn't end up in jail. Oh, well.

Annie and Leo ride around aimlessly, first through the South End, then on to Land's End along Penzance Road. She parks the car at the turnaround out on Loblolly Point and takes Leo along on the cliff walk, where they stand and look out to sea. The water is an unearthly ultramarine at the horizon, lighter blue close to shore. Here and there are turquoise patches where the sand is stirred up by currents. It is a perfect day for the Star boat races. Annie is planning to bring Gianna and Antonio out on the Headlands later, to watch Justin and Judge race—fully aware that Justin had better help win this one. She sees a lobster boat going around the point into Loblolly Cove, and recognizes Tommy Cameron's boat, *Thermidor,* which gives her an idea. She'll invite Sal and Matt for Lobster Thermidor! Maybe right away…like tomorrow, just in case they never find the real killer, and she ends up getting incarcerated for the rest of her life. Annie hasn't *truly* considered this a possibility until this very moment—or maybe she has simply refused to accept it—but suddenly she knows that it is very possible, indeed. After all, with motives galore, in the minds of the public, and

no alibi for any of the misdeeds—Carlo's murder, burning
down his gallery, the attack on Josie, breaking into her own
house and beating up poor Gussie, and then setting fire to her
own house—who is in worse shape than she? Just because, in
her mind at least, she can think of other people who could have
done it (Margo comes most easily to mind, except for her alibi)
and can even come up with motives for some of them, doesn't
mean the police will take any of her suggestions seriously. Why
should they? They've got her, and she's a sure bet.

To avoid going home, she makes another sidetrack, looping
down Marmion Way past Gap Cove. As she drives by Avery
Shattuck's house, she sees him step out of his garage pulling a
lawn mower. She gives him a tentative wave, but he only scowls
when he recognizes her. Oh, well. He has never forgiven her for
joining forces with "the opposition" on the issue of schlock art
when, along with a number of other "anarchists," she signed
one of Carlo's letters to the editor.

Annie drives right by her own house and continues through
town and over the Keystone Bridge to the Cove. She parks off
Curtis Street and takes Leo along onto the conservation land,
walking through the woods over toward Folly Cove. She has
thought of something that she would like to investigate. Annie
is still curious about Stuart's involvement with Margo. Why
did he pick her up? And why would he want Esa to keep quiet
about seeing it? Is it possible that Margo, after leaving Clare, is
now staying at Stuart's house?

Stuart lives not far from the forest trail Annie is on, in an
old stone house in the woods at the end of a long, unpaved
driveway. Behind the house are some old sheds, a small barn,
and a dilapidated garage that will serve to shield her from

view on the way to the main house. Annie approaches stealthily. Stuart would gladly make a big stink about finding her on his property. Leo starts whining, and Annie tells him to hush up. Walking carefully on the overgrown path, trying to avoid any brittle twigs, Annie and Leo end up at the back of the garage. She walks around to the side and steps over and peeks in through the cracked and cobwebbed window. In the gloom inside stands Carlo's old green Scout.

Suddenly Leo starts barking and tugging at the leash.

"Easy, boy. What's the matter?" Annie says, and that's the last thing she remembers.

CHAPTER 47

"For in that sleep of death what dreams may come."
(from *Hamlet*)

Annie wakes up in the dark and thinks it must be night, until she realizes she is in a windowless space. She has been bound and gagged, and her head hurts at the slightest movement. She tries to roll sideways so she can sit up, but instead she rolls off the cot or chest or whatever it is she has been lying on and hits the cement floor, unable to use her arms to brace herself. Her head hits the concrete, and she passes out again briefly. Waking up, she waits for the sharp pain in her head to abate and lies prone for a while, maybe minutes, maybe hours, she can't tell. She falls unconscious in between brief moments of awareness. As she floats in and out of consciousness, her mind wanders. *Willie,* she thinks. *Willie, where are you? I need you... "To be, or not to be..."* No, no, not that...

"Madam, yon young fellow swears he will speak with you. I told him you were sick, he takes on him to understand as much, and therefore comes to speak with you. I told him you were asleep, he seems to have a foreknowledge of that, too, and therefore comes to speak with you. What is to be said to him, lady? He's fortified against any denial."

"Tell him he shall...he shall...he shall not speak with me..."

Dimly, she sees Carlo approaching, a white shadow in the darkness. *"Yes, yes, he shall speak with me now..."* she amends. And then she loses consciousness, never knowing whether Carlo speaks with her or not.

When she is aware of being conscious again, she decides to make no movements, just lie perfectly still until she has a plan. The first thing she wants to do is get rid of the gag so that she can breathe normally—and scream if she has to. But she can't twist her head or squirm her way out of it without excruciating pain. She uses her tongue and teeth, and laughs, twitching with pain, when she realizes that whoever gagged her picked up an old, soft rag that easily shreds apart once she gets it wet enough. Now she has two weapons: her voice and her teeth. Will she be as lucky with unbinding her legs and hands? She tries tentatively to wrench her hands apart, but they are tied with rope, and her ankles are, too. As she begins to scooch around in the dark, she feels nauseous, and wonders if one can get vertigo lying down. She has a concussion, certainly, and decides that moving around is not the thing to do.

After a while, a thin stream of light shines in through a crack in the wall, and she can faintly make out her surroundings. She tries to remember what happened, but her mind is still not functioning right. She remembers passing through Stuart's back yard. Maybe she is in a shed? Wasn't there a garage? Oh yes, the Scout, she had seen the Scout through a window. But this is not the garage; there is no Scout and no window here. And where is Leo? Wasn't she out for a walk with Leo? She must have let go of the leash. Thoughts flash in her mind about what horrible accident may have happened to Carlo's dog, but she forces them away. Nothing happens for the next hour or so, and Annie slumbers off and on.

When she wakes again she is still surrounded by darkness, and wonders if she has slept through the night. She hears the sound of a car in the distance, doors slamming, a voice far away. Tempted to scream, she is still afraid to—what if the voice belongs to whoever conked her on the head? Then she hears Leo barking. He appears to be right outside the shed.

"Shhh, Leo, hush," she hisses. Leo barks ever wilder. She begins to panic when she hears Stuart's voice, coming nearer as he speaks.

"I have no idea where she might be. Not around here, anyway," he says.

"Someone told us she might be here," another voice says, drifting in from further away. Annie tries to clear the cobwebs from her brain. She recognizes the voice, but can't remember who it belongs to. The voices seem to trail away again, as though Stuart and whoever it is are going back toward the house. Annie calls up her courage and cries out feebly:

"Help! I'm in here." But they don't hear her. Then Leo barks again. And again and again.

"What the hell? That damn dog is back again," Stuart says.

"Isn't that Carlo's dog?" the other voice asks.

"Well, it was, I guess."

"What's he doing here, then? What's his name again, Leo, isn't it?" Annie hears a whistle. "Here, boy, come here, Leo." The voice is coming closer again, and suddenly Annie recognizes it.

"Billy! I'm in here!" she croaks hoarsely, jubilant.

Officer Hale breaks open the door and sticks his blond head into the murky interior.

"Annie! What in heck are you doing in here?" he says, treading carefully to avoid stepping on her crumpled body. "Give me a hand here, would you?" he says to Stuart. When he sees Annie's contusions he changes his mind. "Go and call for an ambulance. We're not moving her," he says. Stuart, wordless, runs off toward the house.

"Annie, what happened here?" Officer Hale asks.

"I don't know. I was... I was out in the woods for a run with Leo... Oh, thank you, thank you, Leo," she says, as the dog, hearing his name, comes scampering over and licks her face.

"You just happened to be out in the woods right here behind Cogswell's house? Or was there some other purpose here?" The initial concern Officer Hale showed after finding her seems to give way to suspicion again, or maybe he is just annoyed.

"Well, uh, I don't remember too well, Billy... My head hurts. Oh, but I had some sort of idea, I think... I was looking for something."

"I thought so. Wish you'd leave that sort of thing to us, Annie. Look at all the trouble you keep getting into."

"Yes. Sorry. Oh, Billy, at least you were out looking for me. Thanks."

"For you? No, actually I was out looking for Margo Valenti. Someone said she might be here."

Now they hear sirens coming up the road into the woods, and then, as the technicians bring a gurney, the sound of twigs breaking and men swearing as they crash through the shrubs and thorny undergrowth. Stuart is leading them to the shed, and they quickly have Annie fitted with a neck brace.

Then they untie her limbs—she cries out as the rope comes off her left wrist—and lift her out into the daylight, which is fading. She hasn't slept through the night, after all. As she is being alternately carried and wheeled to the ambulance, she suddenly remembers something. Anxiously, she reaches out for Officer Hale's sleeve.

"Oh, Billy, if you look in the garage back there, you'll find Carlo's Scout," she says weakly. She feels woozy again. In a fog, just before she is lifted into the ambulance, she can barely see him turn around and stare dumbly at the garage.

CHAPTER 48

"This is the silliest stuff that I have ever heard."
(from A *Midsummer Night's Dream*)

Justin, Judge, Josie, and the Valentis are all sitting around her bed in the hospital. Annie is installed in a bed in the ICU until they decide whether to let her home. The room has two beds, the second one being currently empty.

Judge is looking grim. "Now, Annie, that takes the cake. To go and hit yourself on the head like that, and then tie yourself up to boot, and lock yourself in a shed. What will you think of next?" he asks sternly.

Annie laughs, then winces as it makes her head hurt. "You forgot to include 'gag yourself.' But of course, I had gotten the gag off by the time Billy found me," she says.

"Gagged too, eh? Well, was that before you hit yourself on the head, or after?"

"Must have been after, because I don't remember it."

"Allright now, enough hilarity." Judge's thick eyebrows come together. "Who hit you on the head, Annie?"

"Don't know, Judge. Came from behind. Believe me, I wish I had seen who it was. I have had enough of this," she mumbles.

"When are we ever going to get a break, here?" Judge throws his hands in the air.

"Can't all the questions wait? Annie has been through a lot." Josie gives Judge a warning look.

"It's okay, Josie. I'd like to tell Judge what I know and remember in case I die of my wounds." Annie passes the back of her hand over her forehead, pretending to swoon. Gianna looks anxious.

"They must have given her something," Josie whispers, trying to explain Annie's peculiar, droll mood.

"No more jokes, Anna, we so worry about you," Gianna says, and Annie nods.

"Fine, let's have it. Tell me all you remember," says Judge Bradley.

"I hate to admit it, but I don't think Stuart knew I was in the shed. He seemed truly surprised. I have no idea whether he knew that Carlo's car was in the garage. He was gone when I told Billy."

Judge rises out of his seat, totters alarmingly, and Josie takes his arm to steady him.

"They've found the Scout?" he says, in a voice too loud for the ICU, even if there is no immediate roommate to consider.

"Yes, I was looking at it through the garage window, just when whoever-it-was knocked me out."

"Well, I'll be darned. Nobody told *me*," Judge says huffily. "I'll be leaving then, to check on a few things. These people can have a turn at you—unless there was anything else you remember?"

"That's it—except for two things: did you win the race, and where's Leo?"

Judge harrumphs proudly. "We won, but I have to admit that it was close. Justin did a fine job—too bad he lives so far away, or he could crew for me permanently! We didn't know you were gone, of course, so Gianna and Antonio never got to see us race. They were quite worried, naturally."

"And Leo's at your house, Annie. Came whining at the back door just as I was leaving," Justin says.

Judge looks to be satisfied with that piece of news, too, as he leaves.

Annie tells the floor nurse she feels fine and that she wants to go home. The doctor finally arrives to check on her, and advises her to stay overnight in the hospital, but when Gianna promises to accompany and take care of her, he reluctantly agrees to release Annie. Her fractured wrist has been stabilized, and she is told in no uncertain terms that because of the concussion, twenty-four hours of bed rest is necessary. Annie nods assent and winces at the pain caused by the nod.

At home the telephone is blinking like a Christmas tree, but she doesn't want to listen to any messages.

"Justin, could you turn off the ringer, please? I don't want to talk to anyone," Annie says.

Justin hits the silent button but asks, "What if Judge calls?"

"I'll call him in a while. Right now, all I want is a couple of hours of peace and quiet," Annie says.

Gianna enforces silence in the house while Annie rests. When she wakes up she lies briefly looking around her, satisfied to find herself back home among Willie's books and her own rustic furnishings. Then she reaches out for Gianna.

"Could you get me the phone, Gianna? I need to make a call."

"But you need peace and quiet, Anna," Gianna protests.

"I have to make this one call. Please, it's important, Gianna."

Gianna gets the phone, and Annie dials the police station. "Could I speak with Officer Hale, please?" She should probably address herself to the chief directly, but the mere thought makes her head pound.

"This is Annie Quitnot, Officer Hale. I have a request to make of you. I'm afraid I can't do it over the phone, it's a little complicated. Could you come to my house? They've just brought me back from the hospital, otherwise I would come to the station." The reason she can't do it over the phone is that she doesn't want to have the conversation recorded.

"I'll see what I can do, Miss Quitnot. I'll call you back and let you know in a few minutes." Annie is about to breach a solemn promise.

CHAPTER 49

"To unmask falsehood,
And bring truth to light."
(from *Rape of Lucrece*)

Gianna lets Officer Hale in, then disappears out to the kitchen to let Annie speak to him in privacy. Annie decides to start by telling him about Stuart and Margo, suggesting subtly that Hale might check with Esa again.

"Esa is Margo's alibi, after all. And now that you know where the Scout was kept, maybe Stuart Cogswell knows more than he has told. And Esa mentioned something that it would be better if he told you directly, I think. Just remember that he isn't quite like the rest of us, and don't scare him," she says, trying not to break her promise to Esa if she can help it.

"You're not giving me a lot to go by, here. Are you sure this is not just another wild goose chase?" Hale looks dubious.

"What do you think happened to me up there, Billy," Annie asks in frustration, "just some innocent hiker walking by and knocking me on the head, tying me up and throwing me into Stuart's shed?"

Officer Hale looks thoughtfully at her. Then he nods and gets up.

"I'll look into it, Annie, I assure you," he says. "I'll let myself out, you just stay put. I'm glad to see you're on the mend, by the way."

After an hour he calls Annie back. Gianna hands her the receiver with a shake of the head, before disappearing again into the kitchen. Moments later, Hale stops by, and Gianna lets him in.

"A few minute only, agente, Anna need to rest!" Gianna stalks off to the kitchen, mumbling to herself and Annie smiles and shrugs her shoulders.

"She means well."

Officer Hale sits down next to Annie, considerately pulling his chair around so that she can look at him without twisting her head. Annie takes this to mean that he's not planning any more questions of the third-degree type.

As Annie suggested, he has double-checked with Esa, who was the first to say he saw Margo step off the train. Hale tells Annie that, since then, a second witness has stated the same thing, but you never know. Sometimes people read things in the paper and want to feel important, be in the news, and end up become supporting witnesses.

"When I asked Esa about Margo again, he was reluctant to talk at first. 'I don't want no trouble,' is what he said."

Annie giggles. "I'm not surprised."

"I promised him there wouldn't be any trouble, just as long as he told the truth. Then he said, 'But Mr. Swell, he might get mad at me again,' and I asked him why Mr. Cogswell would get mad at him. If Esa had actually seen Margo step of the train, he was just telling the truth, I said."

"What did he say to that?" Annie asks. *Not only cops can ask leading questions.*

"Esa said, 'No, not about that, about the ride.' And when I asked him what ride that was, he said, 'The ride that Mr. Swell gave Margo from the library,' and I asked him to please tell me about it. I promised him that as long as he told the truth, I would make sure that nobody got mad at him for it."

"Poor Esa. He hates to make people upset, you know." Annie can imagine Esa's anxiety during this examination.

"Anyway. In short, he told me that it was on the day when she got off the train, but later in the day. He didn't know where Cogswell had taken her, but he was late for work after lunch, and Esa had to watch his desk for a while, 'so the kids wouldn't take no books that hadn't been checked out,' he said. Apparently Cogswell was gone for at least half an hour, according to Esa. I don't know how accurate Esa's ability to estimate time is, of course. And Stuart never told him where he had taken Margo, Esa said. But he did tell him that the whole thing should be their secret. So then, finally, I had to promise Esa that the truth never hurts someone who is innocent. And Annie, I wouldn't have told you any of this, but you obviously got it all from Esa yourself, so I wanted to compare our stories, in case Esa's memory has holes in it. Is this the way he told it to you?"

"I think you got everything the way I did, Billy," Annie says.

Just then, Officer Hale's phone rings. He turns off the speaker and puts it to his ear.

"Yes Chief, I'll be right there." When he puts the phone away and stands up to leave, he doesn't explain what it was all about, but Annie thought she heard something about *search warrants*.

Drowsing on the sofa about half an hour after Hale leaves she hears sirens. Gianna comes in to check if she is awake, and turns on the radio softly.

"Cinque minuti di riposo, Anna, twenty minutes, just rest a leettle more! I will come sit with you soon." The sirens are fading, going out of town, and Annie falls asleep.

CHAPTER 50

"Away, you scullion! you rampallian! You fustillarian!
I'll tickle your catastrophe!"
(from *Henry IV*)

Gianna joins Annie in the living room soon after Officer Hale leaves. Annie is lying prone on the sofa in the lower part of the living room, facing the harbor. She is following doctor's orders, hoping her headache will go away. Gianna pulls up a chair next to her, "I will sit here next you and read one of your many, many books, Anna. A library, you live in a library, I think. What you suggest?"

Annie points in the direction of the Shakespeare section, which resides on the shelves right behind Anna's chair. "There's even one in Italian there," she says. "Carlo used to read to me out of it sometimes." *O, Carlo, Carlo mio...* She pulls the blanket up over her face.

Quietly, Gianna goes over and pulls out a book in worn red leather binding. She sits down and turns on a little Victorian lamp with a red shade next to her before she starts reading. Slowly and in a rich, well-modulated voice, she enunciates the Italian in such a way that you might think it had been Shakespeare's native tongue. After a while she looks at Annie, who has uncovered her face. She is calm now, as her friend Willie would surely have wanted.

"I think you my daughter-in-law, Anna," she says.

"Thank you, Gianna. You and Antonio feel like family to me, too." Annie tries to stifle a yawn. The long day and the visit of Officer Hale have taken a toll.

"And Judge Bradley...*Joseph*...and Josie also. We nice, big family now. Despite it all," Gianna says. Annie nods and falls asleep listening to Gianna read aloud. She is startled awake when Gianna drops the book on the floor and utters a surprised cry. Someone has entered the room, but Annie lies with the back of the sofa shielding the visitor from view.

"Margo," Gianna whispers.

Margo, again dressed in her artsy long skirt and peasant shawl, shoulder bag swinging, has quietly walked in through Annie's unlocked back door. Justin is gone; Gianna sent him out for groceries, and Antonio went with him. Annie and Gianna are alone with Margo in the living room. Annie sits up, despite Gianna's efforts to keep her down. Pain sears her brain, and she feels faint. She watches Margo step closer, keeping her right hand stuffed hard into her pocket. A gun? A knife? Annie tries not to think about it.

"Why...Margo. What are you doing here? How did you get in? Were you looking for me?" Annie says. She tries to stand up, but her head hurts when she moves. Gianna forces her back down.

"Margo, this not good time visiting, Anna not well," Gianna says firmly, but without rising.

"Hah, well, I should think not," Margo says. Then she looks angrily at Annie. "You have something I want," she says.

"Really? What's that?" Annie asks, truly curious.

"You know what it is. The will."

"The will?" *So, Margo knows of the will.* "You mean Carlo's? Why should *I* have his will?" Annie tries. Maybe Margo doesn't know what the will contains.

"Don't be cute. Carlo showed it to me. Josie didn't have it. I know you must have it hidden around here somewhere," Margo retorts.

"You mean, you already looked for it but couldn't find it?"

"Just give it to me, and I'll leave. As Carlo's widow, the document is mine. I need it in order to handle my husband's estate," Margo says, a little haughtily.

Annie doubts that her handing over the will—even if she had it—would satisfy Margo. Margo looks like a woman on a mission, and Annie does not even want to imagine what that mission is. Can she stall her long enough for Justin to return?

"Maybe you haven't heard, but someone broke in to my house last week and went through all my papers. Made a real mess, too. I haven't had time to go through everything yet..." Annie rambles on. Margo rolls her eyes and cuts her off.

"I'm sure you have a special place for important papers. A safe, for instance." Margo casts her eyes around as if she expects to see one.

"I'm afraid I don't have the kind of valuables you would need a safe for," Annie says.

Margo is losing her patience. She runs around looking behind frames and drapes, throwing cupboards open, shoving books off shelves. When she gets to the Shakespeare section, Annie tries to get up. Gianna reaches over and puts a hand on her arm to stop her, shaking her head vigorously.

"Don't touch those books!" Annie growls. Margo, feeling victorious, rapidly starts pulling volumes off the shelves, rifling through the pages, and when nothing falls out, tossing them on the floor. Annie moans. Margo is getting close to Annie's greatest treasure, a first quarto edition set of Pope's *"The Works of Shakespear,"* bound in calf-gilt with raised bands and red-and-black morocco labels. Annie inherited this set from her grandfather, who was a man of modest wealth until the Depression struck him down. He had refused to part with his books, however, and Annie had inherited his library—and along with it, his love for books. And that set is the crown of her collection.

Now Annie can't stand it any longer. She throws her legs over the side of the couch, shakes off Gianna's restraining arms and hurls herself at Margo, knocking her down. She starts pelting her with blows, but Margo easily pushes her off and gets up. Her hand is back in her pocket, and she leans over Annie, angry, menacing. Gianna screams, trying to pull Margo back.

"Go get it! Just get it and give it to me, Annie!" Margo shouts. Annie moans, putting her hands to the back of her head.

"Wait, I can't get up...oh God," she mumbles. She tries to turn over and raise herself onto her elbows, and Margo kicks her in the side to hurry her up. Slowly, Annie gets up on hands and knees and reaches for the bookshelf. She draws herself up, one shelf at a time, groaning in agony at the effort it takes. When she is upright, she leans against the shelf for support, resting with her head against the books for a moment. Suddenly there is a great banging and crashing, and the shelves seem to be shaking. Is her house coming down?

Thumping and heavy grunts of fighting make her turn around, expecting to find Margo and Gianna locked in battle. Instead she finds Margo lying facedown on the floor, with a burly fellow straddled across her back pinning her arms down with his knees. It's Ned Mazzarini, who has arrived to work on repairing her storm windows. *Good Old Ned.* The banging and crashing must have come from Ned's entering through one of those windows, which no doubt will need some extra attention now. Gianna stands by watching anxiously, wringing her hands for a moment before running over to the phone. Annie, exhausted, face drawn with pain, flops down on the couch.

"*Polizia*, Anna...we must call police, *che numero?*" Gianna pleads.

"Here, Gianna, bring me the phone," Annie reaches for the receiver and dials. She listens, exultant, to the brief message that her call will be recorded. When the desk sergeant answers in person, she quickly explains the situation and hangs up.

"For Gawd's sake, Annie, gimme something to clout her on the noggin with," Ned says—mockingly, as he is not having any difficulty holding Margo down. Margo groans in anger. She looks up at Annie. All Margo's young prettiness is gone, replaced by a hateful, repulsive scowl. Her blond hair lies streaky against her forehead and cheek. The sun slants through the window, throwing a harsh light on her face. The thickly mascara'd lashes and the heavily lipsticked mouth show a woman who looks older than she claims to be. Annie rises and walks unsteadily over to look down at her, her feet only inches from Margo's face.

"Why did you come here, Margo? You know you won't get away with this. So, *why?*" Annie asks.

Margo laughs derisively. "So you won't get anything either, of course." She tries to wriggle out of Ned's grip, still running on adrenaline, fuming with anger and frustration, but he has a lock on her. "Carlo *promised* that when we came here he would help me, said Josie would support me...but *nooo*, the bitch didn't *like* me. And then he told me that *Josie* was his mother, yeah, not you, Gianna. Then, the night before he... you know...died...he pulled out these old photos and letters from you, Annie—to make me jealous, I'm sure—and the *will,* which he bragged he had just rewritten. I'm sure it was just so he could show it to me and hurt me. As if I didn't know he was still sweet on you; I saw you two at Clare's. So I lay all night thinking about everything. Early in the morning when I woke up, I sat down on the landing outside his bedroom." She wriggles angrily, trying to get out of Ned's grip, but to no avail, and angrily, almost proudly, continues her litany. "When he got up to go to the bathroom, I tried to make him change his mind. He just stood there in those old shorts he slept in, yawning and scratching his chest. I told him *no way* you loved him. I saw you turn him down at Clare's, didn't I? Anyway, we argued for a while, then he just ignored me. Told me to get lost. Like he could *fire* me, or something. And then he turned his back on me and went to the bathroom. What a big ox," she says, with an involuntary shudder.

Gianna, who has been weeping silently, utters another sharp wail. Margo takes heart from this, and continues her sputtering, remorseless unveiling, as though reaching for some final, cathartic climax. She has managed to turn sideways a little, so she can at least glower at Annie while she talks.

"I was real mad. 'Get lost?' After he promised to help me! So I left. I just walked down the street. I had no idea where I would go. I got to the top of Broadway before I remembered that all my stuff was still at Carlo's, even my wallet. I turned back to get my bag, at least. When I got there, I didn't see Carlo anywhere. I ran around looking for my stuff, and then I went out on the deck. That's when I saw him. He was just lying there, like he was sleeping...." Her voice trails away.

Annie sinks back down on the sofa and puts her face in her hands. *Margo is not the killer. If she were, she would have admitted it. Proudly. Wouldn't she?*

CHAPTER 51

"Those that much covet are with gain so fond,
for what they have not, that which they possess
They scatter and unloose it from their bond,
and so, by hoping more, they have but less."
(from *Rape of Lucrece*)

Annie listens, transfixed. Is it possible that Margo is trying a last-ditch great lie? Annie has believed—or has at least wanted to believe—all along that Margo could be the murderer.

Ned is the only one aware that Gianna has opened the front door to let someone in. With a shushing finger to her mouth, Gianna motions Chief Murphy and Officer Hale inside, with Sergeant Elwell sliding in right behind them. Margo, who is completely focused on Annie and oblivious to anything else, continues her tale. Ned makes sure she can't turn her head toward the hall.

"I went out on the rocks…and I knew before I got to him that he was dead." She pauses for a moment and closes her eyes. Ned is still securely lodged on top of her, keeping her pinned down as she unloads her furious complaints. Margo's features are momentarily distorted when she remembers Carlo's dead face. Then she juts her chin out despondently. "I also knew right away that everyone would think I did it, so I ran back inside to get some stuff, packed the car, and took off. I drove across the bridge to the mainland, and just kept on going, trying to think of what to do. I couldn't stop thinking about that will, though. *God, Annie would end up with everything!* So I decided to drive back and look for it. If I could only get my hands on the will, and destroy it. It was still early in the morning, and where Carlo was lying nobody could see him from the street. I stopped next to the railroad station in Gloucester to get gas, but I didn't have any cash, so when I heard the train roll in I thought, *I'll just take the train, won't be hard to hide from the conductor, it's only one stop.* And then when I got off the train in Rockport, that stupid kid from the library saw me. Oh, well, ha-ha, it gave me an alibi for the killing anyway, right? When I got to Carlo's place, I went out on the deck, and I saw him, still lying there, two hours later, so I went back inside to look around. I didn't find the will, only a folder with Carlo's passport and stuff. Then I caught sight of a neighbor who must have just seen the body from his house. He was walking over toward Carlo, so I ran out. Screaming, of course—the shock, you know—and later, when the police came, I told them I just got back from Boston."

"But you came back again later that day to look for the will, didn't you, only the police wouldn't let you in? And you were the one who set fire to the place, weren't you," Annie says, trying to puzzle together the order of events. "And then you remembered Josie, and panicked when you thought that *she,* Carlo's *mother,* probably had a copy of the will. So you went up to her house to look for it, and when she discovered you, you slugged her—but you didn't find it at her house either, did you?" Annie's brain is racing now.

"Which was why you came here, to Annie's house, wasn't it?" Annie cranks her head around, disregarding the pain, at the voice of Officer Hale. Chief Murphy stands just next to him, his hair an orange halo in the sun, and Sergeant Elwell is behind them in the background. Margo groans as Ned grips her arms tightly to keep her forced down.

"Billy! Oh, thank God!" Annie says. Officer Hale steps forward and relieves Ned of his prisoner. He pulls Margo up from the floor and handcuffs her. She tries to fight him, but the adrenaline is finally wearing off.

"*You* were the intruder that beat up on Miss Quitnot's little dog, weren't you? And then you came back and tried to burn down *her* house, too, when you didn't find what you were looking for." Officer Hale shakes his head in disgust.

Margo tries in vain to twist out of Officer Hale's hold.

"But if she's telling the truth, we still don't know who killed Carlo," Chief Murphy says thoughtfully.

"Well, we've got enough reasons to take her in as it is. Maybe she'll change her tune," Officer Hale says.

Now Gianna steps forward. "Officer, you must not forget notify Margo's husband, Signor Buonarotti," she says, looking steadily at Margo. Margo wilts. Officer Hale looks confused as he tries to force her toward the door.

"Buonarotti? I thought her name was Valenti?"

"Don't worry, Billy, we'll explain it all later, if she won't," Annie says.

Officer Hale leads Margo out to the cruiser, accompanied by the chief and Elwell. Chief Murphy turns around in the doorway.

"Miss Quitnot, I'll be talking to Judge Bradley shortly. In fact, he's on the way over to the police station right now. I just called to tell him you are fine, in case he had the scanner on. I'm sure he'll keep you informed." Murphy touches two fingers to his forehead as he leaves. Some sort of salute?

Ned is rubbing his hands together to get the circulation back after holding Margo stoutly pinned down. "Well, Annie, that powah Mahgo shoah got some nehve, ain't she? Hahd to believe. Sorry abaht them windahs, now. Gawd, wohse than evah, now. I'll fix 'em up befoah I go, to keep out the weathah, an' be back tomorrah mahnin' to do 'em up good faw ya."

"Ned, I can't thank you enough. I owe you a lot, maybe even my life," Annie says.

"Wasn't nuthin', Annie. She tuhned out to be some kinda' loonatic, that Mahgo, eh? I nevah figge'd it. Seemed lahk a nahs kid at fihst. Aw, an' powah Cahlo. D'ya think she could'a did i'm in, despaht what she says? Well, gotta get on with the cahpentry, don' I, or else you're gonna have a herrican in heah tonaht. Easy now, Annie, go get some lie-down, eh?"

Gianna forces Annie to lie down and leads Ned out into the hall, where she gives him a great hug before she pushes him out the door. Ned walks around the outside of the house to the broken window and starts nailing up plywood to keep the house tight to the weather until he can make proper repairs. Annie's head is spinning. With all the things that Margo had willingly owned up to, the killing of Carlo had not been on the list. Was she devious enough to get away with murder, or was Carlo's killer still at large?

CHAPTER 52

"O, what a goodly outside falsehood has!"
(from *The Merchant of Venice*)

The police and Margo have been gone for less than an hour when there is a knock at the door. Gianna looks at Annie, who is lounging, half awake. Annie shrugs her shoulders, grimacing at the pain it causes, and Gianna opens the door to let Judge Bradley in. As the chief promised, Judge is here to bring Annie up to date. He sinks down in an easy chair next to where she is resting. Gianna fusses, covering Annie with a blanket while giving a warning look to Judge. He blithely ignores it, and Gianna goes out to the kitchen to get him a cup of coffee.

"A couple of hours ago, Sergeant Elwell was sitting in the cruiser in his favorite spot up by the information booth," Judge starts. *No doubt,* Annie imagines, *looking in the rear view mirror now and then to admire the future police station rising behind him, and reading a paperback while munching on his lunch.*

Judge continues: "Elwell had just taken a swig from a can of soda when he saw the Scout coming up Main Street toward Great Hill. Elwell peeled out after the speeding car, turned on the flashing blue light, and when that didn't slow it down, the siren. That actually made the Scout speed up instead of slow down, would you believe it? Calling in for backup, Elwell kept up with the Scout until they got to a section of Nugent's Stretch where he could pass the car. He floored the accelerator to put himself in front of the Scout, which was still speeding, then slowed down to a stop just before the Gloucester line and stepped out of the cruiser. As he walked toward the Scout he saw blue lights in the distance already, so he waited for the backup to arrive. Officer Hale had secured a search warrant, you see, and gone back up to Cogswell's place, only to find nobody home and the Scout missing from the garage. That's what sent Elwell to his lookout spot, and when the call from him came in at the station, Officer Hale hit the door in record time."

"Who was driving the car?" Annie asks, dying of curiosity.

"Cogswell."

Annie's eyes open wide at this. *Stuart? What would Stuart be doing driving Carlo's Scout?*

Judge smiles, pleased to have amazed her. "'What am I being stopped for,' Cogswell asked. 'Well, speeding, for starters,' Elwell said, 'and not stopping for flashing lights or sirens.' Cogswell tried to worm out of it, of course, saying he just meant to get out of the way. Good try. 'Also, for driving a vehicle reported stolen.' Elwell added. Then Officer Hale assisted the passenger out of the car. Care to guess who it was?" Judge peers at Annie expectantly.

"Who? Margo?" Annie assumes.

"Nope. Miss Draper, that's who," Judge says with a rather smug smile.

"Clare? *Clare* was in the Scout with Stuart?" Annie frowns, nonplussed.

"Yes, my girl." Judge takes a sip of the coffee that Gianna has just brought, and motions for her to sit down and join them, but Gianna shakes her head and goes back out to the kitchen. "And then," Judge continues, "the Scout was towed to the police station. Cogswell and Draper were taken in for questioning, naturally. Cogswell got called in first. I managed to advise Miss Draper not to answer any questions without counsel being present, but Cogswell went ahead rather brazenly, figuring he could hornswaggle the police, I suppose. Now Annie, can you imagine what was under the cover in the back of the Scout?"

Annie shakes her head. "No idea, Judge. Margo's clothes, I suppose? She just told us she picked up her stuff. And maybe stretchers and tools and all kinds of junk that Carlo used to keep there?"

"Wrong again. Stacks of canvases, that's what, tightly jammed into every possible spot."

"But Judge, she said she had gone in to pick up *her* stuff..."

"She lied, my dear. Now, can you imagine Cogswell's face when Murphy told him what he had been transporting?"

Annie has to laugh. Then she gets serious. "So, all Carlo's paintings haven't gone up in smoke after all. These must be the ones slated for his retrospective show, if Margo was smart enough to tell the difference." Annie bites her lip at the thought that she might own the crowning achievement of Carlo's work.

"Which brings us to another point. The chief mentioned to Cogswell that they were going to get in touch with Margo's husband, Mr. Buonarotti. 'Buonarotti?' Stuart said. He was really confused, as you can imagine, when he was told that the marriage to Carlo was bogus. At that point, he apparently decided to tell them everything he knew. He explained that he had felt sorry for Margo, who seemed just like an innocent kid to him, he said, not the devious person she turned out to be. She asked him to bring the car to a safe place in Gloucester. Apparently Smythe had made her an offer for Carlo's place, didn't even care that it was burned down since he was planning to level it anyway. Meanwhile, Smythe had an empty studio apartment on Rocky Neck that he told her she could use for free, with a garage where she could park her car."

"Dear old Fred. What a sweetie," Annie rolls her eyes. "Boy, she sure couldn't wait to try to unload, could she?"

Judge grunts. "Well, she'd have a hard time, legally. But that's another story. Anyway, Cogswell seemed quite deflated when he finished. Hm. I'm sure that will pass soon enough." Judge leans back and closes his eyes for a moment, looking exhausted.

"But Judge, none of this gets us any closer to finding out who killed Carlo. And what about Clare?" Annie asks.

Judge looks at his watch. "Clare should be here any time, now. I asked her to stop by," he says, covering a yawn.

CHAPTER 53

"Hasty marriage seldom proveth well."
(from *Henry VI*)

A few minutes later, Gianna lets Clare in.
"Not to stay long, please. Anna very tired," Gianna says, giving Clare a stern look. Clare nods and walks into the living room. Annie has fallen asleep, and Judge shows Clare over to the fireplace area, where they both sit down, Clare in Annie's well loved old settee.

"Now, Miss Draper, let's have a friendly little chat, you and I," Judge says, cool and businesslike.

Clare looks down at her hands. "What will happen to Margo, Judge Bradley?"

"I think that depends, don't you? I mean, at this point, do you think that she told you everything there is to know? Came clean with every detail?" Judge is careful to keep his voice even and not scare Miss Draper. He wants all the information out of her first.

"I don't know, Judge. I thought I knew everything, that she explained it all to me. I thought I was just helping her to what should rightfully be hers." Clare looks over at Annie, wondering if she is really asleep.

"Well, let's start with what you actually know, shall we? Why don't I just ask you some direct questions, and you answer them? First, you didn't know when she came to stay with you that Margo DeVoe was married to an Italian named Paolo Buonarotti?"

Clare shakes her head. "No, she didn't tell me that."

"And how did you find out about this marriage?"

"Stuart told me about it at the police station, but Annie had already told me. Stuart and I were both fooled, I guess."

"What else did he tell you?" Judge hopes they didn't have time to share too much information.

"Nothing else. He left. He was pretty mad, I think. Mad at me, mostly, for getting him involved in this mess."

Judge nods. That would be true to form for Cogswell, no doubt. "Okay, Miss Draper. Now, I understand that the marriage between Miss DeVoe and Mr. Valenti was never recorded. In other words, *officially,* the marriage does not exist. The only evidence is a document acquired under false pretenses, which, if it were filed, would make Miss DeVoe guilty of bigamy? Miss Draper, am I right so far?" Judge looks at Clare, waiting for her answer.

"Yes, I think that is correct," she says thoughtfully, "but—"

Clare wants to unburden herself completely, but Judge won't let her. He only wants the salient points, and puts a hand up to quiet her, then smiles. Clare relaxes her tense pose, sits back, and puts her hands on her lap.

"Well now, Miss Draper, where were you and Mr. Cogswell going in such a hurry today?" Judge has an inkling that Clare

Draper has more knowledge than she understands the importance of.

Clare looks worried again. "Stuart called me and said we had to get the car out of his garage."

"So, you both knew it was there?" That would be interesting.

"Of course."

"Do you know how long it had been left there?" Softly, softly. *Don't get scared, Clare.*

"Yes, since the day Carlo died. Margo told me that Carlo had parked it in Gloucester the night before. He'd been to a bar with friends, and someone else drove him home. Maybe he'd had too much to drink, I don't know."

"But Miss Draper, could you explain to me why Carlo would drive off in a car containing Margo's clothes and belongings on the night before they were to get married?" Judge reaches for his coffee, which has gone cold.

Clare remains thoughtful and silent for what seems a long time. "I don't know, Judge," she says, timidly.

"I'd like to ask you about something else, Miss Draper. Do you know the real reason why Miss DeVoe told the police that the car was missing? After all, the car did not belong to her, did it? Let's think about that for a moment. At the time of the murder, the false marriage to Mr. Valenti had not yet taken place; in fact, we don't even know when she came up with that scheme. So, at first she was just trying to have the use of a car that didn't belong to her, and that's why she wanted it hidden, don't you think? And if she really were in Boston on the night of the murder, how would she have known that Carlo had parked the car in Gloucester? I mean, she says that he was dead the next time she saw him. You see what I mean?"

"Maybe she talked to him on the phone, in the evening?"

"And he told her that he had come home drunk and had left the car parked in Gloucester? Packed full of his paintings? How does that sound to you?" Judge is relentless now, exhausted and not caring any longer to be gentle with Miss Draper.

"Full of his paintings?" Clare turns her large, beautiful eyes on Judge.

"Yes, Clare. And that's what you and Stuart were asked to transport to Gloucester today. A large number of Carlo's best paintings."

Clare has been rendered speechless. A sudden rustling sound makes them aware that Annie is awake and has tossed her blanket off. Slowly, she rises and makes her way over to them, before sliding down carefully into the chair beside Judge. She smiles and looks at Clare.

"It's okay, Clare. There's something else I'd like to know, though," Annie says, looking from one to the other. "Do you know who put a certain note on my door?"

"It was Stuart. He told me. I know it was a rotten trick. It was just a joke, really, he said. I think maybe he wanted to unsettle you a little. You know how he is." She looks pleadingly at Annie.

Annie can believe this typical Stuart tactic. "Well, thanks for clearing that up, anyway. Still, there's a lot I'm not clear on. Clare, you were very quick to tell Stuart about Carlo and me. Did you lie to me before, when you said you never thought I was guilty?"

Clare looks down.

"Yes. I guess so. As soon as I heard that somebody had killed Carlo, I thought it was you. Who else, Annie? Margo had already told me about you and Carlo, by then, you see…I mean, sure, lots of people had issues with Carlo, but you—God, you must have been so jealous—and then, when Margo came to stay with me, she reinforced that feeling, and I talked to Stuart about it, not knowing what to do. He said we should call the police and tell them what we knew. Stuart thought at the most it would be a nuisance to you, nothing beyond that."

"Well, it was that," Annie admits. "And then *he* knew where her car was the whole time. He did drive her to the car—to where *she* had parked it, not Carlo. So he *knew* she hadn't been in Boston. What was he planning to do, I wonder, let me get convicted so he could get my desk? Doesn't that make him— maybe each of you, for that matter—an accomplice after the fact, or something?"

"Well, Margo told Stuart and me two different stories, you see. It never once occurred to either of us that Margo could be so sneaky. We were sure that in the end the murder would turn out to be a robbery, or a dispute gone bad with one of Carlo's enemies. Carlo had enough of those…." Annie has never seen Clare as discouraged as she appears at this moment.

"Annie, I promise you, I honestly don't believe you killed Carlo. I'm ashamed to admit that I did, for a while," Clare says.

"Even though, as Chief Murphy said, we still don't know who killed him?" Annie asks.

Gianna comes in and resolutely makes circular waving motions with her hands toward the door. *"Basta.* Anna too tired. Enough today. Good-bye, Clara."

Clare rises and is herded out the door like a black sheep. She waves to Annie, but Annie has turned away. It has gotten windy, but the sky is clear and radiantly blue. There should be a grand sunset later. They watch through the front window as Clare hurries off, pulling her sweater tight around her. Annie lies back down on the couch. Judge takes a few turns around the room before deciding he'd better get going, too.

"I'll be checking in again with you later, but right now I'd better get back to Josie with all the happenings of the day." he says as he shuts the door.

"Oh, look, Clara forget pocketbook." Gianna picks up a shoulder bag from the floor.

Annie looks at it. "That's not Clare's. That's Margo's. Let me have it, Gianna."

CHAPTER 54

"What's mine is yours, and what is yours, is mine."
(from *Measure for Measure*)

When Justin and Antonio get back, Annie tells them about Margo's unexpected visit and arrest. Antonio pales, but Gianna nods reassuringly that all is well. Annie tells Justin she has something new to tell Judge, and Justin says he'll call him.

Judge arrives, accompanied by Josie, and they all voice disappointment when the days' events don't add up to finding the murderer.

"Of course, Margo *could* be telling the truth. On the other hand, now it turns out she might have had both motive *and* opportunity. But the thing that has bothered me the whole time is, why would she have wanted to kill Carlo in the first place? They weren't married; that idea came later, so there was no inheritance to be gained at the time of the murder. Anger at being told to leave? Doesn't sound like enough. Jealousy? She's turned out to be such a cool, calculating customer, somehow I don't think there's enough passion in her for that."

Gianna takes Josie with her out to the kitchen to get supper organized. Annie reaches for Margo's shoulder bag and hands it to Judge.

"This was left behind when the police took Margo away," she says.

Judge looks at her sternly. "Have you looked inside?"

"Yes."

"Find anything interesting?"

"Nah."

Judge purses his lips, and Annie closes her eyes. He leaves her to sleep—if that's what she's doing—and joins the others in the kitchen. Gianna and Josie tell the men to go outside and enjoy what's left of the sunset while the women cook.

Justin turns the ringer back on, and the phone rings immediately. Josie takes the receiver. It is Duncan, asking how Annie is feeling. Josie, without checking with Annie, tells him to come and see for himself, and suggests that he join them for supper in an hour.

When Annie wakes up, she goes to the bathroom. She takes Margo's marriage certificate out of her pocket, rips it to shreds, and drops it into the toilet. *Just where it belongs,* she thinks, as she flushes it down. She does not want it in existence, false or not. Margo might come up with another sob story and find another dope to help her file the paper. If she doesn't end up in jail, that is. And maybe Annie will tell Clare that she has destroyed it, maybe she won't. She'll think about it.

At the appointed time, Duncan arrives, bringing a surprise: Gussie. Annie is ecstatic, and so is Gussie. Leo comes running, barking wildly, and he and Gussie have a bit of a tussle, followed by a sniffing session. It ends up in an uneasy truce, with Gussie suspiciously eyeing Leo and placing himself possessively by Annie's side. Annie knows in her heart what she must do before the evening is over. It will be hard, but not as hard as she had thought when it first became obvious to her.

Duncan has brought flowers, too, but Annie recognizes the selection and knows before Duncan tells her that they come from Esa. Today's bouquet consists of pink snapdragons and a calla lily. Annie laughs.

Duncan, avowed lover of all things Italian, is in for an unexpected treat. Gianna has outdone herself (with Josie's aid) and serves up a feast from her native region. *Tatra,* a flan made with onions, rosemary, and Parmesan cheese is the appetizer. A main dish of *Osso buco* with *risotto* follows, served with a glass or two of a lovely Barbarolo. Finally Gianna sets out a dessert of poached pears with chocolate sauce, sprinkled with chopped hazelnuts. The hazelnuts were grown in Piedmont and brought along in Gianna's voluminous pocketbook. They bring their espresso and dessert bowls into the living room to keep the still-prone Annie company. Duncan sits down next to her. When everyone is occupied in lively conversation, he leans towards her.

"I hope to see you back at work soon, Annie. You are sorely missed," he says.

"By whom?" Annie asks.

Duncan looks at her. "By me, of course. And I think Jean will be particularly glad to see you back," he says with a chuckle.

"Well, you'll have to wait a little longer, it looks like," Annie says, patting her head. Duncan puts a gentle hand on her shoulder, and Annie doesn't draw back. After a moment, he removes his hand with a smile.

"I don't mind waiting," he says. Annie doesn't know whether there is some sort of hidden message there, but she decides to just let it hang in the air. Duncan looks at her thoughtfully and leans down over her again.

"How poor are they that have not patience! What wound did ever heal but by degrees?" he whispers. Annie nods. They understand each other now.

Antonio and Gianna invite Duncan to come and stay with them next time he visits Turin, which he hinted at the supper table that he would love to do.

"It's very kind of you to offer," Duncan says, smiling.

"Annie is also to coming, she promise." Gianna says. "Perhaps you can go in company?" she adds, innocently. She has noticed the kind of attention Duncan is giving Annie—the looks, the gentle touches. Duncan reddens slightly. Annie says blandly that she would love to come and visit some day, when life has returned to normal.

It is time for the guests to leave, and Annie calls Judge over. Now is the time to do what she knows is right.

"Judge, I want you to take Leo. I have Gussie back now, so I'm safe again," she says.

Judge shakes his head. "Oh, no, Annie—Leo belongs with you. He's so fond of you!"

She smiles at his generosity. "I insist. He'll be much happier with you up at the ranch. Besides, I could never take these two out for a walk together! Leo would be the death of Gussie. But he can come and visit us any time."

After a great deal of dickering, Judge relents, and when he leaves, Leo is trotting happily behind him. Annie will miss Leo, the last live and tactile remnant of Carlo, but she also knows that that's exactly what Leo will be for Judge—who never had Carlo himself.

CHAPTER 55

"The wounds invisible
That love's keen arrows make."
(from *A Midsummer Night's Dream*)

The following morning, despite the fact that the whole town now believes that *Margo* is guilty of the murder of Carlo Valenti, Annie still has not been cleared. However, she is feeling much better today; in fact, she gets up and goes out to the bindery before Justin is awake. There she pulls out a carved wooden box from the wall cupboard. She opens it and takes out a beribboned bundle of photos and clippings, and begins to paste them into the book, which is finished and temporarily covered in brown paper. There are pictures of Carlo as a child, which she had laughed at and begged him for, and some of Carlo in his studio, taken by Annie. The rest are of Carlo and Annie during their years together. Carlo was a good photographer, and had taken a number of photos of her; and also of them together, setting up his camera with a timer before rushing to Annie's side. How young, how happy and innocent they look. Annie pastes the pictures on the page with trembling hands. Oh, how can she go on? She closes her eyes and leans on the table.

But yesterday will not return, no matter how hard you bid it. Nor will today. Time will not stop, nor must she, and she returns to the task at hand. A photo of Carlo, standing between Josie and Judge (how could she ever have missed the likeness between father and son?) goes in next. In the photo, Judge is officially handing Carlo the first check from Josie, his new benefactor. Josie and Judge are looking at each other in the picture. Is there a longing in their eyes, or does Annie only imagine it? A clipping from *Time* magazine of Carlo accepting the prize at the Biennale and some local clippings follow. Annie refuses to put the obituary in the book. Instead, she finishes with a picture of herself and Carlo, arms slung around each other, walking among the dunes on Wingaersheek Beach. A strong breeze is pulling at their hair and clothes. Both of them are smiling broadly. *Finished.* Without leafing back through the book, she closes it and puts a weight on top.

Once she has cleaned up in the bindery after her project, she goes to sit on the little rickety porch that hangs over the harbor wall. Seagulls are screeching madly somewhere out beyond the headlands, a sure sign of a lobster boat returning to harbor. Judges Star boat lies ready at the dock, alongside two or three others. Summer will be coming to an end soon, better make use of the good weather while it lasts.

The Valentis are off with Judge on a sightseeing tour—a short one, as their plane will be taking off from Logan in the evening. They will return for lunch before Judge sends them off in the airport limo. Gianna and Antonio have declined his offer to drive them to the airport, sensing that he must be just as exhausted as they are. The invitations to come to Torino have been renewed with reinforced vigor and no excuses will be accepted.

Justin finally wakes up and, after searching all through the house, comes running out to the bindery looking anxiously for Annie, and finds her seated on the porch with her elbows on the railing.

"Here you are. I thought you were supposed to be resting!"

"I haven't done anything but, Juss. This is far more restful than lying in bed with all this muddle going round and round in my brain." Annie gives him a relaxed smile, and once he has calmed down, he takes Annie out for a little spin. Less than an hour, including a stop for coffee, takes them all around the island. When they return, Annie says she'd like to look in on Josie. Justin says he will drive her there and come back to pick her up in a while. Josie will babysit his sister and, hopefully, keep her out of trouble.

CHAPTER 56

"The 'why' is plain as way to parish church."
(from *As You Like It*)

Justin drops Annie off at Josie's. Josie winks at him as he leaves, letting him know that she understands that she has been elected to guard Annie and keep her from embarking on further adventures.

VALENTI WIDOW ARRESTED, the morning's headline said. Then follows a jumble of speculation and misinformation worthy of a tabloid. The information about Carlo's parentage has been leaked, which is not surprising. It was only a matter of time, in this small town. Carlo is now listed as having been the presumptive heir to two fortunes.

This very fact is what strikes the two women who study the article together. Josie is sitting in her kitchen reading the paper when Annie arrives, and Annie sits down and glances through it with her.

"Oh, dear. How complicated it all seems," Josie says.

"Does that mean that *Margo* some day might have been the heir to two fortunes? I mean, she wouldn't have known that at the time of the murder, but if somehow she had gotten away with the fake marriage, could that have happened?" Annie wonders aloud.

"I really don't think that could have been a reason for the murder. I was the only one who knew who Carlo's father was. If only... oh, what's the use of 'if only's.'" Josie says, and her chin trembles slightly.

Annie suddenly looks at Josie. She hesitates, but then utters what has just come to her mind.

"I just had a strange thought, Josie. Carlo would have replaced Dot as Judge's heir, wouldn't he?" Then she shakes her head. "It's a pretty awful thought, I admit. And she couldn't have known about that either, not then."

Josie folds the newspaper carefully. Her hand shakes slightly as she puts the paper on the table.

"No, I don't think so, Annie. You said she came and asked you for some information about Grant, so she could impress her Grandpa?" Josie asks. "Well, she asked *me* questions, too, said she really wanted to impress him by knowing something about Grant. We'd looked in some old photo albums, you see, from the days when Grant and I were first married. Dot always takes such an interest, you know; it's why people like her. Well, then we went on and looked at some of my other albums. I took a lot of pictures in Italy, of course, and there were pictures of Carlo as a baby in them. She didn't recognize him, of course, he was just a baby. In a later album, from when I was sponsoring him, there were pictures of Carlo as a grown man, you know, clippings, and exhibition notices, that sort of thing. And I told her about you two...how I was hoping you would get back together."

Annie looks at Josie. They are both thinking the same thing: Dot might have put two and two together—but what conclusion could she have reached? She could possibly have guessed that Josie was Carlo's mother, of course—but then, what? Annie frowns, concentrating.

"You know, I never thought of it before now," Annie says, "about Carlo being Dot's uncle, I mean. Dot could never have figured that out, could she? It's a pretty awful and unjust speculation, too. She could never have guessed that Judge Bradley was Carlo's father, when Judge didn't know it himself."

Josie stares off into space. Her hands lie trembling on her lap, like small, anxious chicks in a nest.

"Oh, no. Oh, Lord, please no," she mumbles, and the chicks start fluttering. She gives Annie a worried look, then stands, looking determined. "Well, let me show you something," she says. She goes and gets a photo album, opens it to a page, and puts it on the table in front of Annie. There are several photos on the page, but one immediately draws Annie's attention. She sucks in her breath.

"Oh God," she says. It is a photograph of Judge Bradley—he would have been in his fifties, perhaps, at the time it was taken. He looks the image of Carlo, or at least as you might imagine Carlo would have appeared a few years from now. That same Hemingway-hero look: the well-sculpted face with those clear, intense eyes; the broad, manly chest. Annie looks at Josie, shocked, and with a sense of awful dread. "It could be a picture of Carlo," she says. "And Dot saw this?"

Josie nods. "I didn't think anything of it at the time, of course; there was no reason for me to. I was so familiar with that photo, having looked at it often, but it was always Judge I saw, not Carlo. But I remember now that Dot suddenly became quite agitated when her eyes fell on it. She just slammed the album shut, said she was late for her next visit, and ran off. I didn't see any significance at the time; Dot is so conscientious, you know, never wants to be late."

"And then she didn't even come in to pick up the information I had collected for her," Annie says. "She was probably still trying to learn about Grant, to impress her grandfather, when she saw that picture of Judge, looking so like Carlo. And when she tried to determine if Carlo could have been Grant's child, she found out that he was born well after your husband's death. And with that picture of Judge...well, she must have felt pretty sure." Annie pauses, considering. "Josie, she has been acting sort of strange, hasn't she? She never even knew Carlo, yet she refused to go to the funeral home to say a final good-bye to him. Remember how she shuddered when Judge asked her to go with you? And how catatonic she seemed on the day of the funeral? How she was leaning on Judge like a child needing comfort?"

They sit quietly pondering, trying to understand the full significance of what they are saying, and the possibilities.

Annie speaks first. "Obviously, she could have realized, even back then, just what it said in the paper today: Carlo stood to inherit not only the Valentis, but if things came to light, also you and Judge Bradley. Carlo, not she, would be her grandfather's heir. And since she and Carlo weren't that far apart in age, she might not even outlive him...."

The women exchange looks. "Oh, Josie, do you think it's really possible?" They are both distressed, casting about for some idea that would prove them wrong. "What are we going to do? Call the police? They'll only think it's another brainless idea of mine."

But Josie suddenly looks determined. "I'm calling Judge. If it's true, it'll kill him; he loves that girl. She's been like a daughter to him, ever since George and Lily died. Judge and Pauline brought Dot up as if she had been their own child. Judge spoiled her, in his fashion. I know he seems gruff with her, but that's his manner with everyone, as you know. He has a heart of gold, though. That girl has never lacked for anything, neither love nor whatever money can buy. She takes after Lily, that's all. Lily was always unsure of herself and starving for everyone's affection." Josie sighs. "Judge took George's death awfully hard, and ever since Pauline died, well, Dot's been his entire family. And then, finding out about Carlo...and too late...oh, it'll kill him, Annie."

"We could still be wrong, Josie," Annie says, knowing it might be wishful thinking.

Josie looks at her solemnly. "I don't think we are, Annie. I'm calling Judge." As she reaches for the phone, her hands do not shake. She knows what it will mean to Judge, but she cannot avoid this sad duty.

CHAPTER 57

"Be sure of it; give me the ocular proof."
(from *Othello*)

There is no word from either Judge or Josie all day. Annie knows Judge well enough to know that he would take whatever action necessary, and feels that she cannot intrude on what must be a terrible moment, if Josie and she are right in their suspicions. Justin has picked her up and brought her back home. She walks around the house on pins and needles, waiting for a call. She hasn't told Justin, feeling that she must wait for word from Judge first. What if they were wrong?

Justin finally walks in and shakes his head at her apparent agitation. "What's the matter now, Sis? Come on, we're going out for a ride." They end up on Wingaersheek Beach and walk among the dunes. Annie remains sullen and closemouthed. She isn't used to keeping things from her brother. Finally, she gives up and blurts the whole thing out. Justin stands aghast at the water's edge, while wavelets swirl across his feet.

"Dot? I can hardly believe it. Really, Annie, it can't be true. She'd never get up the guts." He steps out of the water before his jeans get soaked. In a discouraged mood, they walk back to the car.

By the time they get back home, Judge and Josie are on the way to Logan airport with the Valentis. They have left no message. Justin and Annie eat a supper of leftovers from Gianna's dinner in silence. As promised, Sally comes to pick Annie up after dinner, to take her to the concert. The program tonight includes works by Satie, Bruch, and Dvorak. An eclectic evening, in other words. Annie pours punch into plastic cups that she hands to the paying guests. Some people recognize her and look a little surprised, but no one makes a fuss. Then the lights dim, and it's time to get to their seats. The Satie is charming; the Bruch, stirring; and, amazingly, Annie survives the Dvorak. The musicians are excellent, and the concert is recorded and will be heard at a later date on NPR.

At the end of the performance, a certain amount of socializing and meeting with the musicians takes place before the guests depart. Annie is still leery of chatting with the townies and instead walks around the small refreshment room to take a look at the recently hung exhibition. At the moment, this little room features "student works." Member teachers each have an area of the room where their students' efforts are displayed. On the main wall, the students of Priscilla Pettengill are presenting their "Harbor Sunrise" paintings. Annie walks closer, caught by an image. She gasps, then covers her mouth with her hand.

Sally comes over to see what is wrong, fearing Annie is not feeling well. "What's the matter?" she asks, putting a hand on her shoulder.

"Look, Sally, look there!"

Sally looks, uncomprehending, at an amateurishly painted harbor scene. Seagulls that look as if they were painted by a child fly like Vs across a bright orange sky, and boats perch oddly on top of water as thick as blueberry jam. In the background, Bearskin Neck seems to be levitating in air above the Sandy Bay Yacht Club, and a throng of disproportionally large people stands at the end of the Neck, admiring the sunrise. On the rocks along the harbor side of Bearskin Neck, below some boxlike shapes that must represent the fish shacks and cottages, are a man and a woman. The man is seated, the woman stands in a stiff pose, wearing a baseball cap with a ponytail sticking out through the back.

"What is it that I'm supposed to see?" Sally asks.

"Don't you see? That's Carlo and...doesn't that look like Dot?" Annie says, pointing at the pair.

"Oh my God, you're right," Sally says. "Gosh, that's her all right, with that baseball cap. What does it mean, Annie?" She looks in bewilderment at Annie, then back at the painting.

"I wonder when it was painted," Annie says carefully.

They look at the little tag beside the painting, which only bears the title "Rockport Sunrise." But further over on the wall is a larger sign, which reads "Harbor Sunrise, students of Priscilla Pettengill paint at Star Island Park, June 2."

"That's the day Carlo died, Sal."

A man steps up behind them, looking a little annoyed, trying to get a better look at the painting. He is wearing a nice suit and carrying a straw hat under one arm.

"Ah, yes, this is the one," he says, and when Annie steps aside to let the man look, she sees that Priscilla is standing beside him.

"I see. Well, I think the artist might be willing to sell it, but of course she isn't here at the moment. Shall I ask her, and then contact you?"

"That would be fine. I feel I *must* own this painting. I collect primitives, you see. This painting will hang in the same room as my Grandma Moses. Nowadays I limit myself to living artists, of course; one should support them, don't you agree? Now, I hope you will get back to me soon? I'm leaving Rockport at the end of the week, you see; I'll be staying at the Sandy Bay Inn until then. Here is my name and room number." He hands a card to Miss Pettengill, and walks out to the main gallery.

Annie walks up to Priscilla. "Priscilla, I couldn't help overhearing…but you mustn't let this painting go yet."

Miss Pettengill looks suspiciously at Annie. "And why not, Annie? If someone wants to buy it, I owe it to my student to facilitate the sale."

"I'm sending someone in to look at it."

"Are you telling me that someone else is interested in buying it?" Priscilla is looking at the painting, somewhat surprised.

"No, but it might be evidence, you see."

"*Evidence?* Evidence of what?"

"Murder."

"Oh dear, that's the silliest thing I ever heard. It sounds pretty farfetched to me. Besides, it could probably tie it up for a long time, right? And the customer is only here until the end of the week."

"Well, then the police might have to issue a subpoena, I suppose," Annie suggests.

Miss Pettengill doesn't like the sound of that. "What's so significant about this painting, then?"

Annie walks her over and points.

"That's Carlo Valenti. And this was painted on the morning Carlo was murdered. In fact, the murder probably took place during your class."

Miss Pettengill looks at the painting again, stunned and horrified. Naturally, she wants no part of a scandal involving the Art Society, and without further discussion, she agrees to hold it.

Annie and Sally leave soon afterwards. Before Sally drops her off, Annie has an idea.

"Sal, do you have any plans for tomorrow night? I'd like to have you and Matt over for dinner before Justin leaves. Josie and Judge will also be there, I think...and I might ask Duncan, too, actually," Annie says, casually. Sally looks at her with a large question mark written in her face, but Annie pretends not to notice.

"Love to. Have to check with Matt, of course," Sally says.

"Oh, and another thing, Sally. Lisa—you know our page at the library—just graduated, so we need a new page. Why don't you have Ben apply? He's a bright boy, and I think he'd do well. I'll put in a good word for him."

Sally gives her a big hug. "Oh, Annie, I can't thank you enough! That would be great."

"The boys *will* grow up, you know. It's only a matter of time!" Annie laughs.

As soon as she gets inside, Annie gives Johnnie a call at Roy Moore's lobster shack.

"Lobsters for tomorrow? Sure thing," he promises.

CHAPTER 58

"Leave her to heaven,
And to those thorns that in her bosom lodge,
To prick and sting her."
(from *Hamlet*)

VALENTI KILLED BY HIS OWN NIECE, reads the morning headline. Annie can imagine both Josie's and Judge's pain. Now they have each lost the last member of their family. But Annie senses that the two may have grown close again, and so perhaps will have each other in the end. Josie calls Annie early in the morning to relate the events of the previous afternoon.

Dot's arrest was surprisingly quiet, Josie tells Annie, in a voice that is heavy with tired sadness. Judge picked her up, telling her he was taking her to say a final good-bye to her uncle before the body is sent to Italy. Again, Dot tried to object, but this time she was given no choice in the matter. He stood by her, a solid, calm presence. Dot did not open her mouth until the sheet was lifted. Then she broke down and sobbed wildly. Jaws clenched, Judge supported her, and when Dot calmed down she confessed in a quiet, trembling voice, all passion spent in that terrible moment when she objected to the *unfairness* that had entered her life. On that long, awful day, she had dragged herself out onto Bearskin Neck, simply to see the sunrise, trying to lift her spirits out of their black depression, and afraid that her grandfather would find out about Carlo, after which Carlo would surely take her place in Grandpa's heart. That, to her, was more important than the fact that Carlo would replace her as Judge's heir. And then, by chance, she had seen her uncle sitting out there on the rocks—such a handsome man, so lucky, with a future as bright as the sun that shone on his upturned face. She had walked through the open door into his house in a trance, her hand had picked up a knife without her even knowing about it, and she had continued out onto the rocks, where in a white heat of anger and resentment she got rid of the rival that stood between her and her grandfather.

Dot hadn't even winced when handcuffed, and didn't object to being led away. Perhaps she felt relieved. How had she lived through the two weeks since that gruesome, unimaginable act of violence? The funeral, the time spent with her grandfather, with four devastated parents, and with Annie? It passes understanding.

"'We may pity, but not pardon thee,'" Annie mumbles to herself when she hangs up after Josie's phone call. *Poor Dot, indeed.*

Dot is charged with Carlo's murder. Margo is also facing a long list of charges: attempted murder of Josie, assault and battery, two cases of arson, and breaking and entering are among them. The charge of falsifying documents is dropped when no documents are found (nor have any been filed), but no doubt making false claims and the possibility of bigamy will be looked into.

How timely Carlo's death must have suddenly seemed to Margo…and what a surprise it must have been for Dot when someone joined in and struck at the very targets, Josie and Annie, who could shed light on Carlo's background! However, despite Dot's horrific deed, Annie somehow feels that Margo is the more evil of the two.

Stuart and Clare may face some charges, too—"aiding and abetting" and "after the fact" are words Annie hears bandied about by Judge in a phone conversation with Chief Murphy. But some leniency is possible, since it is quite obvious that they were duped. A fact humiliating enough, at least in Stuart's case.

All charges against Annie have finally been dropped, and she has had a phone call from the library trustees assuring her that her "temporary suspension" is over. And, immediately after that, she receives a call from Duncan, asking if she feels ready to come back. Annie answers that she would like a couple of days to recover fully from her concussion but that she is eager to get back to work as soon as she is well. To which Jean, according to what Duncan tells Annie later, exclaimed, *"Hallelujah!"*

Judge and Josie at Annie's request take her to say her final farewell to Carlo. At the last moment she changes her mind and turns around before the sheet is lifted. When they get outside, she turns to Judge.

"That would have been the clincher, wouldn't it? If the chief had seen me try to avoid facing Carlo's dead body, he would have pronounced me guilty then and there. Oh, but Judge, I still want to remember Carlo alive. I couldn't look. I'll get over him when I'm ready."

CHAPTER 59

"Now our joy,
Although our last, not least."
(from *King Lear*)

Justin picks up the lobsters. Annie steams a few, then deftly picks the meat out of them. The meat will be used to stuff the other lobsters later. Then they will be baked, with plenty of butter and some breadcrumbs on top. Annie scoops out the loblolly and puts it in a small pottery bowl. The appetizer is ready.

After all preparations are made for the dinner, Annie goes out to the bindery. The table has been cleared, and the book lies there in all its glory: the leather gleaming, the gold leaf glinting in the sunlight. In an act of faith, she has inscribed the first page with a dedication.

To Josie & Judge
"The setting sun, and music at the close
As the last taste of sweets, is sweetest last,
Writ in remembrance more than things long past."

My dears, in remembrance of things long past,
Do not forget that there is still the present.
With all my love,
Annie.